IGNITE

A NOVEL

BRE BARTELL

For anyone who has ever felt hopeless after a heartbreak.
You are enough.
Don't ever let anyone extinguish your flame.

Note from the author

Thank you for choosing *Ignite* as your next read ♡
As this is a first time, self-published novel, there are some editorial
imperfections that will be addressed in future editions. So, thank you
for your support in my growth as an indie author!
-Bre

IGNITE

Chapter One

Mystery Girl

At some point you're just going to have to get over her and move on." Harsh words from my brother a moment ago, ruminating through my head as I down this glass of whiskey. Both burning as they go down.

He's right though of course. It had been over a year since my brutal divorce.

Leaving me with no money, a broken heart and a coping mechanism of dive bars and brooding. I was beginning to think there was no such thing as true love and happiness. I voiced as much a minute ago to my older brother Jack.

We are sitting at my favorite local dive, *Map Room*. Filled with all matters of personalities here in Cleveland. Slightly dusty, a film of grime from all the alcohol, on the people, not the bar. The sound of some moody rock playing over the scratchy speakers. I frequent here so often, the bartenders all know me by name and drink choice. "Hey Landon!" chirped one of my favorites coming in for her shift, Stacey. Her usual grin meeting up to her brown eyes matching her long curly hair and wearing one of her go-to quirky Hawaiian button-up shirts.

"Hi Stace," I reply gruffly with a polite but hindered smile as I sip my drink, feeling the icy cold condensation dripping off the side.

"Woah, Mr. Broody," she says in return while filling up someone's glass. "Has he been like this all evening?" Stacey asks my brother.

"Pretty much, you just missed his monologue about swearing off love and happiness all together," Jack responds with a chuckle under his breath as he finishes the last of his pint of beer.

I've been about two drinks ahead of him all night, per usual. Jack and I tried to make it a habit of getting together at least once or twice a week outside of work. Unfortunately, most of our nights end up in me feeling worse about my life rather than helping, probably of my own accord if I'm being completely honest with myself. I would never admit it though if my brother called me out.

Jack and I's relationship is the best out of my siblings, my whole family actually. He is ten years older but we have always been close, even as children. Minus the time he locked me in a chest in our Grandparent's basement. Hours had passed before my mom found me and proceeded to shout about how I shouldn't have been down there to begin with. We got closer after I grew to be taller than him when I was entering eighth grade. He tried picking a fight with me, ending in him being knocked out in the snow. We've been inseparable ever since.

"Well, I've got to get going, Nancy and the girls are wanting to have a movie night tonight," Jack says as he puts on his leather coat and slaps a twenty-dollar bill down onto the bar.

Nancy, his wife, and daughters Isabelle and Emily, have been the best thing to have happened to my brother. Nancy calls him out on his shit and the girls are always keeping him on his toes. They make me long for the true happiness I see in them. I have no desire for kids of my own but the joy and love I see from Jack and Nancy make me hold onto some small tether of hope that feeling is out there for me. Somewhere.

I order another drink after telling Jack good-bye. Probably not the wisest decision since I need to walk home and it's starting to snow. The frigid bite of early winter in Cleveland is starting to come sooner than usual. I stupidly forgot my jacket at home too, leaving me only in my green long sleeve shirt and jeans to brave the cold. Maybe the satisfying burn of this whiskey will ignite the warmth in me long enough to make it home before I freeze to death.

Listening to all of the conversations in this bar is one of my favorite forms of entertainment. I always choose the same spot at the wooden L shaped bar. The back corner, where I'm able to see the front door and almost every patron in here. Some girls are laughing maniacally at a joke one of the guys in their group is telling. The couple closest to me, at a table right behind me is arguing. She accused him of texting a picture of his dick to her co-worker, and then had the gall to deny it was his. Even though you could apparently see the Prince-Albert piercing he has in full view, his girlfriend yelling as much back in response. Glad I'm not that guy.

Chuckling to myself and wondering if maybe it is a good thing I am single, listening to all of the horror stories around me about relationships. I'm sure mine tops any of them though. A marriage that started on a whirlwind, my ex was supportive and caring when

I met her, up until we uttered *I Do.* Too long after is when I realized all of the red flags I had skimmed over.

Glancing around, I don't have a desire to attempt to start a conversation with any woman here. I haven't in the past year actually. Until I look directly at the figure walking in the door.

I have never seen anyone as luminous as her. Her long chestnut brown hair sweeping across her shoulder as she laughs at something someone said near her. That sound is the best thing I have ever heard. She somehow is wearing a short dress in this cold, granted she has an oversized leather jacket and some tall boots on. I haven't gotten a full look of her face but something tells me she is the most stunning woman I have ever seen.

The mystery girl is making her way through the room, continuing to look back towards someone at the front door. She settles at a spot in the middle of the bar, trying to get the bartender's attention. The guy next to her is blocking her full view from me. I have never felt this strong desire to know who someone is. To catch a glimpse of her. I start standing, my body on auto-pilot. Feeling like if I don't speak to this woman I might very well fade away from existence here in this bar. I catch a glimpse of myself in one of the smudge covered framed mirrors lining the walls. My brown hair tousled from running my hands through it, a nervous habit. I'm in need of a haircut for sure, also should probably trim my beard some. Hopefully she isn't into more clean cut guys.

She is a couple feet away. One foot. I swear I am able to smell the perfume on her. Crackling embers and Jasmine. She is petite, only coming up to my chest as I stand right behind her. She hasn't turned around, still trying to order a drink. I politely step in between her and the group of men on her left, distracted by their conversation on golf to notice the stunning woman. I shout my favorite bartender Stacey's name, getting her attention immediately.

The mystery woman finally looks my way, her hauntingly steel blue eyes piercing through my soul. I forget everything else in this world. I don't think I even breathe. Her face, the perfect blend of unarming beauty mixed with a softness making her the most sexy and adorable person I have ever seen before. I open my mouth to say something, introduce myself, but she cuts me off.

"I am perfectly capable of ordering a drink for myself thank you," she says with such a bite in her words it takes me aback.

"I - I'm sorry, I wasn't-" I start to say, getting cut off again by this sassy, beautiful woman next to me.

"I don't need you to shout at the bartender for me." Her voice sounds like honey.

Stacey appears in front of us, "Hey Landon, what can I get you?" she says with a slight smile which probably means she is finally glad to see me interacting with someone other than my brother or her.

"Landon, is it?" the mystery girl says, "Do you make it a habit of buying girls drinks at the bar?" Stacey and I exchange a look. If only this girl knew I haven't actually attempted talking to a woman in who knows how long.

"I'm sorry, I didn't mean to overstep. Can I buy you a drink to make up for it?"

Probably the wrong thing to say since she clearly doesn't want anyone taking care of her but I can't help myself. I need an opportunity to find out her name. To find out more about her. Glancing between Stacey and I, she looks me up and down. Completely disarming me, as if she could see all the way to my soul. Luckily, she seems to assess I'm no threat

"*Whiskey*. On the rocks," she finally responds, with a slight smirk.

I swallow hard, looking at Stacey. "Two, please," I say as I turn back towards the mystery girl. We don't speak a word while we wait the minute it takes Stacey to pour the amber colored liquid in our glasses. After we both grab our drinks, the bar starts to feel a little crowded. I head over to a small high table in the back, hoping with everything she follows and doesn't leave me alone.

Luckily, she's right behind me as we arrive at one of the tables covered in discarded beer bottles. She smiles at me and takes a drink from her glass. I do the same. This wonder woman will be the death of me, I know it.

But I can't stop myself from knowing her more. "What's your name?"

She studies me again, as though debating on if she should tell me anything about her.

Finally, with a side smile she says, "My name is Lilah."

Chapter Two

First Spark

*L*ilah. How does a name sound so damn good? I could listen to it on repeat and never get tired of it. The name fits her perfectly. Beautiful but mysterious. I realize I've been lost staring at her, as the song on the speakers changes. *Heroes* by David Bowie, my favorite. I'm lost in my own thoughts when she starts to sing with the opening lines. Her honey voice laces through my thoughts.

"Do you like Bowie?" I ask her with a smile, taking a sip of my whiskey.

"I don't *like* Bowie... I *love* Bowie," Lilah says in between singing. "This is my favorite song."

I feel like this girl was made specifically for me, not in a territorial type of way, but as if she was molded from my soul. God, I sound like a complete romantic nutcase. What the hell is happening to me?

"You seem a little lost in your head," she says as the song ends. "Penny for your thoughts?"

"Sorry," I laugh and run my hand through my hair. "I just haven't met anyone like you," I say with a tentative smile, setting my glass down on the chipped wooden table.

"Well then it is your lucky day Landon, I'm a catch," she responds with the most beautiful grin and wink, completely disarming me.

"Someone is a little full of themselves huh?" I add playfully.

"No." She shrugs. "I am sure of myself. Big difference," Lilah retorts with a slight tilt to her head, adding, "So are you from here?"

I debate on giving her the bullshit short answer or going deeper, I tend not to tell people about all my woes, only speaking about them with Jack or some of my coworkers. Something pushes me though, to want to open myself up to this girl I only just met.

"I'm originally from South of Cleveland. I've lived all over though. I actually moved back up here from California a little less than a year ago..." I trail off, trying not to think about the events prior to my move.

"What brought you back up here?" Lilah asks as she sips on her drink.

I again consider keeping my explanation short, non-complicated. But I find myself responding fully. "I went through a pretty rough divorce a year ago, she was the only person I really had out West so I decided to come home." I down the rest of my drink. "My brother lives here in Cleveland and I have always considered this city to be my home."

A few beats pass, hopefully I haven't scared this poor girl away by immediately talking about my ex-wife.

Luckily only another second goes by before she says, "I'm sorry you went through that, I've never been married but I believe everything happens for a reason and you had to go through that time to learn some lesson to ultimately help you find who you are meant to be." She finishes with a small shrug.

Wise words from such a young looking girl, but I don't doubt her wisdom as I look into those piercing blue eyes, filled with such knowledge of life.

Wanting to lighten the conversation away from my past, I ask her, "How about yourself? Where are you from?"

"Oh, I'm from pretty much everywhere. I've lived all over. Recently moved back up here as well because I was bored with where I currently lived. The city has always been a favorite of mine too," she says with a slight smile, finishing her drink.

"Are you normally a Whiskey drinker?" I swirl around the ice in my glass. "Or did you just want to impress me?" I ask her teasingly.

She smirks then replies, "Oh yes Landon, I so deeply wanted to impress you I forced myself to drink a whole glass of bourbon." She rolls her eyes, somehow making that action one of the sexiest things I have ever seen, then adds, "No, I do love me some good Whiskey but I go through phases and it depends on my mood, you happened to catch me on a chilly night and in need of some liquor to warm me up." Laughter fills the air from a group near us.

Realizing she hasn't looked back at anyone since we came over to the table, I ask, "Are you here alone?"

"I was waiting on my friends but I don't think they are going to show up," she answers with slight annoyance then adds, "But that's okay, seems I might be in better company now." Her smile is doing devastating damage to my psyche.

Lilah starts swaying with the music as she continues to sing along with each word. I was about to ask her if she wants another drink when she blurts out, "Would you want to go sing *karaoke* with me?"

I chuckle, "Um, sure, but they don't do karaoke here."

"No I know, but I found this cool karaoke place down the street and it is so much fun!" she says with excitement lighting her eyes.

I haven't sang karaoke since I was young and drunk at a college party, this is probably an awful decision on my part but I say, "Well, alright. You lead the way."

———

She was slightly understating how far this karaoke bar is. We have been walking for what feels like a mile in the brisk cold before stopping in front of this slightly sketchy looking place. Illuminated with a blue light up sign outside, called *Moonlight*. I might have doubted what this place is if it wasn't for the giant yellow neon bulbs saying *Karaoke*.

"How often do you come here?" I ask as I follow her inside the dimly lit hallway.

From around the corner I see a small wooden bar off to the side, a giant mirror behind it. In fact there are mirrors on all of the walls around us. As if they wanted you to have a full 360 view of your embarrassment on the small stage at the opposite end.

"Oh, only a few times a month," Lilah responds, as if that's a common amount of times to frequent a hole-in-the-wall karaoke bar.

We walk over to grab a drink. Passing by a larger crowd than I would expect, all smelling of beer and mixed shots. I was about to ask if she wanted to stay at the bar or find a seat in one of the few round tables circled by velvet topped stools, when she glances up at me with those bright eyes.

"So what song are we going to sing?" she asks with a wink. Completely catching me off guard. Being honest I fully intended on watching her take the stage, not for me to sing. Zero desire in me to basically ensure she will never want to speak to me again if I get up there.

For some reason though the look she is giving me, one of reassurance, laced with a subtle challenge. As if she is sizing me up to see whether my bravery matches hers. That look alone makes all the bullshit fear subside and I find myself answering, "What song is your *go-to?*

"Oh it is definitely '*What's Up*' by the 4 Non Blondes," Lilah says with more confidence than someone of her size should have.

"Interesting choice," I reply with a slight chuckle. This is going to be very, very bad.

No turning back though, as I go to tell the short older woman by the equipment on stage our names and song choice. The woman gives me an incredulous look, probably wondering how bad this performance will be.

Lilah heads to the bathroom while I sit here downing my drink, half-debating if I should order a shot too. I anxiously fiddle with my rings on my right hand, getting more nervous by the minute while she's gone. Finally I spot her making her way back to the table I chose near the front of the stage. Her chestnut brown hair swaying over her bare shoulder, she deserted her giant leather jacket when we first walked in. Leaving me with my mouth dry as I admire her in that short red dress.

"Why are you looking at me like that?" Lilah asks with amusement.

I didn't realize how lost in thought I was. I swallow, clearing my throat as I glance up at the disco ball covered ceiling, "I just have never seen someone as beautiful as you."

She glares at me, but smirks at the same time. Rolling her eyes in her sexy way again as she sits down, leaving her thighs a bit more exposed as her dress moves up with the movement. I'm trying to think of some more questions to ask her when I hear our names being called.

"Give it up for Landon and Lilah everyone!" The short older woman says into the microphone, garnering the small crowd in the bar to clap for us as we make our way ten feet to the stage. I catch a glimpse of the audience, some are involved in their own conversations, the others are staring up at us with a questioning look on their faces. Probably wondering what this gorgeous woman is doing with a guy like me.

Our song begins, Lilah starting off as I build up my courage to chime in. The crowd murmurs, waiting for me to start singing too.

For some unknown reason though I feel completely at ease and confident standing next to this fearless woman.

We manage to get the whole crowd to join in as we finish singing. Warranting a standing ovation from the whole bar. As we exit the small stage back to our table, gaining a few high fives from the drunken patrons closest to me, I can't help but wonder if this night is actually happening. My confidence had been beat down out of me throughout the last year, hell, more like over the last five of my marriage. In a million years I wouldn't have allowed myself to have as much fun as I did, singing *majorly* off-key for the hell of it.

The rest of the evening goes by in a blur of ecstasy. Being next to Lilah is easy. I feel like I've known this woman my whole life, though I have much more to learn. Most of our conversation is flirty banter, laced with her sexy sarcasm. Sitting closer than we have all night, I feel the warmth radiating from her as her thigh brushes up against mine.

Not wanting to scare her off I try to keep my questions light. I've learned Lilah is an editor at a small independent magazine. She lives in Ohio City, not far from my downtown loft. I try to inquire more about her life when she chimes in to ask, "So Landon, what do you do for work?"

Another question which should be simple but my complicated past makes it a longer answer than I would prefer. The urge though, to tell my whole life to her, overcomes the need to remain simple and vague.

"Eh, well it's slightly a long story but I worked at a corporate run marketing company back in California, your typical nine to five soul-sucking desk job working for someone else," I sigh as I continue on, shifting slightly and resting my arm on the back of her stool.

"The money was good though, which is how I lasted five years there, but when I got divorced I kind of hit a dark point and quit. When I decided to move back to the city, I wasn't sure what I wanted to do. Resulting in me currently helping my brother Jack out at his commercial construction company here in the city."

She studies me for the thousandth time tonight, "That doesn't sound like what you want to be doing though." Tilting her head to the side with an inquisitive look, she blinks a few times then adds, "What drives you Landon? What sets your soul on *fire*?" She places a hand on my thigh, making me lose all thought for a second.

I don't think I've ever had someone ask me something so specific, no one besides my brother has seemed to care about what I do. Especially not my ex, it was always about her and how I could help her fuel her dreams. Which is why I took the marketing job, to earn more money because she would drain any savings I would start to build. I open my mouth to answer but then stop because I honestly don't know how to answer her question. Seeming to sense as much she smiles at me, grabbing my hand and pulling me up from my seat.

"Let's go for a walk," she says as she starts to put her jacket back on.

As much as I don't feel like braving the cold outside, again cursing myself for forgetting my own jacket, I couldn't tell her no. We make our way out of the bar, starting the walk back towards *Map Room* in the same direction as my loft.

Snow falls slowly down, some of it sticking to the streets and sidewalk. Lilah strolls next to me, somehow not letting it show she is cold. I wish I had a jacket to give her, half tempted to ask her to share hers. Craving some warmth, I grab her small hand in mine, she studies the tattoos covering my left. I got them recently after my divorce, something I would have never been able to do before as my ex thought hand tattoos were tacky. My left hand is covered in a dark inky mountain, trailing up my fingers. About ten years ago in my early twenties I took a solo hiking trip, one of the only moments in my life I truly felt at peace. I've been meaning to go back there for a while.

"Do you always wear rings?" Lilah asks as she plays with the one on my pinkie.

I'm taken back to a time my ex told me I looked like an idiot when I wore jewelry. She hated most of what I chose to wear. Always wanting me in a suit jacket and pressed pants, when I preferred jeans and a leather jacket.

"I stopped wearing any for a long time but found them in a box I recently unpacked and decided to try them out again. Do you hate them?" I ask her warily.

A subtle look of concern crosses her face as she replies, "No I *love* them, I think it's sexy when men show their personality in the things they wear."

I smile with relief, "Do you have any tattoos?" I haven't seen any noticeable ones.

"None which are visible right now," she says with a glance over to me, smiling coyly. "But yes, I have a large piece on my back."

"What is your backpiece of?" I ask without trying to sound like I would love to see that part of her bare.

She looks at me, almost as if she could hear the suggestive thoughts playing in my head, "It's kind of hard to explain, but it's a mix of flowers and flames wrapped around a phoenix." She lets go of my hand to tuck a lock of hair behind her ear, snow sticking to the strands. "I got it when I was eighteen, it felt like an empowering choice even though I was young and had no idea who I wanted to be, but I'm glad I got it. I feel like the phoenix has helped guide me to where I'm meant to be. *Cheesy* I know," she says with a slight smile.

"I love it," I say without realizing. "Well I love the idea of it." Holding myself back from

saying I hope I'll be able to see it one day.

We finally get back to my street, a few blocks away from Map Room. I debate on asking if she wants to come back up to my place, but I don't want this to be a one night stand. I also haven't been with anyone since my divorce. The thought does terrify me slightly.

So instead I say, "I'm not going to invite you back up to my place. Not because I don't want to. I just don't want you to get the wrong idea. I hope to see you ag–" She stops me with a finger over my mouth, shushing me.

"Just shut up and kiss me," she says as she moves her finger away from my lips.

Standing next to the front door of my building I look into those blue eyes, reaching my hand up to grasp the back of her neck firmly. I lean her back up against the wall feeling the warmth on her lips as I kiss her gently, but with such a fierceness I think we might melt into each other. She opens up to me, letting me take full control as our tongues collide together in a rhythm coursing through to my bones. Minutes go by. Everything seems to freeze. The snow sticking to both of us as I pull away, holding her face in between my hands. A snowflake lands right on her delicious mouth, melting as I kiss it away.

We stand there for a moment longer, staring into each other's eyes, both at a loss for words. Not wanting her to freeze anymore, I order an uber which conveniently happened to be across the street. We stand there looking at each other while the car pulls up. I open the door for her as she slips inside.

"I would love to see you again," I say as I hand her my phone to put her number in.

"Me too, good-bye Landon," she says with a smile handing me back my phone, turning to sit fully in the backseat of the black vehicle.

I shut the door, not wanting her to go. The car hangs around for another moment. I start to wonder if she is going to get back out. But after another minute they finally drive off.

I turn to head back into my apartment but feel frozen in thought standing there in the snow, looking in the direction she went. All I keep thinking is how electric that kiss was, how it sparked something missing in me.

Ignited a flame that would burn this world down if we aren't careful.

Chapter Three

Morning After

Waking up the following morning is rough. I guess it's more like the afternoon, I somehow slept until noon. My head feels like someone took a hammer to it, my mouth parched. It feels like swallowing sandpaper. I passed out on my unmade bed as soon as I got back up to my apartment, not even bothering to take my boots off.

I dreamt of her all night.

One of the three giant windows on the wall next to my bed blinds me with the morning sunlight while I chug a large glass of water I must have left on the nightstand. I keep meaning to get curtains. I hate to obscure my view of the city though. Lake Erie to my right, the bustling downtown surrounding the rest of the brick faced building. I was lucky in getting this place, located in the complex connected to some newly renovated luxury lofts. I got one of the last semi-out-dated units. Covered in brick walls, giant air ducts, old appliances and probably some lead paint, making my rent way less than the fancy new units in the adjacent building. The only connecting point between me and the fancier tenants being a small market and a coffee shop. I'm in desperate need of the latter for sure.

Making my way through my normal morning routine I keep finding myself getting lost in thought. About the magnificent woman I met last night. Lilah... I am almost certain none of it was real. Until I hear the annoying chirp of my phone. Finally getting a response from the text I sent her last night. I had only sent one word, not wanting to appear too desperate or clingy.

Amazing.

Her response is short as well, a smiley face. I'm starting to think she doesn't feel the same. Maybe she woke up this morning and regrets kissing me. My brooding thoughts interrupted a few minutes later by my phone again. Another text coming through.

I had so much fun last night. I would love to see you again soon.

I let out a deep sigh of relief staring at the screen. Debating on if I should wait a little longer to respond. That's what people do nowadays right? Ultimately my impatience kicks in and I respond only a few moments later after throwing my clothes from last night into the hamper, exchanging them for a t-shirt and jeans.

Tomorrow night?

I would have said today if I hadn't promised my brother I would come over for some family time. Especially since I skipped out on their invitation for Thanksgiving next week. The holidays are a weird time for me after this past year. Her reply comes in a minute later.

Sounds good to me. Where do you want to go? Tomorrow being Monday night and all.

Luckily there were things to do pretty much every night in the city, but I want to get to know her better. Somewhere quiet would be best. I hope I don't sound too forward when I ask,

How about my place? I'll cook you dinner.

Another minute passes, anxiously waiting on her response. Then the three little dots on the screen appear, her reply following shortly after.

Mhm, I see what you're trying to do, Landon... trying to get me all alone in your apartment, huh?

Shit. I was worried it was too forward. How can I turn this around? I'm ruminating on a couple responses when another text from her comes in.

Can't wait. 7pm sound good?

This girl is going to be the death of me. I type my response,

7 is perfect. See you then beautiful.

She doesn't respond, not that I expected us to text back and forth all day like we are a couple of teenagers. I honestly hate texting. Part of me is a little sad though as I realize I'll have to wait a whole day until I see her again. I'm genuinely concerned for my sanity at this point. I'm being completely ridiculous. I need some caffeine in me. Maybe it will cure me of this craving I have for her. I put on my shoes, grab a lightweight zip-up jacket and head out my door for the coffee shop a few floors down.

———

The headache of last night's alcohol is finally starting to subside as I pull up to my brother's quaint house just west of the city. The fall leaves on the front lawn crunch under my boots. Everything is starting to have a slight grey hue from the cold, especially with last night's melted snow. Fortunately, it's a beautiful crisp day out, perfect for grilling. My brother and I's usual activity on Sundays when I come over. That and entertaining my nieces, Emily and Isabelle. They're twins but couldn't be less alike. Emily is obsessed with anything her father is doing, fixing his motorcycle, watching sports, you name it.

Whereas Isabelle is a mini version of her mother, a complete girly girl, interested in ballet and anything pink.

I'm making my way inside when I hear screaming coming from the house, the cream colored door flinging open as Isabelle runs outside in a pink tutu and bare feet. She almost runs right into me. I see Branch, their tan giant shaggy dog, charging straight for the seven year old. Behind Branch is Emily, chasing him with a plastic sword and wearing an eye patch.

Isabelle flies right past me, with the other two not far behind. Nancy, my brother's wife, is shouting out the front door at them to put shoes and jackets on if they're going to play outside. Nancy has always liked me, she is definitely the better half of my brother. Kind and patient, but also strong-willed enough to not take any shit from him. The twins look exactly like her, brown hair and eyes the color of dark honey.

"Hey Nancy!" I say as I reach the front door, going in for a hug.

"Hi Landon, Jack is in the back. I'm glad you could make it, we're definitely going to miss you on Thanksgiving," Nancy says as she hugs me, pulling away to grab the twin's shoes and jackets to force them into since they decided to start running in circles through the front yard, their laughter echoing through the trees as Branch hops into a pile of leaves.

I head into the house, aiming for the backyard through the side door in the kitchen. Jack is already halfway through grilling the various meats and veggies as I walk up behind him. Scenting the air with subtle spices and the smell of the small flames in the grill.

"Didn't want to leave any grilling for me, huh?" I ask.

"Sorry, the girls have been extra wild today because they knew their Uncle Landon was coming over. I retreated back here early to avoid being trampled by them," he replies with a chuckle as he flips a steak over with the spatula in one hand, sipping on his beer from the other.

"They definitely seem very wound up today," I say with a laugh as I grab a beer out of the large cooler on the deck behind me.

"Glad you didn't dip out on us again, it being close to the holidays and what not," Jack says with a slight bite to his words.

He understands why I despise this time of year but never presses the issue. Probably a good thing I didn't plan to come for Thanksgiving anyways, since the rest of my family accepted their invitations. That would be a shit show. I haven't spoken to any of them in what feels like months, the last conversation turning into me listening to my mother yell at me over the phone about how she wants me and my ex back together.

"How late did you stay out after I left?" My brother casually asks.

"Eh, only a few more hours or so," I answer with a side smile I fail to hide as I reminisce about last night again.

Picking up on the insinuation, Jack asks, "Meet someone?" Raising his brow as he flips a steak over.

Glancing down with an idiot grin that doesn't fully leave my face, I debate telling him about Lilah on the off chance I screw up anything with her.

"Maybe." Is all I say back with a shrug.

Jack studies me for a minute then decides not to push further for more information, and turns back to finish up the steak he was almost done grilling. Thankfully my brother never pries too much into my personal life but supports me and my decisions. With our family dynamic growing up it made each of us independent, careful not to overstep with anyone. Definitely makes it harder to get close to people. Even in my marriage, I never wanted to dig too deeply into something she would tell me, for fear of her snapping or pushing me further away. Thinking back to last night, I'm shocked I let any details of my past slip to Lilah, but somehow I felt no fear in exposing my messiness to her. I'm going to keep some cards close to my chest though.

The rest of the afternoon into the evening goes by in a blur. After finishing our food, the twins wanted to show me their new video game. Walking me through every detail they could, until Jack finally told them they were putting me to sleep and it was in fact getting to be time for them to get ready for bed.

Me and Jack retreat to the basement after making sure Nancy doesn't need help cleaning up. My brother turned the basement into his haven. A bar, giant TV, a pool table, your stereotypical man-cave. We always found ourselves down here at the end of our family get-togethers, him drinking another beer, me opting for a glass of whiskey from his impressive collection. Landing on a nice rye on ice before settling into the couch in front of the TV.

Jack sits next to me, taking a drink before he says, "I know you hate the holidays brother, but you're going to have to suck it up eventually, you can't let her ruin everything for you."

"Thanks for the sound advice," I say sarcastically, taking a swig from my glass. I know he's right but I'm not ready to admit it fully. Instead I get up to start a game of pool so I don't have to start talking about my feelings, Jack follows. We played the rest of the night, until it got late enough the twins and Nancy had long gone to bed.

I say bye to Jack, getting into my car. He has the garage open, I spot my black motorcycle sitting right next to his in the corner, covered and untouched since this past Spring. I know all too well the weather is venturing to be too cold and dangerous to ride until the warmth comes back around. I'm definitely not looking forward to full-on Winter.

As I pull out of the driveway though I have a feeling for some reason it won't be as bad this year.

———

Mondays used to be agony back at my old job. Always dreading my alarm going off to go into that hell hole. It's definitely a nice change working for my brother's construction company, Stone Construction. I mostly help with scheduling for his projects, setting the timeline and making sure everything goes according to plan at the job sites. Sometimes on smaller projects, lending a hand with the carpentry. The past few months we have been working on a big project in the heart of the city. I have been on calls working from home most of the morning, coordinating everything for some deliveries this week. I've been busy all the way up to lunch, finally getting a break to go get some things I need for dinner tonight.

Making my way down to the market, I'm hoping Lilah doesn't end up canceling on me. We haven't spoken since yesterday morning when we texted.

She hasn't given me any reason to think she won't show. Then again, I don't know her all that well. I try not to get too in my head as I walk through the market doors, immediately met with the smell of freshly baked bread and coffee. I planned to pull out all the stops tonight, homemade pasta, fresh bread, some nice wine. Hopefully she likes fettuccine alfredo.

I'm in the line ready to check-out with a full shopping cart. I'm probably going a bit overboard but I want to impress this girl so bad for some reason. Apparently, the middle of the day is the worst time to go to the market. I have been waiting in this line for about ten minutes. Standing behind a man debating between two variations of diet soda and an older lady buying five large tubs of kitty litter.

At least I'm able to keep myself busy by trying to find Lilah online, first looking on social media, no luck. It would probably help if I knew her last name. I tried looking up the karaoke bar, *Moonlight,* we went to. No luck finding either. Finally the line moves up so I give up my search.

I head back up to my apartment with seven bags in hand, almost to the door when my phone starts ringing. Thinking it's work, I'm about to ignore it but then wonder if it's someone else, maybe Lilah calling. I hope she doesn't cancel, if she does, it looks like I'm about to eat a shit ton of pasta by myself.

It's not Lilah.

I debate answering. Anger and frustration start roiling through my veins. I go numb as I hit accept.

"What is it, Rachel?" I don't try to hide my annoyance, shifting my phone to my shoulder to try and pull my keys out.

"Woah, so snippy Lan," she replies with condescending amusement.

"I'm a little busy, what do you want?" I haven't managed to unlock my door. I'm standing in the hallway, debating if I should hang up before I drop all of these bags.

"I just wanted to check in on you, I miss your voice," she says in that viper tone of hers, the voice of someone who is used to always getting what she wants. Not this time.

"Rachel, you're my *ex*-wife, you don't get to randomly check in on me," I respond. Finally unlocking my door and setting the bags down on the floor inside.

"Oh Lan, don't be like that, you know you miss me too," she says with mastered condescension.

"I'm serious Rachel, I don't have time for this. We haven't spoken in months and we have been divorced for almost a year. Was there a point to this call?" I'm about to pull the phone away from my ear and hang up when she responds.

"So, mean," she says with a tsk. "I wanted to call you because my friend Lorie had something very interesting to tell me over the phone yesterday. You remember Lorie, short blonde hair, lives in Cleveland. Well, she said she was out Saturday night and swore she saw you."

"Your point Rachel?" I've had enough of this pointless conversation.

"Well even though you were alone as Lorie mentioned, she swore she heard you ordering drinks for someone else," Rachel says, not holding back her amusement.

Exasperation is taking over, why the hell would she bother calling me for this?

"So she heard me order two drinks but didn't tell you if I was with someone? Sounds to me like you and Lorie have nothing better to do than gossip about whether I was drinking one drink or two." I *need* a drink after this conversation, that's for sure.

"Well she thought maybe you were there with someone and she didn't see your brother. I thought maybe you were out with a girl." Sounds like she is implying it would be a problem if I had been.

"I'm hanging up, thank you for the pointless-ass phone call," I say as I pull the phone away from my ear to hang up but I hear her trill voice come through again and go against my better judgement.

"Lan, you know I just want the best for you and I don't think you're ready for someone else. I know you still think about me." I hear the narcissism oozing from her mouth as she speaks. I've had enough.

"Good-bye Rachel, please don't call me again." I hang up, not giving her a chance to respond.

I toss my phone onto the couch, picking up the bags I left on the floor to bring into the kitchen to put away. It's only two o'clock. So much time until I'm supposed to see Lilah. That conversation making me grit my teeth. I need to get out of this mindset before I let it get the best of me.

I make sure there are no other work calls I need to make, then change into my gym clothes. Dressing only to end up sweating through my clothes is always hard this time of year. I opt for sweatpants instead of my usual shorts. Going to the gym always helps when I can't deal with the thoughts in my head.

I'm about to head out the door when I hear the chirp of my phone, a text coming through. I curse out loud that it better not be Rachel. It's not.

I'm so excited for tonight.

The text from Lilah instantly brightens my mood. I respond,

Me too, come hungry. I hope you like pasta.

Only a minute passes by before her response.

Oh I LOVE pasta. Fettuccine alfredo is my favorite.

I swear this girl has the ability to read my mind. I can't wait for tonight. I need to hurry and get back from the gym and get cooking. I keep my answer short.

Good. See you tonight, Beautiful.

I can't wait to see her gorgeous face, wondering if she will wear another short dress. Hopefully she doesn't hate my cooking. I head towards the front door, turning around to lock it as I think to myself. *Tonight is only the beginning.*

Chapter Four

First Time

"*Shit!*" I say out loud as I burn the hell out of my hand trying to grab the bread out of the stove. I've been cooking for the last hour, feels like twelve. I should've opted for store bought noodles. What devil in me decided it was a good idea to make this girl pasta from scratch? Maybe if she has a couple glasses of wine before we eat, she won't be able to tell if it's awful. I should probably freshen up some before she gets here. It's six thirty, I wonder if she will be right on time or will get here a little after seven.

I hurry to go throw on a new shirt, since the white long sleeve button up I had been wearing has pasta sauce all over it. Luckily Alfredo shouldn't stain. I opt for a black t-shirt this time, unintentionally showing off more of my tattoos. I hope I don't look too rough. I trimmed my hair last night, it's a little messy but I don't look completely as if I just got out of bed. The thought crosses my head for the hundredth time on if she will be wearing another dress like the other night. I have no expectations for this evening though. I honestly just can't wait to see her again.

I go to look at my phone to see if she's texted that she changed her mind and can't make it, when I hear a light knock at my door. Six fifty-five on the clock. I hurry and chuck the discarded shirt from earlier into the hallway closet, forgetting I left it on the couch after the scalding hot pasta sauce splattered on me. A quick glimpse in the mirror by the door to make sure I don't look as frenzied as I feel. I brush the hairs of my trimmed beard down and shrug, this will have to do. When I open the door my breath catches. She's somehow more beautiful than the last time I saw her.

"Hi gorgeous." I don't try to hide my excitement.

"Hi, Landon," she replies with a mischievously sexy smile not quite touching her stormy eyes.

She is wearing a white blouse under her coat, tucked into leather pants flowing out slightly at the bottom above her heeled boots. How does she look even more captivating than she did the other night? Her long brown hair in loose curls draped over her shoulders, her lips painted a subtle shade of red. I would give anything to kiss those lips. I restrain myself though, not wanting to push my luck.

"I hope you're hungry. Can I get you some wine?" I say as I open the door for her to enter the loft.

I spent the few minutes I had in between cooking earlier to tidy up some. Records and books are scattered throughout my small living room though. Music on the record player, *The Goo Goo Dolls*. My brown leather couch is worn with a small tear on the side, I got it second hand off someone when I moved back here. An old man moving out of the unit right next to me. I managed to make the bed in the few minutes I had after changing, realizing I neglected it. I like to think I made my place somewhat homey for it being a studio loft. Although the bed is right on the other side of the kitchen, there are big beams to divide the space up some. The lights outside coming in through one of the three giant windows facing the street, letting in some of the city's luminance.

"I'd love a glass of wine," Lilah responds as she walks inside while I close the door behind her. I can't help but notice the view of her walking from behind is almost as mesmerizing as the front, even beneath her layers of clothes. "I love your place," she adds as she takes her long tan jacket off, abandoning it on the side of the couch.

I had already poured a glass of white wine, hoping she would be right on time. My fingers brushing against hers as I hand her the long stemmed glass I grabbed off the small entryway table.

"Food is about finished," I say as I remove my lingering eyes from those lips sipping her glass.

"Good, because I'm famished," she replies as she wanders over to the bookshelf near the TV, inspecting the assortment of books, records and miscellaneous items discarded there.

"What's this?" she asks as she picks up an old coin on one of the middle shelves, flipping it over a couple times in her hand.

"Oh, that's nothing, just a trinket I picked up from somewhere." A complete lie, but I wanted tonight to be fun, no need to get deep into some old family shit.

"Do you like to take pictures?" Lilah asks as she points out the black, long lens camera sitting on the shelf. The model is a few years old but does the trick.

"Eh, more of a every now and then kind of hobby. Nothing special," I respond.

The food is finally done cooking. I waited to toss the noodles in the sauce until she got here. I'm plating everything as she walks over to the kitchen taking a seat at the long concrete bar on the other side of the island.

"That smells amazing," she says, getting a whiff of the pasta sitting in front of her as garlic and cream scent the air.

"Fresh parmesan?" I ask her as I hold up the block I bought from the market.

"I didn't realize I was coming over to a Michelin star restaurant tonight," she quips with a small chuckle, holding her plate out to me for the cheese.

"I had to pull out all of the stops for you, granted I burnt myself and spilled some sauce on my shirt in the process," I say as I look at the small red crescent already starting to scar on my left hand from the stove.

"Giving me the princess treatment huh?" she says with a smile, but a look of concern crosses over her face as she notes the burn on my hand.

"Oh I'll be fine," responding to the look she's giving me. "But yes, for someone as beautiful as you, I am definitely going to give you the princess treatment," I add with a joking dramatic bow.

"I see, you're only interested in me for my looks huh?" she says with a roll of her eyes, picking up her glass of wine and taking a sip.

I put a hand to my chest, pretending to be offended. "Even though you are the most stunning creature I have ever laid my eyes on, no darling, I am interested in every part of you."

She gives me a smirk as she swallows her sip of wine, a bead of it collecting on her bottom lip. It takes everything in me not to be disarmed at the sight of her licking it off.

I make my way to the other side of the bar, grabbing my glass of wine on the way. Sitting on her right, we both dig into our pasta. Thank God, it's actually good. I haven't made handmade pasta in forever. The fact that Lilah hasn't put down her fork tells me she's enjoying it too.

"This is delicious, I don't think I've ever had a man cook for me," she says as she finishes her mouthful of noodles.

"I'm glad you like it, would have been awful if I went to battle with the stove to make you a terrible dinner," I say with a laugh. Genuinely relieved that she thinks it's halfway decent. "So tell me a little about yourself, I feel like we mostly ended up talking about my life the other night," I add as I take another bite.

"Oh, not too much to tell," she responds as she wipes her mouth off with the napkin I gave her and takes another sip of her wine. "Only child, moved around a lot. Especially as I became an adult, I tend to get bored with where I'm at a lot. Probably a deeper meaning there we don't need to get into." She lets out a chuckle as she continues, "I never know how to talk about myself when people ask."

"I completely understand," I reply, finishing my glass of wine. "I never know if I should give the long or short answer. Whether I should dive deep into trauma and bullshit or if I should give a shiny, easy answer."

"I didn't think anyone else understood, that feeling I mean," she says, her eyes glowing at me.

———

We finish our food, not bothering to clean anything up as we move the short distance to the couch in the living room. Lilah discards her boots, cheeks flushed as she starts on her second glass of wine. I refill my glass before I go to put Bowie on the record player. I mostly listen to music on my phone or through my TV, but there is something about vinyl that sounds better.

Lilah is sitting with her feet under her on the couch, looking like she has always lived here. I love that she is comfortable around me already. I go to sit next to her, sinking into the cushion, the leather crinkling under the weight of my body.

"So tell me more about what you do for work, how is it being a magazine editor?" I ask as I put my arm over the back of the couch, sitting close but not crowding her space.

She shifts closer to me and takes a drink from her lipstick rimmed glass. "Eh, it's not all that exciting, it has its high and low moments. It's worth it when I get to work on a piece for the magazine that isn't filler nonsense."

"Do you have a favorite piece you've worked on?" I ask, trying not to pry too much, but am genuinely curious.

"I do actually, it's a little sad though." She pauses. I sense she is debating if she wants to elaborate more.

"There was this anonymous writer who submitted to our column about uncommon advice. They wrote about never experiencing love, talking about how many partners they had. All ultimately ending in heartbreak, only to realize they never truly loved anyone before. They ended up meeting someone and fell deeply in love. Then their partner left abruptly, with no trace of where they went or what happened." She looks down at her wine before she continues.

"They wrote the article to give advice on never falling in love. However, reading their words, the passion behind them. I couldn't help but think it would have been a shame, if they never went through any of that." She takes a deep breath before she finishes.

"Because even though they were sending a warning against it, the *love* and passion I read shining through in their words made me believe in it stronger than I ever had before," she says, "As if maybe experiencing heartbreak was the truest sign of love."

She stares off in front of her like she is remembering every word this person had written. I can't help it, I have to be closer to this beautiful soul, I put a hand on her knee. Leaning closer, I gently grasp her chin, turning her to face me.

"I think that is the most beautiful thing I have ever heard," I say as I look into those mesmerizing stormy eyes. Wanting to lean in.

Thankfully, she wants the same, moving in before I can, meeting my lips with hers. I taste the wine she finished from her glass.

I pull away reluctantly, not wanting to push her too far. Especially after Lilah shared something incredibly intimate. I feel like I should tell her something personal so she doesn't feel like the only one exposed. "I lied earlier," I say.

She looks at me, brows scrunching together as curiosity crosses her face.

"When I told you the coin you saw was meaningless." I look down at the small drop of wine left in my glass. "It belonged to my grand-father, my dad gave it to me after he had passed. It was supposed to bring me luck throughout my life, I don't think it's ever worked though. My family and I aren't close, we don't speak at all actually. The only member of my family I am close with is my older brother Jack. The rest of my family is toxic, my dad not as much though. Unfortunately, he is wrapped up in the poison my mother spews at him." I let out a sigh, realizing I am not ready to go any further into my family drama.

"Anyways, my dad gave me that coin when I was a teenager, about fifteen years ago. I haven't felt any luck but I can't get myself to get rid of it." I consider before I finish, "Maybe it is starting to work though..." I trail off as I look at her.

Maybe that coin has brought this girl to me. She might be my undoing but maybe she is what I have been waiting for my whole life. I realize I sound ridiculous, thinking these things about someone I literally met a few nights ago. Lilah looks over at me. Moving to set her glass of wine down on the coffee table, swinging her leg around to straddle me. Looking deep in my eyes as she leans down to kiss me.

Gentle, but deeper than earlier. I taste the sweet tang of wine on her tongue. Which sets me loose.

I wrap one arm around her waist, pulling her closer to me. As I grip the back of her head with my other hand. Kissing up her neck, making my way to her lips. Our mouths are a tangle of passion. Each movement in sync. I've never been with someone who matches with me entirely. We are a set of flames, burning together.

She lets out a subtle moan, moving up slightly on her knees. She reaches forward to grasp my face in her hands, pulling her lips from mine. The look in those eyes, holding all of her secrets and passion. I need to know more, to have more. I stand up with her on my lap. She obliges by wrapping her legs around me as I spin to set her back down on the couch, hovering over her.

"Stop me if we are moving too fast," I say breathlessly as I move down to kiss her again. She nods in response.

Her hand moves underneath the edge of my shirt, touching my torso. She tugs the fabric upward, gesturing for me to take it off, I oblige. A moment of self-consciousness takes over as her piercing eyes scan me from my waist up, but she bites her bottom lip, liking what she sees. I go to kiss her more but she scoots up slightly on the couch, unbuttoning her top. Her fingers making swift work of the small buttons. I'm glad she doesn't seem to want or need my help, my hands are shaking too much to make the task quick.

My breath catches as I take in the sight of her. Wearing a thin black lacey thing barely covering her amazing breasts. We are a tangle of mouths and hands. Both roaming over each other like we are trying to unwrap the thing that will save us. As if we stopped, our very lives will cease to exist. I could stay in this moment forever, my mouth on hers, my hands touching her remarkable body. I don't want to stop, my body is on full auto-pilot, but my brain finally catches up to me. Before things go further than I think she would want, I sit up reluctantly, my hands at her waist about to undo her leather pants.

"We should probably slow down some, yeah?" I ask with a slight breathless chuckle knowing lust is burning in my eyes as I stare down at her.

She looks up at me with a smirk, "Oh, Landon. Don't try to be chivalrous, I don't want or need you to protect me, I need you all over me. I need you to bury yourself deep inside me."

Fuck.

I think this is the first time I have ever been disarmed by a woman in bed. It's been so long since I have been with anyone. Not since my ex, granted we hardly had sex at all within the last year. Dismissing those thoughts. I look down at this magnificent creature, wondering where she came from.

I move down to kiss her plump lips again. She feels like fire in my bones, a fire I can't extinguish if I wanted to. I make my way to undo my belt. Obliging her wishes.

Chapter Five

More

I *really need to get curtains.* The morning sun shines through the loft windows, illuminating Lilah's face with golden light. I could stare at her forever like this. The small curve of her nose. The way her plump lips are slightly parted as she breathes deeply with sleep. The silhouette of her body under the sheets, her back exposed, with her phoenix tattoo in full view. What is she doing here with me? Last night was more than I ever thought it could be, more than what I thought she would want from me. Yet here she is, in my bed.

We were entwined in each other all night, breathing and moving as one. I've had plenty of experiences with other women when I was younger, and of course in my five-year long marriage up until that final year. Last night though, was electrifying. I don't know how long I've been staring for when her eyelids flutter open, looking directly at me.

"Good morning, beautiful." I reach over to tuck a lock of her chestnut-colored hair behind her ear.

"Good morning," she replies with a sleepy smile, turning over on her back to stretch as she yawns.

"Can I get you some coffee?"

"Yes please," Lilah responds as she rubs above her eyes with her thumb and forefinger, hopefully she's not too hungover. We both only had a few glasses of wine each. But before I let myself think we drank too much and that is the only reason why we had sex last night, I get up to grab her some coffee. Throwing on a pair of loose black sweatpants as I stand, I make my way the short distance to the kitchen.

"We may have a problem..." I say as I notice the few grounds of coffee left in the canister.

I meant to restock yesterday when I went to the market but must have gotten distracted with getting supplies for dinner. I look over at Lilah, lying on her side and resting her head on her hand. Looking at me with raised eyebrows and a concerned, yet amused look in her eyes.

"Get dressed, looks like we are going out for coffee," I say as I discard the empty tin into the trash. She chuckles as she removes the sheets from her bare body, making my brain empty of all other thoughts, except a replay of last night. Almost as if she is inside my mind, she smirks and then throws my t-shirt at me that was on the floor next to the bed.

"This is no laughing matter, caffeine is a necessity," I say with complete seriousness, throwing on the shirt that just hit me in the face.

"*Ohh*, I see. You're Mr. Grumpy in the mornings huh?" she replies mockingly, laying bare naked in front of me.

I glare at her as I respond, "Well I see it one of two ways, either you get dressed so you don't freeze outside, or I throw you over my shoulder. Just. Like. That." Nodding my head in the direction of her delicious naked body. She matches my glare, sticking her tongue out as she moves to find her discarded clothes on the floor from last night.

We definitely left the loft in shambles. I spot her lacey bra which I nearly ripped from her body discarded on the kitchen island. Her boots lay where she took them off after dinner. Her pants thrown over the couch. I go to grab them when I notice something looks a little wonky. The back leg completely knocked off the base of the old leather sofa. It is in fact very much broken. I laugh as I grab Lilah's pants, turning to find her right behind me, she found her shirt somewhere and is working on the small buttons.

"What happened?" she asks with amusement.

"Looks like we broke my couch," I say as I hand her the leather pants in my hand.

She reaches for them, responding with a laugh. "Just the sign of a good night, I'll help you find a better one," she adds as she slides into her pants, buttoning them, "You ready?"

How does she look so damn good this early in the morning? Especially after last night.

The wind is slightly brisk off the water today. We decided to venture down to the area of the city called *The Flats*. There is a West and an East bank on either side of the river flowing into Lake Erie. The latter is a short walk down from where my loft is located. Filled with restaurants and bars on one side and the river on the other. We haven't had any more snow since the other night, but an almost grey haze taunts us in the sky. Walking along the rail of the walkway you almost see the steel colored reflection on the water. We headed this way after grabbing some much needed caffeine and bagels from the coffee shop in my building so we could have a little longer to talk before we go on with our mundane days.

I wonder when she has to return to work, it being a Tuesday morning at eight thirty. I texted my brother and the rest of the crew at *Stone Construction* to let them know I would be in a little later this morning. My brother responded by asking if I was with the girl from the other night. I didn't respond, which brought on the rest of the crew blowing up my phone asking who he was talking about. I decide to turn it off.

"Your girlfriend blowing up your phone?" Lilah asks nonchalantly as she looks sidelong at me.

"You're funny, it's the guys I work with hounding me."

"Mhmm, sure." She smiles playfully as she takes a sip of her coffee.

I take a drink from mine too, the warmth a welcome friend against the cold November air, December being a little over a week away. Heading into my least favorite time of the year. It's been colder this month than I remember. Maybe because last year I was in the sunshine of the southern part of California, or maybe because the weather is taunting me.

I realize I've been lost in my own thoughts. I look at Lilah and say, "You know, you very well could be hiding a boyfriend from me. Or maybe a whole other family, you *are* very mysterious." I add with a side smile and wink, hoping she doesn't think I'm being too serious.

"I don't have the time to juggle multiple lives," she says, considering, "and I'm not *that* mysterious."

"Oh, you are very elusive Lilah, you're like a puzzle I can't figure out. You're confident and so sure of yourself, yet I hardly know anything about you."

"Well, ask away," she replies.

I consider asking her the numerous questions in my head, even though she responded to a few of them previously. Her answers are always simple or vague, I want to know more about her. I want to know everything about this magnificent woman, but I don't want to scare her or pry too deeply. I know I hate it when people poke too hard into my life.

"I'm a patient man, I can wait to figure you out. Besides, I want as much time as I am able to get with you. My luck is I would figure out the riddle you're made of and then you would disappear, I'd rather keep the mystery, at least for a little longer."

"That's why I like you, Landon. You get me," Lilah replies with a slight tilt of her head, looking at me as if she truly believes I understand exactly how she feels.

We've been walking for a while, making our way around the bend near the railing against the water. Listening to the wind and distant sound of freighter ships out on the lake. She goes to sit down on one of the steps on the opposite side of the walkway.

"Let's play a game," she says as I follow her.

Raising an eyebrow, I respond, "Uhh, sure. Should I be scared?"

She laughs. "No silly, it's a question-and-answer game. I ask you something and you have to answer as honestly as you can. Then *you* ask me a question. Let's keep it to two questions each though."

"So, I should be scared," I say with a laugh but then add, "You go first."

Who knows what this woman is going to ask me. I hope she doesn't go too hard on me.

Lilah pauses for a second, to think of what to ask. "When you were a child, what did you want to be when you grew up?" she asks as she raises her chin slightly, putting her thumb and forefinger against it like she's truly pondering the answer I'm about to give.

I let out a small sigh, slightly relieved she didn't ask a deep question. "That's an easy one. I always wanted to be a firefighter growing up. Not sure why I never went for it though, I guess it just wasn't the path I was supposed to be on."

"You'd be a sexy firefighter," she responds with a suggestive smirk, "Okay, you're turn to ask me a question."

Wanting to keep mine equally as playful, I ponder before I ask, "What is your favorite color?"

"Oh, that's a tough one," she squints her eyes, looking off towards the water as if I asked the most serious question she has ever heard before she answers with a nod, "Red. It's definitely red."

I laugh and shake my head as she adds, "Ooh yay my turn again!" She bites her bottom lip as she considers what to ask me next.

"How come you don't talk to the rest of your family anymore?"

Ouch. She went right for the jugular. I agreed to this game though, I would be honest with her this time. Maybe I won't give all of the details, just an overview of all the bullshit regarding my family recently. But as I look in her eyes, I feel safe enough to answer fully.

"It's kind of a long story, but I will give you the main points." I let out a long sigh as I continue, "Honestly, it's mostly centered around my ex. My mother is also bat-shit crazy which doesn't help. My ex, Rachel, always liked to start issues with my family. They ended up hating her, until we got divorced. Somehow, she clawed her way in after, convincing them of lies about me. She said I cheated on her, that I was abusive and narcissistic. All traits I would like to think are the opposite of who I am."

I glance over to make sure I haven't scared Lilah yet, but find her looking at me, waiting for me to go on.

"A week or two before Christmas I came home from work and I found her with our neighbor. She tried to turn it around on me, saying I didn't love her and she could tell I was cheating so she went ahead and tried to find *"her own happiness"* or something. About a month later we filed for divorce. The next thing I knew my mother was calling me and shouting at me about how bad of a person I am and how I didn't deserve a nice girl like Rachel."

I shake my head, reliving those moments as I go on, "It's crazy, literally the month before, at Thanksgiving, my mother was trying to convince *me* to leave the marriage, saying I could come home and live with her and my dad. My ex must have been pretty convincing though because everyone in my family except for my brother Jack wrote me off."

I'm lost in my own story when I hear Lilah ask, "How come Jack didn't go with what they were all saying?"

I think for a second, honestly not fully sure as me and my brother never dove super deep into this conversation. "Maybe because he knew me better than the rest of them did. He also knows how crazy my mother can be."

She studies me for a second, "What about your dad?"

I sigh. Thinking about my father, a truly selfless person who always put my mother's wants above his. "Unfortunately, he is wrapped around my mother's finger. He never let on that he believed what they were all saying was true, but he also never stood up for me."

Realizing this story doesn't paint me in the best light I add, "I know this is a lot, and I'm sure it probably makes you think differently about me, but I want you to know I never cheated on my ex. I was never abusive in any way, I truly did love her during our marriage. I don't know what I did wrong to make her and my family turn on me so drastically."

She blinks at me with those steel blue eyes. "I believe you," she replies with a nod. "Sometimes shitty people are just what they show to be. *Shitty*. They do things to hurt other people and don't have to face any repercussions while good people get the short end of the stick. Just because she said you did terrible things, as long as you know your truth that's all that matters, and if it helps, I believe you didn't do those things either."

"I appreciate that," I say, a little taken aback but relieved.

"You get one more question," Lilah says with a smile not quite meeting her eyes.

I completely forgot we were playing this little question game of hers, lost in my own mind. "Oh, right, I almost forgot. Hmm, let me think."

I debate going for a more serious question but I want to change the tone of the conversation. Keeping it light, I ask, "I got it. If you could be anywhere in the world at this moment besides here, where would you go?"

"Ah, but there are so many places though, hmm I guess I would probably want to go somewhere I've never been before." She pauses for a second, "Colorado! I've always wanted to go to the Rocky Mountains," she says excitedly.

I blink for a second, not missing the humor. Considering those mountains are exactly where I went on my solo hiking trip when I was eighteen, a little over a decade ago.

"I love Colorado, the mountains tattooed on my hand are inspired from there. It's beautiful," I reply, holding out my left hand to show her the tattoo again. Though I am certain she remembers the ink there since I had the same hand all over her body last night.

Before I'm able to start fully daydreaming about her body on top and underneath mine less than twenty-four hours ago, Lilah's phone starts ringing.

She answers hastily and with slight annoyance, "Hi Nancy."

"What do you mean? Didn't he tell you I was busy?" she replies to the woman on the phone, "Okay fine I'll be right there."

"I am so sorry Landon, but I have to go," she says as she hangs up.

We stand up from the step we were sitting on and make our way towards the road. "That's okay, I understand. I should probably get to work here soon too." I say, trying not to sound too sad.

She must have ordered a car while we were walking back. She goes to open up the door of a black SUV in front of us. I move to open the handle around her before she gets to it.

"Such a gentleman," she says with a smile and an eye roll.

I hope I don't sound too desperate when I ask, "When can I see you again?"

"This weekend?" she asks in response.

"Sounds perfect. I'll call you later," I say as I lean in to grab her hip, pulling Lilah into me and kissing her goodbye.

"Bye Landon," Lilah says with that beautiful smile of hers as she hops in the car and I shut the door. I watch her drive away, wishing it was the weekend already.

Heading back up towards my apartment to change for work, not aware of what time it is. Last I looked it was close to nine but then I shut my phone off. I turn it back on as I make my way up the hill.

Every moment with Lilah leaves me wanting more. I want more of her lips on mine, more of her body tangled in mine, more of her life and what makes her, *her*. I'm almost back up the long hill to the coffee shop entrance of my building when my phone starts going crazy. It's ten o'clock, we had been talking for a while then.

I glance at the notifications continuously coming through since my phone was off. *Holy shit.* Ten missed calls. One from my brother, then a text from him asking if I was alright. One from an unknown number, and five from my ex. I'm thrown off by the amount of calls from Rachel but it's the other three unsettling me more.

All of them from my mother.

Chapter Six

Restless

The dim lights of the hallway are flickering. Giving me a headache as I sit here on this scratchy out-dated chair. I have always hated hospitals. "Want some?" Jack asks me as he reaches out to hand me a small styrofoam cup of some shitty hospital coffee.

"Thanks. Casie or Dad, tell you anything?" I ask in regards to my younger sibling and father, grabbing the warm cup from his outstretched hand.

My younger sister hasn't said a word to me since my divorce. We rarely communicated much before anyways. My mother isn't any better, only speaking to me when she gets in a mood to call and tell me I should get back together with Rachel. It hurts the most not getting to speak to my father as much. He doesn't have a phone which means the only opportunities I have are at get-togethers, all of which I haven't been to since last year.

"They're being ridiculous. Casie is saying mom had a heart attack while dad is trying to comfort her. I spoke with the doctor though. Mom is completely fine. He said she must have had a panic attack because her vitals and EKG are perfect. Are you going to try and see her?" Jack asks as he takes a sip of his coffee.

I contemplate. Already frustrated about being here. The voicemail from my mother worried me enough I immediately drove to the hospital she usually frequents when she's having an episode. Despite our complicated relationship. Casie flipped out as soon as I arrived, Jack had to hold her back because she threatened to spit in my face.

I am not sure why my sister hates me so much. Sure we've never been super close but Casie chose to side with Rachel after the divorce, despite not liking each other to begin with. One day maybe she will be decent enough to explain why, today was clearly not that day. My father, on the other hand, gave me a hug when he saw me and said he was glad I came. I've been sitting here in the waiting room since, even as they all went back to check on my mom.

The initial call she left definitely took me aback, but she's done this kind of thing before. Cried wolf. Even before the fall out with my family. My mother would find any way to make the day, night, family gathering, you name it about her.

I learned from a young age, life is her show and we are side characters here to fulfill whatever storyline she wants. Therefore I never tried to push her, never argued for the fear of being snapped at or being shunned. Because when you disagree with my mother, she treats you like the devil until you tell her you are sorry and beg for forgiveness. Unfortunately, my sister has followed in our mother's footsteps. Hence why she is hysterical even after the doctor said there is genuinely nothing wrong with our mother physically, implying she might need some help in other departments. Debating on if I should just leave rather than allow her to seep into my head. Though part of me continues to crave a healthy relationship with her.

"I guess I will check if she wants to see me," I reply to Jack as I get up to leave this depressing beige waiting room.

I start towards the blue swinging doors leading to the hospital rooms and chuck my empty coffee cup into the trash. As soon as I pass through the threshold I face a death stare from my sister down the hallway, in front of the room I assume my mother is in. Before I start walking in her direction, I get stopped by a doctor.

I instantly remember him, Dr. Alex. I was never sure if Alex was his first or last name. He looks to be in his early to mid-forties. Dark hair slightly greying, small rimmed glasses and a friendly composure. He has always been good to us anytime we've had to make a trip here.

"Hi Landon, how are you doing?" Dr. Alex asks me in his go-to casually, friendly voice.

"Hey Doc. I'm okay, glad to hear my mother is alright," I reply with a small shrug.

"She physically is very healthy, especially for her age." He sighs, "However, I am concerned about the frequency at which she tends to pay us a visit here. I tried to have this discussion with your other family members but they dismissed it. Your mother needs to see someone regarding her constant fake illnesses. These always seem to be a cry for help. I've known your mother and your family for about five years, never actually needing to do anything to help besides confirming she is healthy. Your mother says she has never been to a therapist but I believe one could help her way more than I can," he finishes with another sigh.

"I know, unfortunately though, my whole family hates me at the moment. I doubt anyone will listen to me," I reply.

Dr. Alex seems to consider, glancing down at his clipboard before asking, "Did your mother start another argument? Not trying to overstep but I know when she gets to the point of coming back to the hospital usually it is surrounded by a fight or disagreement of some sort."

"A big one not too long ago over the phone, about my divorce and regarding my ex-wife." Before I go on further, Dr. Alex's eyes widen, a look of concern flashing across his face.

"I'm so sorry, Landon, no one told you, did they?"

Confused, I ask, "Tell me what?"

Dr. Alex lets out a breath before he responds, "Well, it looks like your mother changed her emergency contact with us. No one was at the house when she called 911 so an ambulance came and got her. When they called her emergency contact..." he trails off, looking over my shoulder. I sense someone is walking up behind me as I follow his gaze.

I don't know what is happening as my ex-wife Rachel puts her hand on the back of my shoulder, coming into my view to get in between me and Dr. Alex. She reaches up to pull me into an unwelcome hug.

"Oh Landon! It was so awful! I was out with my friend when I got the call. I immediately jumped on the first flight out. I was so scared Lan.." Rachel says as she feigns a sob into my shoulder, continuing to cling onto me.

"I'm happy mom is okay," she adds.

I start to finally snap back into my brain, reaching up to remove her arms from around my neck.

"Rachel, what are you doing here?" I ask in disbelief.

She looks up to me with her muted hazel eyes. "I told you silly, I got the call your mom was here." Dr. Alex gives me a sympathetic look as his name is called over the intercom, leaving us to tend to another patient.

"Rachel, you live in *California*. There is zero possibility if you received a call this morning about my mother being in the hospital, that you would be here right now," I reply as I try to do the math in my head. Even if she headed to the airport when she got the call, and came straight to the hospital after landing, it's only been two and a half hours since they brought my mother in. There is no possibility.

She looks up at me with the same expression I've learned means she is trying to think of the perfect answer. Her being here at all has me dumbfounded.

"The hospital called me this morning Lan, when they picked up mom. I called your sister and she called everyone else. You sound crazy, baby." She reaches a hand up to touch my arm.

"You're probably all caught up in the scariness of mom being here," she adds with a forced concern and condescending tone as she reaches around my waist to bury her face in my chest.

I reach up again to gently pull her off me. She obliges but then loops her arm through mine, guiding me down the hallway.

"Let's go check on mom," she says as we start to make our way to my mother's room.

We pass my sister and dad in the hall-way, Jack must still be in the waiting area. Neither of them say anything as we make our way through the door of my mother's hospital room. My mother, laying in the off-white colored bed, a monitor attached to her, beeping a healthy rhythm to the beat of her heart, smiles as we walk in.

"Oh I am so happy to see you two together," my mother says as she places a hand over her heart, glancing between me and my ex.

I go to unhook Rachel's arm from mine, "We aren't together mom."

Both of them look upset at my tone. I make my way over to the side of the bed, Rachel starts to follow me. I look at her, trying to keep my tone as neutral as possible and say, "Can I please get a moment alone with my mother?"

"Landon, I would like Rachel to stay," my mother responds, reaching out her hand to grab for Rachel's.

I let out an exasperated sigh, "Mom, please. I just want a moment to talk to you without my ex-wife in the same room."

"Oh Lan, you know I'm part of this family," Rachel responds in that lilting voice of hers.

"No, you aren't. Not anymore," I respond in a forced neutral tone trying to hold back my annoyance.

My mother lets out a dramatic sigh, "Landon! Don't be like that. Rachel is always going to be a part of our family. I wish you would just put aside your mistakes and realize you two are meant to be together," she says pleadingly.

I have had enough of this conversation. I look over to Rachel, she is mirroring the same pleading look my mother has. I reach up to rub above my eyes, the headache steadily forming from when I got to the hospital tempting to turn into a full blown migraine. I close my eyes for a split second.

"See I told you it wouldn't work. He's too stubborn," Rachel says quietly to my mother.

I open my eyes, confused as to what she is implying.

"What wouldn't work?" I ask.

Rachel glances back and forth between my mother and I, her blonde hair falling loose from the clip holding it back. She looks nervous as she bites her bottom lip.

"Landon, don't be mad at sweet Rachel. It was my idea," my mother says to me.

I look over to her, "What the hell are you two talking about?" I don't bother to hide the frustration in my voice.

"Well Lan, I decided to come visit your mother this weekend– and we got to talking.." Rachel starts to respond before I interrupt her.

"What do you mean you were here over the weekend? You told me you flew in this morning?" I ask, even as the pieces are finally making sense and I see this was another ploy put together by these two. I wonder if it was even her friend Lorie who saw me out at *Map Room*, it was probably Rachel keeping tabs on me.

"Well, I didn't want you to be mad Lan, you know your temper gets wild sometimes." Rachel knows she's been caught in a lie but somehow manages to try and put this on me.

I choose to ignore her jab, "So you planned this then? You never thought you were having a heart attack did you?" I ask my mother.

"Well I might as well have! It doesn't mean you and Rachel shouldn't try to work things out..." she replies with a dramatic fake sob.

My memory flashes through all of the other times my mother has pulled a similar stunt. Faking illnesses to gain attention to herself whenever she wanted something. This is by far the worst. Usually she would admit herself to the hospital because my sister had been fighting with me or Jack and she wanted all of us to be forced to get together and work things out. Or because she disagreed with some choice we made. Jack starting his construction company brought on the first of her *"heart issues."* This pushes past the limits of her crazy.

"I am done with this conversation," I say, shaking my head of the toxic recollections and turning to leave the room. Rachel hurriedly gets up from the side of my mother's bed, grabbing my wrist to stop me.

"Lan, please, mom and I both want the same thing. And I know you want us to be together too so let's stop all this. I forgive you, let's forget everything and be together again," Rachel says in a pleading tone.

"Just stop." I respond, pulling my arm away and heading from the room. I ignore my dad and sister as I walk out those blue swinging doors again into the waiting area. Jack spots me from the front door, hanging up his phone. One look and I know he senses some shit happened.

"I'll see you at work," is all I say as I pass him out the doors and into the brisk wind.

The rest of the day has luckily been not as unhinged as the beginning. I got to the job site shortly after leaving the hospital. The downtown high-rise a welcome escape from my crazy life. We have been working on this site for months, finally rounding out to the end stages. There isn't too much to finish here, just some smaller tasks and clean-up. Probably a couple of months and it will be done.

This building felt almost like a second home throughout the end of Summer into Fall. The main bones and structure were already here but one of the wealthier developers in Cleveland wants to completely revamp this place to make more office space and an accessible first level for retailers and restaurants. I mostly arrange for deliveries and the contractors to show up so I don't usually go to all of the work sites. When Jack asked me to come in person to this project though I fell in love with this building as soon as I saw it. I'm going to be a little sad when it's completed, the skyrise is therapeutic to me. The view from the top floor is magnificent. You almost see the whole city. The bustling cars and people coming and going. Lake Erie to the North. It's especially beautiful at night.

I sometimes would come up here by myself in the middle of the night to think and take photographs with my old camera Lilah pointed out at my place, even if I would never let anyone see them. I love capturing the city and the people in it.

I'm completely lost in thought looking out the window of the top floor when Aaron, the lead carpenter walks in.

"Hey Landon! Jack told me you had a peaceful morning," he says, not hiding his sarcasm as he comes behind me and pats me on the back. I turn to glare at him, I swear he only owns plaid shirts. I've seen him in every color but never in a different variation of shirt and always in jeans. His chest length red-brown beard matches his lumberjack wardrobe and his husky build. Aaron has become a good friend though since I started working for my brother. Always ready to try to make anyone laugh, especially when arguments ensued from working all day amongst the crew.

"Ha, funny," I say as I grab my clipboard from the work table next to me amongst the discarded tools and building plans, "Where are we projected to be at today?"

Aaron looks down at the table, leaning on his hands placed on either side of the plan for this floor. "Looks like we are about done up here, leaving us to clear out any tarps and extra parts."

"Perfect, that's exactly what I wanted to hear after the shitty morning I had." I check off this floor as good-to-go on my clipboard. Looking back out the window as Aaron says,

"You seem extra broody today man," he laughs as he rolls up the paper on the table.

I don't look over to him as I respond, "You would be too if your family was bat-shit crazy."

"I would give anything to have a family who was bat-shit crazy," he says with a forced chuckle.

Not fully registering who I complain to, I look over at him, "Man, I'm sorry, you're right. I shouldn't be complaining."

Aaron's story is brutal. He was married and his parents were super supportive of him. They would always come to visit the city even though they lived out in Montana and hated the hustle and bustle of Cleveland. Him and his wife Natalie, had been trying for a baby for a while. Natalie had just found out she was pregnant the morning of the incident. Aaron's parents were in town so she couldn't hold back her excitement and told them. He was at work on a job site, his phone on silent. Natalie and his parents excitedly decided to surprise him with the good news while he was at work. They went out and bought a cake and balloons to bring to the site he was at. While driving to him they got in a tragic car accident on the way. None of them survived.

That all happened years ago, before I knew him, but apparently he hasn't been with anyone since. You wouldn't be able to tell he went through any of it though, from how Aaron carries himself. He is genuinely the most positive and upbeat person I know. He helps to put things into focus sometimes for me, with my family. I wish I could repay his kindness somehow.

"Want to come out for drinks with me and Jack tonight?" I ask him as we finish clearing off the work table.

"Sure, man. Sounds fun. Around seven at Map Room?" he responds as he starts to head down to one of the lower floors having complications with some wiring in the elevator.

"See you then," I reply, taking one last look out the window before I go home to finish some paperwork. Definitely going to miss this view when the building is done.

Looking around at the crowded bar, I'm slightly surprised how packed this place is for a Tuesday night. Usually, workers early in the week come here to drink away their stress with their friends. I guess everyone needs a drink after today, I know I do. My mood lightened up a little when I got a text from Lilah at the gym right after work, saying she missed me already. I haven't had a chance to respond so I pull out my phone while I wait at the bar for my brother and Aaron to get here. I'm always the first to arrive and usually the last to leave. A fact Stacey likes to remind me of every other time I am here. Tonight being no exception.

"Whose text are you smiling like an idiot at?" she asks as she hands me my usual, not bothering to hide her amusement.

"None of your business, that's who," I reply with a glare. Stacey purses her lips and smiles as she walks away to help another customer.

I miss you too, beautiful. How has your day been?

I reply to Lilah's text, right as Aaron pats me on the back, making me spill my drink in my other hand.

"Whoops! Sorry man!" Aaron says with a laugh, grabbing a bar napkin to clean up the mess he caused. Stacey comes over to get his drink order, there is a girl I've never seen before with her. She looks about mid-twenties, long strawberry blonde hair with freckles and deep green eyes.

"Looks like you guys are up to your typical shenanigans of making a mess," Stacey says with a smirk but laughs. "This is Madison, she's a newbie, and my wife's cousin so be nice." She pats Madison on the back, leaving her with us. I spot Jack walking up to our place at the bar.

Aaron elbows me hard in the ribs as I go to open my mouth and introduce us to the new girl.

"Hi Madison, I'm Aaron and this is Landon. If you see him brooding here don't worry, that's his natural state," he says in a mocking tone, gesturing to me.

I glare at him, about to respond when Jack chimes in, "Seriously, you should be worried if you *don't* see him brooding." Madison laughs and goes to get their drinks, her smile lingering on Aaron for a second.

"I'm going to ignore you both," I reply, looking back down at my phone as it chimes. A text coming through from Lilah.

Eh, it hasn't been too bad. I wish I was spending tonight with you though.

I don't bother to hide my smile as I respond,

I definitely wouldn't complain if you were with me, that's for sure. Would it be crazy

to ask you over tonight? Or I could come to your place, not to invite myself over of
course.

Even though we have already slept together, anxious thoughts of feeling too much or overstepping kick in. Luckily she responds quickly.

I wish. Unfortunately I have a super busy work week ahead of me so I probably won't
be too responsive.

Damn, that sucks. I contemplate before I respond, but I know I need to see this girl again soon.

Ah, I completely understand. When can I see you again then?

Her reply takes a little longer this time.

Friday night?

Smiling, I go to respond but I glance up to find Jack and Aaron looking at me with unmasked amusement. I realize I had been lost in texting Lilah and I have no idea how long they have been looking at me.

"What?" I ask, not feigning my annoyance at their mocking stares.

Both huff a laugh as Jack asks what they both want to know, "So who are you texting making you anti-social and grinning like an idiot?"

"I asked him the same thing!" Stacey chimes in excitedly as she grabs a beer for the old man next to us and pops the cap off. Madison is shadowing her but trying to not look too interested in the conversation. I notice she keeps glancing over to Aaron though.

"Since you all keep hounding me. Her name is Lilah okay?" I say, holding my hands up. Deciding to stop hiding her from them, well, at least her name.

Stacey smiles and turns to go help a group of guys who just walked in. Madison stays by us, leaning over the bar, fully interested.

"Is she pretty?" she says with a playful smile.

I can't help but chuckle. "Yes, she is very pretty," I say, remembering every gorgeous angle of her face.

Aaron looks at Madison, mirroring her smile as he says, "I'm sure she has nothing on you though beautiful."

Both Jack and I instantly turn to Aaron, him looking as dumbfounded as we are. Madison smiles nervously and turns around to help Stacey with the new rowdy group of customers.

"Did I say that out loud?" Aaron asks, staring off at Madison, a look of subtle panic flashing across his face.

Jack and I can't help but laugh as we say almost in unison, "Yes, you did."

Aaron puts his head in his hands, me and Jack are cracking up as I shout to Stacey, "I think we need a round of shots over here Stace!"

I finally go back to answering Lilah's texts, getting restless to talk to her, to see her again.

I can't wait.

Chapter Seven

Magical

Friday couldn't come soon enough. The last two days have been agony. Just waiting until I would be able to see her mesmerizing eyes. To taste her mouth on mine. Barely being able to talk to her this week was killing me.

Lilah tried to maintain at least some sort of contact, usually one or two texts a day. I both love and hate caring about someone this much, this fast. I can't remember the last time I felt this way. Sure, in my previous marriage there was a point when I did love my ex, where it felt like a whirlwind of passion. Yet, it was different. I have never felt something to this depth, I'm scared but ready and waiting to feel, to see more.

Work has done little to distract me. I feel like in every floor plan, in every checklist I made. Lilah's name kept appearing, tearing me away from any concentration I could muster. Aaron and Jack even noticed, telling me to get my head out of my ass and focus. To be fair we are only a few months away until our deadline to have this building finished. The main investor, Dean Wolf, is a nice guy but I have a feeling if you don't meet his timeframe he won't let you forget it. The main issue with finishing this project is something electrical Aaron is continuing to try and get fixed. Well, not him directly, he's no electrician.

Aaron had been assigned that floor when we divvied up the different tasks to be done, the electrician was a friend of a friend so he wanted to personally oversee the section. I have no experience in anything electrical so I've let him deal with it. Luckily everything else is flowing smoothly, making this week drag by slowly. Usually there is some project I'm able to tackle for the day, but with everything almost done in my areas of the building I have had way too much time to spend in my own head.

Lilah texted earlier, letting me know she was excited to see me this evening. I had asked Jack and Aaron if they wouldn't mind me stopping by the job site later on. Both of them slightly confused but not questioning why I wanted to come here. Jack is used to me sometimes coming back here at night to take pictures, even if I never show them to him. Therefore when Lilah asked me where we should meet, I knew exactly what my plan was. I needed to stop by the market nearby first, to get some wine and a bottle of whiskey. I brought a change of clothes to keep here. I wouldn't be wearing only a t-shirt and jeans this time. Just one more thing I needed to get ready for tonight.

———

Nine O'clock exactly. Lilah let me know she would be a little late because she got caught up with something at work. I didn't mind at all though, it took me way longer than I anticipated to set everything up. Finally sitting on a bench in the Public Square, people watching and waiting for her. Downtown always attracted the most eclectic crowd of people. The strangest of tonight was an old man dressed in a striped suit jacket dancing through the falling snow. He seemed to be having the time of his life though so who am I to judge. I'd love to feel that kind of joy again, the joy of not caring what other people are thinking of me.

Still focused on the exuberant man, I do a double take when I spot Lilah walking towards me. Breathtaking as usual. Her chestnut brown hair flowing loose around her shoulders. She's wearing a cream colored sweater, the neck bunching up around her face. Her black jeans hovering around her ankles over black boots. I start to walk towards her. Good thing she dressed for the weather, it's been unseasonably cold and snowy lately and today was no exception. Her long tan coat moving with each step she takes towards me, leather gloved hands in her pockets. Even covered in layers of clothes she steals my breath away.

"Hi gorgeous," I say to her as the distance closes between us.

My heart feels like it stopped beating for a second.

"Hi, Landon." She blinks up at me with those stormy eyes as I reach down to gently grab her chin, planting a kiss on her perfect lips. "So where are we going?" she asks as we pull away from each other.

"It's a surprise," I answer back with a wink, grabbing her hand to lead her down the sidewalk.

The building isn't too far from where we are, maybe a couple minutes to walk. The frozen air makes it seem longer. The warmth from Lilah is welcome as she clings to my arm.

"I love the snow but wish the cold didn't seep into my bones," she says with a small laugh, reaching her gloved hand out to catch a falling snowflake. I can't help but smile as she tilts her head up, snow sticking to her eyelashes and cheeks. "Have you ever made a snow angel?" she asks, pulling away from me to walk over to the grass covered in a thin layer of powdery snow.

"I don't think I actually have," I answer back, realizing I honestly never did even as a child.

"What! Why not?" Lilah asks with a concerned tone and face, as if I am insane for never laying in the freezing snow.

I laugh as I respond, walking over to her, "I guess I never saw the fun of purposely making myself almost go into hypothermia."

I'm not given a second to know what is happening as Lilah suddenly pulls me down to the ground. Both of us lay in the snow, her arms starting to swing above her head and then back down to her sides.

"Come on Landon! Don't be a downer," she says as she tosses a bit of snow over at me.

Laughing again and rolling my eyes, I oblige Lilah's antics and start mimicking her movements. Luckily this doesn't go on too long as she seems to get bored of making *snow angels*. Instead, she reverts to drawing something in the snow.

"You having fun there?" I ask, chuckling under my breath at how someone could find this much joy in something incredibly simple yet uncomfortable.

"There," she says as she stands up, brushing the snow off her gloved hands.

I look down to see a giant heart drawn in the snow.

"Well, isn't that adorable." I say, standing up and reaching for her hand. She turns to me and sticks out her tongue like a child, clearly picking up the subtle sarcasm in my voice.

"You need to learn to have more fun, Landon," Lilah adds matter-of-factly as we start our walk again, almost to our destination.

I gently nudge her with my elbow and add teasingly, "Maybe you'll just have to teach me how."

We finally arrive at the door to the job site, my favorite high rise in the city. I figured since this job will be finished soon I might as well show her the view. A look of confusion crosses her face as I unlock the door and lead her into the dark building. After glancing around for a second she asks unsurprisingly, "So, is this where you plan to murder me?"

I laugh and grab her hand to lead her to the stairs, the elevator not fully operating due to whatever wiring issue they were having a couple floors up.

"We have to walk up a decent amount unfortunately but I promise it will be worth it," I tell Lilah as we start our journey up the fifty flights of stairs.

"You're lucky I didn't wear uncomfortable shoes," she says as she laughs and heads up the first set of steps.

———

The majority of the assent wasn't terrible. I let Lilah walk in front of me for a bit until she realized why. Playfully slapping my arm and telling me not to be a pig and to stop staring at her ass, making the rest of the walk up not as bearable as I took the lead. It's worth it though to see her reaction when we finally reach the top floor. My favorite floor.

I came back after the crew had all left, before meeting her down in the square, and set up what looked to be hundreds of twinkle lights. Luckily there is no wiring issue on this level. There weren't too many places to attach them to. Some were strewn about over a few fixtures along with some work tables. I filled the extra space with thick blankets and big pillows. A small tray lay in the center of one of the blankets closest to the window. Lilah is silent as we make our way over but I see she is happy by the look in her eyes.

"When did you do all of this?" she asks, waving her hand around gesturing to the room.

"Eh, earlier today. I wanted to show you my favorite view in the city," I hold back being corny and saying it is my second favorite view, knowing Lilah would only roll her eyes.

She walks over to the window, looking out towards the city. With the early night sky the lights in the buildings around us are visible, adding to the small bulbs inside this room.

"This is amazing," Lilah says as she takes in the view.

"I know, I'm lucky to be able to see this when I'm at work. I'm going to be sad when I can't come up here all the time when we are finished with this project," I reply, looking out the window next to her.

"No, I mean all of this," she says as she gestures around again. "I've never had someone put this much effort into a date before."

"Oh it was nothing," I shrug, turning around to grab the bottle of wine and bottle of whiskey I set out on the tray with two glasses. Lilah turns and puts a hand on my arm, grabbing my attention.

"Don't do that," she says, looking up at me.

"Do what?" I ask, confused.

She drops her hand and takes off her coat and gloves. "Don't sell yourself short. I've only known you for a short while and don't know everything about you but from what I see you are a genuine person with one of the kindest hearts. You don't deserve anyone making you feel less than, especially not yourself," she says as she stands up on her toes to plant a small kiss on my cheek before she plops down onto one of the big pillows by our feet.

"Wine or whiskey?" I ask her as I hold out both bottles. Changing the subject because I'm not sure how to accept what she just said.

She taps her pointer finger to her pursed lips, deciding on which one she was feeling this evening.

"I'm thinking whiskey tonight," she responds with a short nod.

A girl after my own heart. I go to sit down, handing Lilah her glass, filled a third of the way with amber colored liquor. She is the most beautiful creature I have ever seen, lost in my thoughts I don't even realize she is staring directly at me. I look down, nervously sipping from my drink.

"Penny for your thoughts?" Lilah asks me with a tilt of her head, chestnut locks falling in front of her shoulder as she blinks at me with a mischievous smile.

"If I tell you what I was thinking you'll just roll your eyes at me."

"Try me," she replies.

I take another swig of my whiskey, swallowing hard before I respond, "Honestly, I was thinking it's crazy that a woman as beautiful and mysterious as you would want anything to do with me."

She seems to consider, narrowing her eyes in a subtle glare as she says, "You are possibly one of the sexiest and craziest men I have ever met. Don't you see how great you are, Landon? Sure, you have your faults, like anyone. But you don't give yourself nearly enough credit."

Before I say anything in response, Lilah moves to sit right next to me, our thighs touching. Putting her hand on my cheek, she gently moves her thumb along the hairs of my beard. The intimacy of this moment feels deeper than sex.

"Landon, you *are* worth it. It's time to start treating yourself that way too," she says as she lifts up to kiss me gently on my lips.

We sit there for a moment suspended in time, taking in the view of the city while we work on finishing the liquor in our glasses.

"Question for a question?" Lilah asks suddenly, an adorable smile on her face.

I chuckle and say sure, hoping she doesn't ask anything I don't feel ready to talk about.

"What is your biggest regret so far in life?" she asks.

"Hmm, well that's a deep one. Where do you have these saved in your head huh?" I ask jokingly, thinking about my answer. I'm surprised how quickly it comes to me, "My biggest regret is probably not trying to follow or even think about what I want to do with my life, instead I focused solely on those around me."

"It's not too late to change," Lilah says in response.

Before I deep dive into a pit of regret for not putting myself first at least once in my life I jump right into my question, wanting, needing to know more about this woman.

"When was your last serious relationship?"

Lilah glances away, lifting her glass up to her lips to take a sip. "It's been a little while, didn't end great. We fought a lot. He was selfish and cheated on me." She finishes her drink.

"Who in the world would cheat on you, he must have been certifiably insane." I genuinely can't believe someone would let this woman go, or hurt her.

"I could say the same to you Landon."

To get us out of this heavier mood, I grab the bottle of whiskey refilling both of our glasses. Looking over at Lilah with the glow from the lights on her face, I can't help it, I need to capture this moment. Something pulls me towards my bag I left off to the side, I take my camera out, removing the lens cap. Luckily Lilah is lost in thought staring out the window, allowing me to get a candid shot.

Lilah hears the click of the lens and looks over. "Don't you know it's rude to take pictures of someone when they aren't paying attention," she says, glaring at me as she sticks her tongue out.

I laugh, "Well, when someone is as beautiful as you, it would be a crime not to capture it." I snap another of her rolling her eyes.

"Well aren't you smooth," she says with subtle sarcasm.

I'm about to put my camera away when Lilah suddenly stands up next to me.

"Well if you're going to take pictures of me, I at least deserve to see them."

Before I pull away, she snatches the camera out of my hands, turning around to block me from retrieving it back from her. I stand and go to wrap my hands around her waist, picking her up and spinning around to throw her off balance. I'm too late though, she'd already clicked through at least the last seven photos I have taken. The one she landed on, a night shot of downtown before the cold and snow.

"Landon these are amazing, why don't you let anyone see them?" Lilah says wide eyed. "You told me this was just a small hobby. You have real talent."

This was the first time anyone has seen my pictures, I'm not sure how to react. I grab my drink and finish it. Lilah sets down the camera and grabs the empty glass from my hand, staring at me with her piercing steel blue eyes.

"Stop ignoring your strengths Landon, you deserve better than being hard on yourself all the time."

I reach down to grasp the back of Lilah's neck, pulling her closer to me as I bend down to kiss her. Not as gently as she kissed me earlier, no, this time I put every ounce of passion into those perfect lips. Losing myself in the ecstasy of our tongues melding together.

My other hand at her waist, she leans into the kiss, arching her back. I pull her as close to me as possible, reaching down to grab both of her thighs while lifting her up to straddle me as we stand there absorbed in each other.

I start moving towards the window, leaning Lilah's back against the cold glass pane, gently letting her legs plant firmly on the ground before I start moving south. Kissing down her perfect neck, I lift up the edges of her sweater to reveal her lacy covered breasts. My hands are all over her, worshipping her body as I end up on my knees. Unbuttoning her pants, revealing her matching thong, I reach around to grab her ass. Kissing and teasing her as I remove the small piece of black lace.

I let my tongue guide me through every angle of this magnificently delicious woman. Moving up each of her thighs until I find her sweet center. Letting out a soft moan she runs her hands through my hair. I grab her left leg and lift it up to rest on my shoulder, allowing me more access. She starts to shake, on the edge of release. I tease her with slow strokes of my tongue until I lift my hand to feel her, allowing one and then two fingers to venture inside. She cries out with pleasure as I speed up my tongue to match the rhythm of my thrusting fingers, her climax sounding through the air with her cries.

I stand back up, removing my shirt. Our mouths find each other again. I let her taste herself as she fumbles with my belt. Lifting her hands above her head to rest on the glass, I use my other to remove both my pants and belt while never breaking from her. I turn her around to look out at the city, hands placed on either side of her head while I find my way to her entrance. I don't waste my time with teasing anymore as I slide myself inside, meeting her wetness with lust filled thrusts.

I want to. No, I need to see her face. We migrate to the spread of blankets and pillows on the ground, pinning her down below me. Her hands are above her head as I make my way back into her, starting gently but picking up with a fervor like this relationship. Heavy with passion, blazing fast and quick. We are swallowed up with the smoke as we find our climax at the same moment, setting my mind and body on fire.

"How can I be falling so hard for someone I just met?" I half say to myself and to her as we lay there surrounded by lights and the city. A magical feeling in the air.

Chapter Eight

Imagine

"*L*andon? What the hell are you doing here?"

I open my eyes halfway, heavy with sleep to see my brother standing over my feet, nudging me with his boot. I turn to crack my neck, the effects of sleeping on the floor hitting in full force. The sun is shining brightly through the top floor windows of the high-rise. I have no idea what time it is but I do know I lie fully naked under these blankets and Lilah is nowhere to be seen.

"Hey bro, uh sorry," I half chuckle as I glance around for my clothes.

"So were you here alone all night or was there a good reason you set up lights and blankets all over our worksite?" Jack says with slight annoyance but amusement slips through.

I find my underwear and pants, holding them up to Jack to give him time to look away as I stand up to clothe myself, wondering when Lilah disappeared. After buttoning my pants I throw on my shirt and search for my phone.

"So? You going to tell me anything else about this girl? She must mean something to risk being fully fucking nude at work. I haven't seen you put this much effort in or look this flustered since Rachel," Jack says as he glances around at the setting of our date last night.

I contemplate telling him anything at all, wanting to keep her to myself. Not wanting anyone or anything to ruin us.

"I told you her name is Lilah," I remind him with sarcasm lacing each word, knowing he will ask for more.

"Yeah, I remember. Anything else?"

"Okay fine, she is 29. Gorgeous. Lives in Ohio City, recently moved back here too. She is an editor for an independent magazine," I say as if listing off the menu selections at a restaurant, nervous to give this information for some reason. Even if it's to my brother, knowing he only ever has the best intentions when it comes to me.

He looks at me, slightly nodding his head as he replies, "See? That wasn't so hard, was it?"

I'm fully dressed, feeling my jacket pockets for my phone to text Lilah.

"Well at least it looks like you had some fun last night huh?" Jack says as he hands me my phone from the table next to him. Great. The battery is dead.

I try to hide my half smile as I look around at the string lights lit up from last night.

"Wait, why are you here on a Saturday morning? I thought as the boss you said you would never work on the weekends," I say, turning the conversation back to my brother before he asks me for more details about Lilah.

"Well when one of our security guys calls me early in the morning because there's some *strange lights* coming from the building no one is supposed to be in, and Aaron is busy with something. Then my brother didn't answer his phone, I had to come check." He laughs, all annoyance gone since he knows the building is fine.

"I did ask you and Aaron if you minded whether I came here last night," I reply as I start to unplug the lights I set up and fold the blankets on the floor.

"Yeah, well I thought you were going to just take some pictures with that camera of yours you always try to hide away when you think no one is looking, not go full on romance mode and turn this place into the night sky." Jack laughs again, helping me fold the biggest blanket.

"My bad," I say as we finish gathering everything and start to head out down the stairs.

"Where is your girl anyways?" Jack asks curiously.

I go to look at my phone, thinking she might have texted or called. Right, the battery is dead.

"I'm actually not sure, I'm sure she had to run out for work or something," I say, although I thought I remember her saying she doesn't usually work Saturdays.

The brisk cold hasn't let up since last night even though the snow stopped. Leaving the downtown square blanketed in a thick layer. The sidewalks covered in a sheen of ice. Jack had to head back home. Making the walk to my loft quiet as I watch people try to navigate through the cold. A little girl is trying to ice skate in her tennis shoes on one of the large patches of ice on the sidewalk opposite me. Resulting in her mother grabbing her arm to keep her from falling on her face. The little girl isn't fazed at all, her curly ringlets bouncing as she starts to skip off. Oh to be a child again and not care about getting hurt.

I've been trying not to let anxiety bubble up in me. There is no reason I should feel nervous about why Lilah disappeared. Yet I have this feeling in my stomach, reminding me of a time not too long ago when I caught Rachel cheating. Not that I thought for a second Lilah would do such a thing. It's just been hard to fully trust anyone after the incident since I never thought Rachel would have stooped so low either.

I'm completely lost in my own thoughts, walking on auto-pilot as I make my way into my building. I stop in the cafe to get a much needed coffee, I keep meaning to pick up more from the store ever since Lilah stayed over. Grabbing my keys out of my pocket I go to unlock my door. That's odd, it already is. Maybe in my rush last night to get everything set up I forgot to lock up. As I step inside and hang up my coat on the rack behind the door. I sense someone else is here.

"Hi Lan."

Turning around I don't try to hide the surprise and annoyance on my face at Rachel sitting casually on the chair next to the still broken couch.

"Rachel, what are you doing here? And more importantly, how the hell did you get into my apartment?"

She shifts in her seat, grabbing for a mug of coffee next to her on the side table. Taking a sip before she answers.

"Oh don't be so dramatic Lan, mom had an extra key she got from Jack. She lent it to me because I wanted to check on you. I don't like how our last conversation went." She starts to get up to walk towards me, I head the opposite direction into the kitchen. Eyeing a new canister of coffee on the counter. Rachel follows me.

"I hope you don't mind, I saw you were out so I went down to that shitty market downstairs and got you some more," she says as she takes a seat at the kitchen island. "And also what the hell happened to your couch?" she adds, pointing to the destruction of the old leather sofa.

I rub the back of my neck, stiff from sleeping on the floor. As much as I can't believe Rachel is in my apartment, or the fact my brother gave my mother a spare key. At least she got me more coffee. I need it to get through this conversation. Discarding the empty paper cup from the cafe I pour myself a fresh one from the pot on the counter. Plugging my phone in after I take a big gulp.

"You couldn't just call me? You didn't have to break in," I say after I finish half of my cup, going to top it off with what is left in the pot.

"Well you never answer my calls for one thing and I did try to call you earlier this morning but it went straight to voicemail," she says as she reaches her manicured hands over to me, "Are you okay Lan?"

I look down at her hand on my forearm, it's always hard for me to trust if she is being genuine. There is usually some agenda when it comes to Rachel, always something she wants and she doesn't care who she hurts to get it. Deep down I don't think she is an awful person. I wouldn't have married her if I thought she was, but where the beginning of our relationship was full of fun and support and love. Over time it twisted into something malicious. She started controlling what I did, questioned where I went or who I was talking to constantly. I initially thought it was just insecurity fueling her rampant moments where she would snap and scream at me. I realized too late though it was her projecting onto me, what she was doing behind my back.

Not wanting to go back there and relive it, I pull my arm away, taking another sip of coffee.

"I'm fine Rachel, thanks for getting me coffee. You didn't need to come out here though, I'm okay," I say, trying to keep my tone neutral since she is actually being civil.

She goes to get up from her stool, grabbing the mug out of my hand and setting it down on the counter, taking both of my hands.

"You know I care about you, right?" she says as she looks up at me with her hazel eyes.

I sigh. "I know you do Rachel, to a small extent you do at least."

"Do you still love me?" she asks as she reaches around my body, pulling me into a hug, her head at my chest.

I'm tired of fighting with her, I would like to avoid any screaming today or her convincing me I'm the crazy one. "Some part of me will always care about you and wish you the best. But I know we aren't meant for each other and I don't think you actually think we are either."

She looks up at me, "Oh Lan, don't say that. I love you, and I know deep down you want me, and want us to be back together. You just need some time."

I'm about to pull her off of me, but luckily, she moves away first. Turning towards the living room and heading to the bathroom. She makes me feel insane. Does some part of me wish everything worked out between us? Yes, of course. I wish I didn't catch her with another man dick deep inside of her. Of course, I wish we hadn't spent months with her not trusting me and constantly yelling at me and controlling my every move. But that isn't the reality we are in. I can't look at her without replaying all of those awful moments. Lost in my thoughts I barely hear the chime of my phone, a text coming through.

Hi! I am so sorry, something came up and I had to leave super early this morning. I tried calling but your phone went straight to voicemail.

I'm relieved, I was starting to think I wouldn't hear from Lilah again for some reason. I start to reply when Rachel walks into the kitchen, staring at me. Her eyes flash with a look I learned to have slight fear of.

"I thought your phone was dead." The viper tone I know all too well is back as she crosses her arms and glares at me. "Who are you texting? And don't tell me it's Jack, you wouldn't be smiling like an idiot if it was just your brother."

I know better than to tell her I am seeing someone, "I'm texting a friend, and yes my phone was dead. You saw me plug it in to charge. You also have no place to dictate who I text. We aren't together, Rachel."

"Well, you tell me enough we aren't. Do you think I'm an idiot!? I'm not going to wait around for you to come to your senses forever Landon. I'm heading back to California on Monday. I hope to see you again before I leave. Maybe you will realize you are the only one fighting this. You know you'll never love someone like you love me." She turns to go into the living room, grabbing her bag and coat off the half tilted couch.

"Rachel," I say as I walk into the living room, looking towards the door at her, "Can I have that spare key please?"

She forces a quiet laugh, "Sure Lan. If you think it's the only copy I have you might actually not be as intelligent as I thought you were."

Rachel slaps the key down onto the entry table, slamming the door as she walks out of the loft.

The gym is packed for a Saturday this close to dinner time. People around me sweating out their own demons. I've been here for almost two hours, my head reeling from Rachel's unwelcome visit. Texting Lilah helped some but I can't get the words my ex said to leave my head. She has a way of making me feel like I am genuinely going insane, she's mastered it at this point. Flashes replay in my head of waking up to find her going through my phone, where there was nothing to find. To her locking me out of my laptop because she couldn't guess my password, ironic considering it was our wedding date. To her screaming at me when I tried to take a day off work to go to the beach with her. She would always tell me I was being suspicious, making her not trust me. I realize in hindsight how much she was projecting, and hiding in return.

Needing to get these thoughts out of my head I changed and immediately came straight here when she left to lift some weights, hoping to rid my head of memories.

Lilah had a work issue she had to go in to take care of this morning, and is going to be stuck there almost the whole day. I wish I could breathe her in, to rid my mind of this morning.

I decided to shower at the gym, wanting to wash away all of today before I went home. Hoping Rachel's perfume of toxic smelling roses isn't lingering in the air. I start to walk towards my loft, passing *Map Room* on the way. I'm almost down the street when I turn around, deciding I deserve one drink today for not fully snapping on my ex.

The bar is slammed, being the evening on the weekend I'm not surprised at all, even for six o'clock. Luckily I manage to find a seat on one of the old wooden stools at my usual spot. Stacey isn't here for some reason but Madison, the new bartender is. I'm half tempted to text Aaron and tell him to come out because I know he has a thing for the strawberry blonde, but I remember Jack mentioned he is out of town this weekend.

"Hi Landon! Good to see you again, are you by yourself tonight?" Madison asks, looking around excitedly, until she realizes who she is looking for isn't here with me.

"Hi Madison, yep just little old me. I'll take a Jameson on the rocks when you get a sec."

She turns to go pour my drink, bouncing with energy. I somehow know she is one of those people who brightens up any room. I make a mental note to try and nudge Aaron towards her. He deserves happiness in his life. I don't think Madison would argue too much about it either, not for how much she kept staring at him the other night. I feel my phone go off in my jacket pocket.

Ugh finally done with work! I miss you. How has your day been? Hopefully better than mine.

I hesitate for a minute before texting Lilah back, not wanting to go into the details of my ex's visit yet, especially not through text.

Eh, my day wasn't amazing either. Better though now that I am talking to you. I would call you but I am out at the bar.

I take a sip of my drink, her response coming in quickly.

Uh oh, out drinking huh? Your day must have been just as bad as mine then.

I let out a small laugh, realizing my day was probably worse. I need to get over it though, I'm sure there are crazier people than my ex-wife.

Ha ha possibly, but it would definitely be better if I could see you again. Any chance you want to come out for a drink?

Another text comes through.

I can't tonight unfortunately but I do need a break from work and desperately need a vacation. Any recommendations?

I think for a few minutes, realizing I too would love a vacation away from the drama of my ex and mother. Starting to imagine where I would go. I have a potentially crazy idea. Before I think too much, I respond,

How do the mountains sound?

Chapter Nine

Mountains

We decided to go the following Thursday evening. Having only seen each other once since our date at my job-site. Work has been crazy this week resulting in me getting back later than usual, around seven. Packed my shit into my scuffed leather duffle bag. Lilah came over with her surprisingly minimal luggage and then we hopped in my car to start our journey. Lilah isn't able to fly unfortunately, otherwise we would already be in Colorado. She has bad flying anxiety and also no driver's license, which explains why she always orders a car. I'll have to ask her more about that sometime soon but I am completely exhausted.

We had initially planned to stop at a motel along the way but stayed up through the night to get into the snowy mountain state as soon as we could.

Lilah is asleep in the passenger seat, her head resting against a small pillow I bought for her at the last gas station we stopped in. I do wish I could have gotten some sleep but I'm too excited to get to our destination. It's almost noon on Friday. I think we will make only one more stop for gas before we make the final two-ish hour trek to

Denver. I managed to find a decent hotel last minute so at least we won't have to worry about getting a place to stay when we arrive.

It's taking everything in me not to roll the windows down and let the cold crisp mountain air in. If Lilah didn't look so cozy next to me I would. Being back here brings back many memories.

Memories of a young boy, who wasn't sure what he wanted in life but filled with hope there was something out there for him. He stood atop that mountain, excited for what was next. First college, changing his major multiple times until he graduated with a generic business degree. Not too long after, he met Rachel. I wonder if he knew then, what I know now. Would he have been so naive and hopeful? Maybe he would have been more cautious in his choices, and chose to stay away from certain people. I can't think like that though, the decisions he made then have got me to where I am. I wouldn't be in this car with this magnificent woman sleeping next to me. Sure, I have no idea what I want to do with my life besides spending every moment I have with Lilah. I would figure it out though, something about her makes me know I will.

"How long have I been out for?" Lilah asks through a long yawn, reaching up to stretch.

Chuckling to myself I glance at the clock, honestly not sure how long I have been lost in my own thoughts, "Only a couple of hours, I think." I say as I grab a red plastic grocery bag from behind my seat and hand it to her. "I ran into the gas station while you were asleep and grabbed some sandwiches if you want one."

"It's beautiful outside," she replies, looking longingly out the window towards the tiny looking snow covered mountains in the distance.

The scenery is definitely breathtaking, but it takes every effort in me to peel my eyes away from Lilah's face, at the wonder in her eyes. I almost miss our exit.

I would be taking pictures if I wasn't driving. I had decided to leave my old camera at home, not wanting it to potentially break on the trip but Lilah insisted we stop somewhere for me to get another one. I have had my eye on a newer model anyways so I didn't argue when we ended up at a shop along the way somewhere in Chicago.

A couple more hours pass listening to the radio and losing ourselves in the view.

"Almost there, beautiful," I say as I click on the turn signal to exit the highway, resting my hand on Lilah's thigh. Trying to keep my thoughts on the road and not her.

The hotel looks a little drabby compared to the pictures online. I was under the impression it was updated fairly recently. From the looks on the outside though this building was older than my loft and lacked much accommodations. I half debate if the pictures online were doctored because there was no way this was the *cozy chalet* described online.

The old creaky door almost closes on us as it shuts behind, sealing us into the dim, stuffy lobby. There are antlers hung up everywhere on the dark red walls and old, slightly creepy portraits of deer. We walk over to the worn looking desk with an even more weathered old man behind it.

"Name for reservation?" says the man, in a deep monotone voice. This place's customer service must also be lacking amongst its need for a deep clean and updated decor.

"Should be under *'Stone'* for two."

"I didn't know your last name was Stone," Lilah says as she looks over at me. I didn't realize I hadn't shared such a minute detail yet. A sudden realization about barely knowing each other hits. Yet at the same time, I feel like I've known her forever. Hopefully this trip will allow us to get to know some of those small details about each other a little more.

We get our key from the man at the desk and head down the long hallway to the last room on the right. I insert the key into the large wooden door, an actual door-key, not one of the new scannable cards. As soon as we step inside, I can't help but look mortified at the gigantic deer head hung right above the bed. Our very small, red velvet comforter covered bed. I look over to Lilah, hoping she doesn't think less of me for booking this place.

"Well, this is... cozy," Lilah says as she turns to look at me. Both of us erupt into a fit of laughter.

I try to reply through breathless laughs, "I promise this place looked much nicer in the pictures when I booked it."

"Mhmm, sure. I knew you were taking me here to murder me. This is the perfect setting." She walks over to the bed, taking a seat and resting back on her hands. "Let me guess, this deer head is going to coincidentally fall on top of me in my sleep while you just happen to get up to go to the bathroom right?"

"Ha ha. Very funny," I set my bag down on the floor, moving to the bed. I stand in front of Lilah, grabbing her hands to push her back on the mattress. Pinning her hands above her as I lean down to kiss those perfect lips.

It takes every effort in me to pull away from her mouth, "So what do you want to do first? Grab some dinner maybe?" I ask, staring down into her blue eyes.

"Hmm, let me think," she seems to consider and then grabs the back of my neck with one hand, pulling me back down to her mouth.

"I think I have a better idea," she adds as she pushes me up, switching places so I lay on the bed as she starts to unbutton my pants.

Chapter Ten

Letting Go

The dawn sunlight beams into our room through the small opening in the curtains, illuminating Lilah's perfect silhouette on the bed. We stayed up late tangled in each other. Only stopping to go to the little diner down the street for some food around ten o'clock last night. I've been awake since five this morning. I never sleep in on trips, I get too excited. I decided to go to a gym down the street and then to a coffee shop nearby to pick up some sustenance for the morning. A couple of bagel sandwiches and four coffees, I would be lying if I said three of them weren't for me.

It's pretty brisk outside today but the fresh air felt amazing on my lungs. It's crazy how being back at a sentimental place adjusts your focus. Lately I have been caught up in the drama of my family and ex-wife that I haven't focused on myself. Sure I have maybe been a little selfish in spending time with Lilah and not letting my brother or friends into our relationship, if we could even consider it a relationship this soon. When we get back to the city though I'm going to make an effort to bring her more into the rest of my life.

I've been lost in my own thoughts staring out the window for who knows how long when I feel Lilah's arms slide around my waist from behind.

"Hi sleepyhead," I say as I turn around to face her, somehow she is so beautiful even first thing in the morning with her tousled hair, untamed with sleep. "I didn't know if you'd wake up until nighttime, you were out cold."

She leans up to kiss me, adding as she pulls away, "It's only seven in the morning ya goof. Are any of these for me?" She asks, grabbing one of the black paper coffee cups from the table.

"Of course," I let out a small laugh, "You think all four of those are for me?"

"I wouldn't be surprised. I know how serious you are about coffee. " She shrugs.

I glare jokingly at her as she takes a long sip from her cup. I grab the other bagel from the table and hand it to her as she takes a seat on the edge of the bed with her feet folded under her.

"So, when do you want to head out?" I ask.

"I don't know..." Lilah replies through a mouthful of bagel, trying to cover her mouth as she laughs.

"Someone's hungry."

"Sorry, it's probably from how busy we were last night," she says with a smile and a wink.

My thoughts flash back to hands and bodies welded together with passion. Breathing each other in like we would die without it. The same passion burning from the first time. I have to shake my head to focus back on what I asked her a second ago.

"We should probably try to head out towards the mountains before we try to ravage each other again, as much as I would love to stay in this room with you the whole time. I also would like to show you how beautiful this place is."

She sticks her tongue out at me in that adorable way of hers before replying, "Fine, I'm excited. I only need like half an hour to get ready, then we can leave."

Lilah gets up and heads towards the bathroom as I move to take her place on the edge of the bed, in full view of the bathroom and the shower she is undressing for.

"Works for me," I say as I lean back with my hands behind my head. Taking in what is an even better view than the one we are going to see in a couple hours.

"Pervert." Lilah glares at me then huffs a laugh as she hops into the steaming water.

———

Snow. I've always loved the snow. Sure, we left Cleveland with an inch of it on the ground but the snow in Colorado is different. Feels more magical. We've been driving for a little over an hour and a half from Denver to the Rocky Mountains. We haven't said much during the drive, both of us taking in the scenery.

"I see why you wanted to come back here," Lilah says as she sits up in her seat as we go around a bend, in full view of *Longs Peak*, near the Front Range of the mountains. I had traveled up this way during my solo trip to the mountains over a decade ago and stumbled upon the quaintest town afterwards.

"It is gorgeous isn't it?" I reply, trying my hardest to focus on the road and not the snowy mountain range around us.

"You okay with a short hike?" I realize I didn't check what shoes she was wearing before we left.

"Of course! I did wear my boots for a reason.." She lifts up her right foot to show me the bulky brown hiking boots she put on, somehow making them look sexy.

We pull into the main parking area. The snow starts to pick up some as we walk towards the entrance of one of the trails. I wasn't trying to make us too winded today after our passionate workout last night. I opted for an easier route which should still give us a beautiful view. I was worried Lilah would be cold or hate having to walk too much but every time I turn around to look at her she is beaming as she stares up at the snow falling down to dust the trees.

We walk in silence taking in the mountain air for about an hour until we come to a small cliff overlooking a clearing. Settling on a large rock we open the backpack I brought, grabbing some water and granola bars.

"When I came here in my early youth, I was so lost. It's kind of fitting being back here. Feeling almost as confused as I was then." I don't even realize I've said the words aloud until Lilah turns to me.

"What is making you feel so lost now?" she asks.

"Honestly? Everything. Well minus you, somehow you make me feel seen. I know we don't know a ton about each other but I'm okay with that for now." I sigh, trying to piece together my words in the right way. "I've gone most of my life worried about where I am going to go next, what the next move is. In my last relationship I was always made to feel like I wasn't doing enough. I needed the perfect job, the perfect house. My family has always made me feel less than too. Like I'm not good enough for them or something. Not with you though, you give me a sense of calm I've never felt before."

Realizing I just word vomited all over this magnificent woman, I open my mouth to start backtracking what I said. Hoping I didn't scare her off and make her want to hitch a ride all the way back to Cleveland.

"Stop that." Lilah puts a hand on my knee.

"Stop what?"

"You have this habit of opening up, only to try and take it back a lot. Like you don't actually want anyone to see who you are. What are you scared of, Landon?"

I take in a deep breath. I definitely didn't mean for this conversation to go the direction it is but I'm tired of playing scared. I want to know this girl more, I'd be a hypocrite if I kept trying to hold myself in.

"I am terrified once you see all of me you will want to run away."

Lilah pauses, looking away at the tree line within our view. "What it sounds like to me, Landon. Is your previous relationship royally fucked you up."

I'm honestly a little taken aback by her brazen words but it's refreshing to hear so I let her finish.

"You are scared someone is either going to leave you, or wrong you so you hold in who you truly are, instead of letting go and showing the world how amazing you can be. Sure we all have faults. Like you said, we honestly hardly know each other and I am sure there are skeletons in my closet that would send you running as well. But that's the beauty in getting to know someone, getting to know their faults as well as their pros. You get to choose once you fully see someone, if they are worth it. It's all up to you, if someone leaves then they're the ones missing out on the wonder of you, not the other way around."

Her hair starts to fall loose out of her ponytail, a brown strand falling in front of her face. I move to push it back behind her ear. Again, feeling fully seen by this woman who came into my life out of nowhere.

"You're pretty magnificent, did you know that?" I say as I reach behind her neck to pull her close as I plant a kiss on her mouth.

"Now if only you saw how great you were, all our problems would be solved," she replies half-jokingly as we pull away and she hops down from the rock we are on.

"How do you make everything sound so simple?" I ask as we resume our steady pace back down the trail. Lilah reaches for my hand, "Years and years of practice."

"Tell me more about yourself. What's your story?" I ask her, wanting her to open up more about her life.

"Not much to know really. I've told you about my family. I was an only child, moved around a lot and have continued to do so." She stops talking. That must be all she is willing to tell me.

"Okay, remain a mystery a little longer Lilah. I'll get you to tell me all your secrets soon enough," I say half-jokingly as she laughs and rolls her eyes.

"Come on, I'm starting to get a little hungry. Didn't you mention a cute town or something?"

"Yeah, it's not too far of a drive from here."

My goal of learning more about her failed again but I won't stop trying. Time to show her Estes.

This place is exactly how I remembered it. Maybe with a few enhancements and added shops but the charm of Estes Park remains. The buildings all have a rustic cabin or lodge feel. Even the chain restaurants. This is a popular tourist destination because of its proximity to the Rocky Mountains. I love it though. I hope my favorite cafe is still here, I probably should have looked it up before we headed this way, too late as we both have no signal.

We opted to park by the visitor center and walk down the main street, taking in the multiple small candy and hot cocoa shops. The smell of both wafting through the air making it taste sweet. The breeze doesn't feel as cold here, the sun helping to thaw both of us from our short hike. The snow is holding off at the moment.

"This place is adorable," Lilah says as we walk past a shop with scarves hung up in the windows.

"There's something about this town that makes me feel like I am home away from home, it hasn't changed much since the last time I was here. Minus some of the shops of course." I definitely don't remember this many chain coffee shops being here. "Oh, there's the cafe I was talking about, *Scrambled.*"

Looks like there isn't a line to get in unlike the last time I ate here. The mom and pop establishment is full of minimal decor, relying on their reputation purely by how great the food is. They offer everything from lobster bisque to pancakes. My favorite type of restaurant.

We walk towards an open table, following the directions of the sign at the door to seat ourselves. Pulling Lilah's chair out for her before I take my seat.

"Thank you," Lilah says with a smile, "Always such a gentleman." Her sarcasm shines through anyways.

"You say that like it's a bad thing," I laugh as I hand her a menu.

Our food arrives shortly after we order. I opted for their house burger, Lilah chose shrimp scampi. An eclectic combination for sure. Lilah went off to find the bathroom right before the food got to the table, an older waitress noting the amount of food, making a joke about one person being able to eat it all. I'm still laughing at her visible relief when I told her Lilah was in the restroom, resulting in her joking about joining me if my girlfriend didn't come back.

"What's so funny?" Lilah asks when she sits back down after the waitress walks away, opening her napkin wrapped silverware.

"Nothing, just the sweetest old lady wanting to join me for lunch," I joke with a wink, "Jealous?"

"Oh, very," Lilah says in the same un-serious tone as she dives into her pasta.

After shoving a few handfuls of food into my mouth I want to see if I can get this beauty savagely eating pasta across from me to give me more details about her life. The realization we haven't exactly discussed our *relationship* yet, ceases to leave my head.

"Question for a question?" I ask as another forkful of noodles is scarfed down.

She laughs as she wipes her mouth off with her napkin, "Shoot."

"We haven't discussed relationships much, when it comes to future ones I mean." I pause, gauging her reaction, she's distracted by her food. Or at least pretending to be. "I know we've only known each other for less than a month, but I was curious what your thoughts were about us?"

I seem to have her full attention, "Well, I am very into you Landon and I hope to see us together for a while."

"But?" I could sense it in her words.

"But..." She smiles and adds, "You need to work on a few things within yourself before you're able to fully invest into a relationship."

Ouch. That stings a little, but it's true. There are definitely a few things I need to let go of before I fully give myself to someone. "You're right. Completely. I kind of just wanted to see where your head was at because it's very easy to fall for you Lilah."

She rolls her eyes. "You're pretty easy to fall for too, Landon."

Leaving it at that, we finish our food in contemplative silence. Neither of us saving any room for dessert.

———

The rest of the stroll through town went by in a blur, the snow started to pick up so we headed back to the car. Grateful for the working heat as we sit here in silence driving back to the dead deer filled motel. Passing the old man at the front desk, who barely mumbles a greeting as we walk through the lobby.

"He seems extra cheerful today," Lilah jokes as we head towards our room.

"Probably a little too cheerful, I think he should calm down a bit."

We both start laughing. I think the small amount of tension after our lunch is finally smoothing out. Lilah plops onto the bed, looking up at the ceiling.

"You know what I could use right now?" I ask as I remove my boots and coat.

"What's that?"

"A good nap." I go to lay right where Lilah is sprawled out, gaining a grunt as she attempts to push me off of her. I don't let her suffer for too long, rolling over onto my side to hold her.

"I'm not a stuffed animal, Landon!" She tries to pry free of my grasp. Laughing, she adds, "If you want to squeeze something to death, grab the deer off the wall!"

I look up above us at the gigantic deer head, frozen and staring at the other side of the room. At least its eyes don't follow you. Lilah sits up to remove her boots. I start to drift in and out of consciousness, her chestnut colored hair the last thing I see before my eyes close with exhaustion.

———

"Landon!"

I hear her yell as I jolt awake. It's dark, must not be morning yet.

"Lan! Wake the fuck up!"

I'm being shaken to wake up. My eyes pop open. I try to get my bearings after being deep in sleep. Her nails dig into my shoulder as she shakes me. I reach over to turn the lamp on. Blinded by the sudden brightness, I blink a few times. She comes into clearer view as I turn to face her.

"*Who the fuck is this!?*" *she yells at me as she sits up in bed, shoving my phone in my face.*

I catch a glimpse of the screen, trying to piece together what is happening through my sleep fogged brain. I see a text thread open, the name reading Chloe on the top. My co-worker who works overseas in the UK.

"*Rachel what's going on?*" *I try to reach for my phone, to see what she's referring to but she yanks her hand back and gives me a stare that pierces through my soul.*

"*Who the actual fuck is Chloe!? And why are you looking forward to meeting her next week!?*" *Rachel shouts as she scrolls through our very few messages.*

"*Rach, it's not anything like you're clearly thinking it is...*" *I start to say before she interrupts me.*

That stare of hers gets somehow darker as she shoves my phone in my face again. "Oh, really? And you expect me to believe that Lan?"

I sit up and reach my hand out to grab hers, to try and calm her down. She jerks it away. In the two years we have been married I've learned how jealous Rachel can be. If a woman even smiles in my direction I get accused of cheating. We used to go out all the time to bars and restaurants when we first met, not anymore. I try to ease her worries, show her how loyal I am and how I would never hurt her. She'll be fine for months and then all of a sudden, I must be cheating.

This is the second time this month.

"Rach, honey. I promise you she is just my coworker." I have already told her this, we went to a work party last week and my boss even mentioned Chloe in front of both of us. She is a senior employee at the UK branch, who is in her late fifties. She is coming to the states to collaborate on a new campaign.

She's finally calmed down, after throwing my phone when she didn't believe me. I had to go on my laptop and open my work email to show her the conversations between my boss, me and Chloe.

I'm finally able to fall back asleep after my heart stopped racing. I hate seeing her like this, I don't know what else to do to show her I only care for her.

Chapter Eleven

Free

Nighttime has reached us as I peel open my eyes. It takes me a second to realize where I am at, to mentally shake loose the shitty dream I had. Even if the memory is ingrained in my mind. I look over at the red digits on the clock, it's seven in the evening. I roll over to find Lilah next to me, reading a book. Stretching out, I reach across her, leaning up on my other arm.

"Favorite of yours?" I ask, pointing to the book.

She turns the paperback around to look at the cover, '*The Great Gatsby*.'

"I found it on the shelf over there. I don't think I've read this since high school. I couldn't get into it as a teenager though."

"Yeah me neither, I think I was too focused on girls in school rather than the reading material." I laugh and stretch out my arms.

I sit up, reaching for the bottle of water on my nightstand. I grab my phone, seeing if there are any messages from anyone. I had texted Jack before we got on the road to let him know where we were going. I haven't gotten any notifications since we got here, or any signal at all. Probably needs to be restarted.

"So, what do you want to do this evening, beautiful?" I ask as I shut my phone off and turn it back on, setting it to the side.

Lilah pauses for a moment then opens her mouth to answer right as an incessant beeping starts coming from my phone. I grab it from beside me, powered back on. I guess I finally picked up some service because there's what sounds like fifty notifications continuously coming in. There are two texts from my brother, one saying to drive safe, the other apologizing. Over ten missed calls from my mother, my father and oddly my sister. Then of course, the rest are texts or calls from Rachel. I start to listen to the voicemails.

The first call from my mother, half screaming and half crying, asking why I would go off to the mountains with someone I just met. The rest were of similar fashion, my father being calmer but holding the same worry from my mother in his tone. The few from my younger sister, Casie yelling at me for causing drama and making *everything about me once again*. I didn't realize going on a vacation for myself would cause such an uproar.

Explains Jack's '*sorry*' text, he must have mentioned it to them or they asked him where I was. I'm not surprised by any of their reactions though, especially not Rachel's. She must have found out too, and found out I was here with Lilah because all of her texts and voicemails were half hysterical. I don't have the energy or want in me to listen to or read all of them. Instead I hit delete. Turning back towards Lilah who is sitting there patiently, a curious look on her face.

"Well, looks like my family and their hysterics followed us to the mountains," I say, tossing my phone to the end of the bed.

Lilah leans forward towards me, laying on her stomach as she rests her closed book next to her. "Did you tell them you were coming here?"

"Ah, yeah." I chuckle, "No I did not. It's none of their business, they can't pick and choose when they want to act like they give a shit about what I do. It's only because I'm here with you they are freaking out."

"Hmm, why would they care who you are with?" Lilah asks, looking up at me.

I let out a big sigh, "Well, I think they are hoping me and my ex Rachel will get back together. At least it's what my mother wants and the whole family goes with whatever whim she is on, except my brother of course."

She seems to consider before responding, "Well that, sucks. Seems like a battle you might lose with all of them on the same side. Not trying to pry too much, but does some part of you want to be with her again?"

I wasn't expecting such an honest question. I would be lying if I said I never thought about the possibility. Maybe it would be the easier route, to let everything go back to how it was. To pretend like the last couple of years didn't happen. I know deep down though, that would be the worst choice I could make. Considering I already let so many things get brushed under the rug with her before.

"No. Honestly, I had mulled over the idea once upon a time. But we aren't right for each other, I could never be the person she is wanting me to be. She needs someone who will bend to her every wish, which isn't me. I also don't think I could ever forgive her for cheating."

"Well that's good for me too then," a small humorless laugh escapes from Lilah as she adds, "I think at some point though it's less about forgiving the other person as it is to forgive them for yourself. That way you can let go of everything in the past."

Lilah moves to get up from the bed, walking around to face me.

"How are you so young yet so wise at the same time?" I say, grabbing her hands dangling in front of me.

"I'm only a few years younger than you, you goof!" she replies as she pulls her hands away and playfully shoves my shoulder back.

"Yes, but technically I am your elder. I should have all the knowledge to teach *you*."

She rolls her eyes at me as she crosses her arms, "Well maybe you do actually have all the knowledge inside of you but you choose to ignore it."

"Hmm, see? More wise words. Please teach me your ways, Lilah." I lace my fists together, pleading to this beauty staring at me like I am a mad man.

"You're ridiculous. You know that?" she says as she turns to go look out the window at the night sky.

"Yeah, it's one of the things I am definitely certain of in this world. Want to know the other?"

She turns back around to face me, "Let me guess, you're about to say something extremely corny?"

Glaring but pressing my lips into a smirk at the same time I reply, "I am almost certain you are the most beautiful thing on this planet and I am falling pretty fast and hard for you." I sense she desperately wants to roll her eyes.

"I told you it would be something corny." No eye roll, but there she goes sticking her tongue out again.

I get up to go stand on the other side of the bed with her, wrapping my hands around her waist as she turns back to face out the window. Breathing in her scent of Jasmine and firewood. I could stand like this forever. I know I want to make the most of this trip though so we should probably figure out what to do for the rest of the evening considering we have to start the drive back home tomorrow. A short but necessary trip.

"We got interrupted earlier. What would you like to do this evening, gorgeous?"

Lilah turns to face me, looking up in thought.

"Well I did have one idea, but you would have to trust me." A mischievous smile spreads across her face.

"That doesn't sound sketchy at all," I say, laughing as I try to imagine what the hell she could be talking about. "Do I get any kind of hint as to where this mystery is located?"

"Nope! Just dress nice. I'm going to get ready," she says as she heads towards the bathroom, grabbing a slinky looking dress from her suitcase. Dress nice? I don't know if I should be offended or not. Nevertheless I start to get changed and comb through my messy nap hair.

Glad I opted for my black button up shirt and leather jacket, otherwise my t-shirts would have stuck out like a sore thumb in this place. The lights and patrons both bumping with excitement. I feel the music vibrating through my bones. The last time I've been to a club was probably in my early twenties, it was never my scene but if this is where Lilah wanted to spend our last night here, then I would oblige. I just need to find the bar.

We head over through the dimly lit hallway towards where I assume the bar is. A large number of people dancing in front of the platform we are approaching. I reach across the surface of the packed bar to try and grab us both a drink, the bartender is young and very unfriendly. He says something about not being allowed to order multiple drinks, I try to tell him one is for Lilah but she abandoned me to go onto the dancefloor. I'll come back for my drink then.

As I approach the lit-up floor filled with dancing bodies, I'm mesmerized by the movements of Lilah. She chose a silky silver dress with thin straps, abandoning her jacket to the coat check as soon as we walked in. Every curve of her body moving to the beat of the music. She's turned around, allowing me access to admire her perfect backside. Then her gorgeous smile as she spins around to face me, almost bumping into the drink I brought over for her.

"I brought you a drink, I'm going to go grab one for myself. You look stunning out here!" I have to almost shout to make sure she can hear me.

"I'm okay! You take this one, come on, dance with me Landon!" She starts dancing around me, grabbing my free hand. There's no way I'll be able to keep up with her tonight. I down my drink and stand there, subtly swaying to the music.

"Oh, come on, that is not how you dance is it!?"

"Dancing is not my forte!" I say loudly against her ear, only to gain a laugh and eye roll from her.

Lilah grabs the empty glass from my hand, setting it on one of the tall, skinny black tables spread throughout the dance floor. The lights above us moving through the crowd like a firework flying through the sky. Colors of red and blue alternate, illuminating Lilah's perfect face and figure.

"You need to let loose!" Lilah shouts as she starts dancing in front of me again, her backside gently gliding across my body. Grabbing both of my hands she puts them on her hips to feel her movements. All logical thought abandons me as I think of the curves of her body.

"I don't know how to move like you do," I say into her ear. She turns to face me as she moves to the music.

"You're thinking about it too much. Stop trying to rationalize your movements or how you look. Let your body feel the music."

Easier said than done. I don't remember the last time I truly felt free, maybe the last time I was here in Colorado. On the mountain breathing in the fresh air, all the possibilities in the world ahead of me. Before I got knocked down and reality slapped me in the face.

I've felt more alive the last month since meeting Lilah though. She's right, I haven't truly let myself just feel.

I start to try and clear my head, only focusing on the beat of the music. The swaying of her body against mine, and then I'm moving. Probably looking a fool. No. I needed to not get stuck in my head, needed to stop worrying about what anyone else around me was thinking. I close my eyes, breathing in the air of this packed club. Smelling of alcohol, perfume and sweat. The music vibrates through my body. I start to find my rhythm, similar to Lilah's. I clear my head, letting all my worries melt away with each beat.

My family, my ex, not knowing what I should be doing with my life. All of it. I breathe in and let it all go. The thoughts eddying away with each of my movements against Lilah's body. Every worry, every doubt, every insecurity disappearing as I fall into a natural rhythm.

Finally feeling free, I let it all go.

Chapter Twelve

Wolf

It's continued snowing in Cleveland. Though it's not as magical as the mountain snow, it's still beautiful. I love how the city becomes a wonderland. The traffic however, not as much. After a long drive back from Colorado yesterday, I'm happy yet a little sad to be back. Jack has me meeting with him and our main investor for the high-rise project today for a late lunch. The restaurant is on the west side, right outside of the city. The highway is packed with people who don't know how to navigate the wintery roads, granted I have had my own spills in this type of weather.

Dean, the main investor for the building, is very well off. Which is probably why we are having this meeting at a fancy steak house in the early afternoon. Hopefully my slacks and button up work shirt are acceptable attire. I've only met him once, nice guy but I never fully trust rich business men for some reason. I guess he wanted to meet with Jack and I to discuss some of the complications with the building. My brother would have brought along Aaron but apparently, he was busy.

The building plans got pushed back slightly from both of us being out for a few days. Meaning I've been fully back in work mode since Lilah and I got back late last night, dropping her off outside her apartment just before midnight after leaving Denver before dawn. Exhaustion fully taking over, I didn't even try to get Lilah to let me see her place. Hopefully this meeting doesn't carry on for too long.

I spot Jack waiting by the front door of the restaurant as I pull into the parking lot, he's standing with a petite younger woman with short black hair and giant glasses too big for her small heart-shaped face.

Jack greets me with an arm around my shoulder as I walk up, introducing me to the woman he is with. Her name is Claire. She is Dean's assistant. She wanted to meet us outside so we would be let in without any issues I'm told after she gives me an assessing look. The work shirt must not be up to their standards of dress here then.

The restaurant is dark, filled with mahogany wood and ornate gold light fixtures. Stuffed mounts of animal heads on the walls, reminding me of the motel room in Colorado. No Lilah here though unfortunately, I'd love to be back in that bed with her. I shake my head to focus, spotting Dean in a glass enclosed room towards the back of the restaurant. Claire holds her arm out, gesturing for us to enter the room as she closes the sliding door behind her.

"Jack! A pleasure to see you again!" Dean says excitedly as he embraces my brother in a wide hug. "And Landon! Good to see you as well." He reaches out to shake my hand.

Dean looks to be in his mid-fifties, ten years my brother's senior. His dark brown and grey hair styled neatly, to go along with his clean shaven face and perfectly tailored light blue suit, the contrast to his dark complexion. Without knowing him, he gives the impression of a scholarly man who grew up with a trust fund. Relying on his money to get him through life. Luckily he doesn't fully seem like a complete ass though, or he at least hides it well.

Taking our seats at the table, Dean at the head, Jack and I to his left and right. Claire remains standing near the door, looking down at her phone.

"So Dean, what brings us the pleasure of dining with you today?" Jack asks.

I glance over at my brother, slightly taken aback by his formality but he's learned to deal with these businessmen quite well, knowing how to almost blend in with them.

We knew why we were there, even if Dean didn't want to give any details over the phone to Jack when he asked to meet today.

He hasn't answered my brother yet. Instead he unfolds his napkin, shaking it once to let it fall free of its fold before placing it on his lap. He raises a hand, signaling for the waiter patiently standing outside to enter the room.

"Three old fashioned's and a couple of waters please," Dean says to the timid waiter who quickly fills our water glasses and retreats from the room.

Jack and I exchange glances, I'm fighting the urge to clear my throat. Feeling completely out of place in this setting.

Finally deeming it suitable to answer Jack, Dean finally looks over to my brother and sighs, "You have been doing great so far Jack, you and your team." He glances over at me, "But as you know we are venturing up to our deadline and there is still a good amount to be done before the project is complete."

"Sir with all due respect, we unfortunately have run into a couple of electrical issues but I am positive Jack and the rest of our team will have things cleared up by our March deadline," I answer before Jack is able to, wanting to stand up for my brother and not have everything rest on his shoulders.

Dean peels his eyes from my brother to look at me, considering before he responds.

"Well, good to hear, my boy. How have you liked working for your brother so far?" An odd shift in question, but luckily, he isn't going to continue hounding Jack about the project.

The waiter is back, setting each of our drinks down beside us. As much as I'd love to down the amber colored whiskey, I wait for our host to start first.

"Oh, my brother is great, I've honestly never worked for a team or job that runs as smoothly as ours. I didn't come from a background in construction but with my brother's and lead carpenter Aaron's help it's definitely been a great project to work on."

Jack gives me a thankful look before adding, "Just as Landon said, I have full confidence we will get this project finished in time despite any issues having arisen."

Dean finally picks up his glass to take a drink. Jack and I follow his lead. Raising ours to clink in unison with his.

"Well that is great to hear! Cheers to future prosperity and success with this project."

I finish my glass before setting it back down.

"Is it just me or did we just have a meal with a Bond villain?" I laugh as we walk out the heavy wooden doors of the restaurant an hour later after the best steak of my life.

"Shut it, we are still here, Landon," Jack says sternly, must be afraid Dean has villain like super hearing too.

I roll my eyes at my brother. I know why he is nervous, Dean has pulled out of projects before simply because he didn't like the team working for him. Which I don't see happening with the high rise. Jack is great at his job and I also have a newfound confidence in my abilities to help him see it through too. Not to mention Aaron is coming back today so we will fully be able to get back to work. As long as I don't let a certain gorgeous woman distract me too much.

"Mr. Stone!"

We both turn around to find Dean's assistant Claire running behind us, a binder in hand. She catches up to us, slightly out of breath.

"Mr. Stone, so sorry, I forgot to make sure you received this when you left. It's a few changes or adjustments Mr. Wolf wanted you to make to the project."

The binder was easily a couple inches thick, a few changes my ass.

"Thank you Claire," Jack says as he grabs the binder and opens it quickly, then closes it just as fast.

"I also wanted to apologize for my boss's bed-side manner, I swear he is a lot nicer than he leads on. He absolutely loves your team and the work you have done," Claire says, adjusting her large glasses with a red painted fingernail.

My brother nods his thanks.

"It was great seeing both of you, if you ever need anything don't hesitate to reach out to me," Claire says as she turns to walk back into the restaurant. Back to the wolf wearing sheep's clothing, or how she implies, the sheep who strategically disguises himself as a wolf.

I turn to Jack, "Well I don't know about you but I need another drink after all of that," I say, gesturing to the restaurant.

"Yep." Is all he says.

Chapter Thirteen

Falling

"Hi, Mr. Broody!" Stacey shouts my way as we walk into the bar. It's only been a little over a week since I've seen her but I've missed her sarcastic, Hawaiian shirt wearing self. Madison finishes handing a customer a beer, the young guy staring off at her a little longer than normal, giving her a wink as he turns around. She doesn't seem to return the interest though and quickly turns towards us.

"Hey Stace, been a minute! Good to see you again, Madison," I reply as me and Jack walk towards our usual stools at the far end of the bar. Madison looks past us, realizing it's only us two and goes off to take another customer's order, her strawberry blonde hair moving across her shoulder.

"The usual?" Stacey asks as she puts down two bar coasters in front of us on the worn wood.

"Yep, make it three though. Aaron should be here soon."

I hear a small squeal and a *"Shit!"* coming from the other end of the bar, Madison. She was filling up a beer from the tap and accidentally let it overflow, shaking the beer off her hand and grabbing a towel to clean up the counter.

Stacey looks at her and lets out a small laugh, "You shouldn't have said that, she gets all nervous when the lumberjack is mentioned."

"Lumberjack? Stacey, are you talking about me again?" Aaron walks up to us with a beaming smile, he must have snuck in while we were distracted with Madison.

"Hey Aaron, your *bros* already got your usual," she says, setting down our drinks in front of us.

I get up to hug my grizzly of a friend, "Hey Man! I missed your *lumberjack* ass while I was gone!" I think Stacey's nickname for him is going to stick.

"Looks like someone else missed you too," Jack adds as he looks towards Madison heading down to our end.

To all of our surprise, Aaron leans over the bar as she reaches us and plants a kiss on Madison's lips. Resulting in a smile and blush on her freckled face.

"Madison, can you grab those guy's drinks for me?" Stacey shouts from the other end of the bar. A hoard of customers is piling in.

"I'll be back," she says to Aaron before sauntering off to help the same guy from earlier, his group of frat looking friends joining him.

Jack and I stare at our friend, questions brewing on our faces.

"Care to explain?" I let out an amused laugh.

Aaron rubs the back of his neck with his hand, looking down sheepishly. I don't think I would have ever thought I'd see my friend look this shy. He's always the loud, funny one of the group. Something about this girl seems to have brought something different out in him though.

"Ah, yeah... that." He pauses and smiles in Madison's direction, "Well... we've kind of been seeing each other for almost two weeks."

Had I really been so distracted with Lilah I completely missed this?

"Did you know about this?" I turn to ask my brother, who looks equally as bewildered as I imagine I do.

"No idea," he replies, shaking his head.

Aaron takes a drink before he explains himself, "Well... I decided to take a note from Landon's book and wanted to keep it on the down low until we knew we wanted to fully start dating." He looks down the bar towards Madison again, true happiness shining in his eyes, "I don't think I've felt like this in a long time, especially not this early in."

Looking at Aaron longing after her, I am so happy for him. This man has been through too much and deserves to find someone who could help fill that void for him. He hasn't been with anyone serious since his wife. The accident nearly ripped his heart out. I don't blame him at all for trying to keep that happiness all to himself.

"Dude, I'm happy for you!" I clap my hand on Aaron's shoulder and smile at him.

Jack shouts to Stacey, "We're going to need a round of shots over here!"

Stacey must have a sixth sense because she already has a bottle of whiskey in hand. She pours us all some, smirking at Aaron. She must know about Madison and him already.

"What's the occasion?" she asks curiously.

"Who says we need an occasion to take some shots?" I say, glaring at the brunette as I grab mine, holding it up to cheers. "Rather judgmental of you, Stace," I give a sarcastic wink as Jack and Aaron lift their drinks into the air.

"I think I like you better when you're entranced by someone Landon, you're a lot more fun than when you sit here and brood," Stacey adds as she picks up our discarded shot glasses and goes to help another customer.

We are a few drinks in, feeling loose and light when my brother and Aaron start their interrogation.

"So, how was Colorado?" Aaron asks.

"Oh it was great," I look to my left at Jack, "You know, until my whole family and ex-wife started bombarding me with texts and phone calls."

Jack's face says how bad he feels for letting the information slip on what I was up to, "Yeah... sorry about that one man. I accidentally said something to Casie about you being out of town and then all the questions started."

I laugh, "No it's fine, just added to the excitement."

"How did Lilah handle everything?" Aaron asks as he tries to peel his attention away from Madison, who is once again helping the guy from earlier at the bar. His arrogant politeness is replaced by drunken aggression as he refuses to move away so anyone else can order.

"Oh, Lilah handled it great, better than I would have honestly. She really is amazing," I reply.

"You planning on inviting her for Christmas?" Jack asks.

Usually, the holiday festivities are held at his house, Nancy is amazing at hosting. Since last year's drama I honestly didn't know if I had planned on attending. After Colorado though I don't feel the same pinching nerve sensation I normally get when thinking about my family. A new sense of ease has replaced any agonizing emptiness.

So, I say, "I'll think about it."

All of a sudden, a commotion breaks out at the other end of the bar. The security usually posted by the front door is working to pull apart the patrons grouped together where Madison had been helping the douchebag.

Aaron beelines over there, Madison is being pulled into the hallway by Stacey at the far end of the bar, out of view of the crowd. I go to follow Aaron, hoping there isn't a fight about to happen I have to be a part of. I can't remember the last time I threw a punch at someone. We make it to where all the action is happening, the douchebag is being dragged out of the bar by security, beer dripping from his hair and face.

"You dumb bitch!" The beer soaked asshole shouts in the direction where Madison disappeared, and then spits on the ground towards the bar. Which is all Aaron needed to witness before he is moving straight at the guy, ignoring the security guard who is trying to pull him towards the door. Aaron lands one impressive punch sending both the security guard and asshole back a couple feet.

He is right on him, grabbing the man's shirt in his hand as he says through gritted teeth, "You EVER call her that again, or even look in her direction and I will make sure you physically aren't able to ever drink beer again, let alone breath."

The man rightfully looks terrified but doesn't say anything as the security guard gains back his composure and finishes leading him outside, telling Aaron to follow him.

"Oh great, now Aaron is going to get thrown out and we just got our drinks," I say looking towards the door where Aaron headed. Madison comes out to see what happened in the aftermath of what seemed like her throwing beer in a man's face. Probably for good reason.

"Nah, Larry won't throw him out," Stacey chimes in from the bar, "He probably wants to ask him if he saw everything that happened."

True, Larry, the security guard never threw out patrons who were standing up for someone, usually only the ignorant assholes got tossed out.

A few minutes later Aaron comes back inside, smiling and laughing with Larry. He definitely isn't getting kicked out from the looks of it. Aaron meets Madison by the side of the bar, grabbing her waist to pull her towards him as they kiss passionately. I look over to Jack as he feigns being sick watching them. I enjoy seeing my friend happy though.

The girls are back to their usual attentiveness behind the bar. The entire place has a much more calm and merry energy once the asshole and his friends were removed.

Aaron is in a special kind of mood after his brief moment of violence he is non-stop buying everyone rounds of shots. After our next round, I step outside to make a quick phone call. It is freezing out, the cold wind nipping at my face. My mind is a little fuzzy but I have to ask Lilah something.

A small part of me hopes to get her voicemail but I can't hold back my smile when I hear her voice, "Hi Landon." I swear I hear the smile on her face too.

"Hi, beauti– *shit…*" I accidentally stepped in a slick ice patch, "Sorry." I laugh, "Hi beautiful, what are you up to?"

She laughs as she replies, "Just reading a book. Are you drunk?" Not a hint of judgment lacing her words, only curiosity and amusement.

"Ahh, maybe a little," I laugh, adding, "There was a lot of excitement happening at the bar tonight, plus Aaron is back so he's the one to blame."

"Oh I see, so did you drunkenly dial me for a booty call then? Considering it's almost midnight."

"Of-course not… but I mean I definitely wouldn't argue if you were offering." I hope I don't sound too much like a dick, realizing I'm stumbling a little on my words.

"I knew it!" she half shouts and chuckles into the phone. Her laugh is the most beautiful sound I have ever heard.

"It's not my fault you're the most gorgeous creature on this planet." I can't help the giddy smile etched on my face, probably looking like a fool to the people passing by, but I don't care anymore. Before I lose my courage, I know I need to get to the main reason I called, besides wanting to hear her voice of course. Seeing as we both have been busy after getting back to the city.

"So I want to ask you something," I hesitate, hearing the silence of her listening on the other end. I rip off the band-aid, "Would you like to join me at my brother's house for Christmas in a few weeks?"

There's a long pause before she replies, "I'm not sure Landon."

Damn. "I understand, I don't blame y–..." I start to say when she interrupts me.

"I do want to, it's just your family doesn't seem like they will be too welcoming to me. Which makes me nervous." I can't blame her at all for feeling that way.

"Yeah, I understand. I wish I could give you more reassurance but unfortunately I am not sure how my family will react to *me* being there. You think about it, don't feel pressure to answer yet or even to say yes. Just know I will be there with you the whole time and if at any point you feel uncomfortable, we leave and go make love for the rest of the day."

Another pause. "Did you say, *'Make Love'?*" She starts laughing again.

"Yes, I sure did. No better way to describe it," I pause, hesitating on what I am about to tell her, wondering if it's the whiskey pushing me to say my feelings or something else, "I think I'm in love with you Lilah."

I start to panic and wonder if what I said was too much. We had mentioned falling for each other but hadn't fully uttered the words we couldn't walk back from. I have to think of something to add, to take away the seriousness. Do I blame it on the whiskey?

"I think I love you too, Landon," she says, adding, "And I would love to spend Christmas with you.

Chapter Fourteen

Kindling

This past week has flown by. After telling each other how deeply we feel, Lilah and I have been inseparable. She is staying at my place more nights than not. Usually only retreating to her apartment to pick up things for work or to switch out clothes she's brought over. Our evenings have been filled with takeout, listening to music and as she openly mocks me for saying, *making love*.

Over this past weekend she begged me to take her ice skating. The small rink in the downtown square filled with children laughing and falling onto the ice, it's funny how as a child you weren't afraid to fall, you just went for it. As an adult I am terrified of falling, at least I was until Lilah stepped into my life. Her fear is non-existent. She flew by on those skates, stumbling as she went but zipping by quicker than a lot of the other skaters around us. I however, kept a hold on the side of the rink, almost falling even as I did so. It wasn't until I saw her standing in the middle of the ice, snow starting to fall down, when I dared to venture from the edge.

She was so beautiful there in the center. The city around us. The night sky. A perfect image. I had gotten into the habit of starting to carry my new camera with me, for such moments.

I took my hands off the side railing, pushing myself off to give me a head start as I stumbled towards her, staring up at the snow. I managed to reach her right in time as a snowflake landed on her perfect mouth. I almost fell into her as I captured the image with my camera, earning a laugh from her and a couple of people around us. Luckily she stabled me and we spent the rest of the night slowly skating around as the winter air surrounded us.

"Hey *lover boy*, you going to help me with this or not?" I shake my head, returning back to the present. At work, with Aaron staring at me, an amused look on his face.

"Sorry man," I laugh and shrug as I glance back down at our plans for the day.

We have been busy this whole week working to get the electrical issue fixed on one of the lower levels in the elevator. Aaron's friend he suggested we bring in had said it was fixed on Monday, but it's not working again. After updating Dean, the enigmatic investor wanted someone he hired directly to come in instead to fix it. We have just been monitoring to make sure everything is running smoothly today.

"If Lilah keeps occupying your brain this much, there's no way we are going to meet our deadline," Aaron says.

Apparently, Dean had given Aaron a serious lashing about how his friend didn't fix the issue like he was supposed to. He's been in a grumpy mood since.

I would point out he is equally distracted with Madison but it's better not to poke the bear. When Aaron is in a mood, he usually gets out of it quickly.

"Looks like Dean's guy should have this thing finished by Friday, leaving us today and tomorrow to tie up any other loose ends before he sends more guys out here to help us," I say, looking at the notes from today. We are so close to finishing this building, and we have another couple of months anyways, but Dean is a stickler for wanting projects done early. Plus with the holidays coming up it delays us some.

"Great. I'll be glad to get these assholes out of here, they act like our team isn't capable at all," Aaron replies with a grunt.

Dean's guys were definitely not as friendly as our crew. Jack has always done a great job at weeding out the troublemakers, making our team run smoothly. The last couple of days have been more rough. Hopefully by the end of next week we will be ready to pick up after the holidays with no issues and get this project completed. Though I continuously think how much I will miss coming here every day for the view.

"Everything is looking good guys," Jack says as he walks into the hall we are occupying. "Oh and Nancy wanted me to see if you both wanted to come to dinner this Sunday?"

"You know I'll be there," I reply. Jack already asked me a couple days ago. We haven't had our normal Sunday dinners since I have been occupied with Lilah so I didn't hesitate to say yes.

"Yeah, sounds great. Can't wait," Aaron says, looking up from the clipboard he was glaring at.

"Awesome, oh and she said to bring Madison and Lilah too. You know she wants to scope them out," Jack adds.

Aaron perks up, smiling like a lovestruck fool. Not that I am one to judge, I've definitely looked the exact same way this past month.

"Oh she will definitely be there," he says.

I have no idea if Lilah will be free or even want to come, considering she already agreed to spending Christmas with my family. I wouldn't blame her if she wanted some solitude considering we are only a week and a half away from the sure to be shit fire.

"I'll check with Lilah and see if she's able to come," I add as we all start packing up our things to head out for the evening.

The gym was packed after work, resulting in a quick session before I got the hell out of there. Lilah said she is waiting for me at my place. I gave her a key when we got back from Colorado, which I realized moved our relationship along quicker than intended but luckily she didn't get nervous when I had handed her a copy. She simply smiled and kissed me.

Stepping into the cold to head home, I'm grateful for the brisk breeze, hoping it will wick away some of the sweat on my body before I see Lilah. The wind picked up a little more, sending a woman's shopping bag almost flying out of her hands on the other side of the sidewalk. The walk today seems extra-long with anticipation, knowing I will see Lilah soon. I fumble with my keys in the lock.

"Hi stranger," Lilah says as a way of greeting from the couch. We finally picked a new one out last week after returning to the city. After breaking my old one on the first night we spent together. She might have been the one to pick it out though. I normally wouldn't have gone with blue velvet, but she said it *fit my vibe.* Whatever that meant.

Lilah is positioned on her back, laying on the couch holding a book over her head. Catching a glimpse of the cover, I read, '*The Great Gatsby.*'

"Did you take that from the motel?" I ask her with a laugh.

She closes the book, setting it down on the coffee table as she sits up and looks at me, "Maybe I did, whatcha gonna do about it?"

"Hmm, I might just have to report you, I didn't realize my girl-friend was a *kleptomaniac*," I say with a shake of my head, pressing my lips in a thin line. Trying to feign disappointment.

She moves off the couch to follow me into the kitchen where I go to set my gym bag down.

"Oh no, please don't report me," she says in a playful voice, a fake pleading in her intense steel blue eyes as she looks up at me.

I reach around to grab her behind the waist, pulling her into me. "What will you do to guarantee I don't expose your thieving ways?" I ask, an equally playful smirk spreading across my face.

She considers for a moment, looking up at me with a mischievous smile, "Oh I have a couple of ideas." She stands up on her toes to grab the back of my neck, bringing me down into a kiss laced with so much passion it stops my breath.

"I'm very sweaty," I manage to say in between kisses, suddenly feeling self-conscious.

"We can fix that," Lilah says as she grabs my wrist, leading me with determination through the living room towards the bathroom.

Once we enter the modestly sized space, big enough for a small but sturdy sink, toilet and a decent standing shower, Lilah has a wild look in her eyes. Immediately making all the blood in my body go south. We don't stand too long looking at each other before we are tangled in each other's mouths again.

I turn to lean her against the sink, lifting her to sit on the hard porcelain surface as she wraps her legs around me. I break away for a moment to turn the shower on, letting the steam start to fill the room. We start grasping at each other's clothes to peel them away from our bodies.

"How are you this fucking beautiful?" I say to Lilah, grasping the side of her face while my other hand ventures down her body, to the place I want to be buried in. Our mouths entwine with each other. I grab her thighs, hoisting her up to carry her into the shower, the hot water falling onto our faces.

I lean her up against the wall, her legs placed on the wet ground as I grab both of her wrists, lifting her arms above her head. She lets out a soft moan as she arches her back, moving her tongue to start gliding along my neck. I move my other hand to gently grasp her throat as she tilts her head back with pleasure.

I make my way down to that most intimate area I want to live in. Tasting every inch of her body on the way. I could devour her whole. On my knees I begin to savor her until I hear her cry out with ecstasy.

She yells out my name as she reaches climax, I look up at her, those piercing blue eyes looking back at me intently. I make my way back up to her mouth, letting her taste herself before I flip her around, placing her hands on the wall. She moves her hips back in response, readying herself for me as I enter her. I don't stop until we are both spent and barely able to hold ourselves up.

—

I could lay like this forever. Lilah resting on my chest, snuggled in bed after spending the rest of the evening laughing and talking over dinner. We opted for ordering in tonight, too tired from our shower to cook anything. Music playing from the record player. This is the happiest I've been in a long time. I grab my camera from the nightstand, just in time for Lilah to look up at me. Capturing her chestnut hair and beautiful eyes.

"How often do you try and sneak pictures of me?" she asks, playfully glaring at me.

I laugh, setting my camera next to me on the bed, "Only when you're looking beautiful. So. Always."

"Smooth," she laughs as she moves to get up, only wearing one of my white t-shirts hanging just below her waist. "I'm going to go to the bathroom, try to resist taking a picture of my ass as I walk away." She turns around, naturally I can't help myself and grab my camera to do exactly what she suggested I not. The shutter clicks at the same moment a knock sounds at my door.

"Did you order more *Chinese food* when I wasn't paying attention?" I jokingly shout towards the bathroom on my way to see who it is. I have no idea who would be here at this time of night.

Surprise and anger fill my body as I open the door. Rachel standing on the other side.

"What are you doing here?" I ask with zero emotion in my voice.

"That's not a very polite way to answer the door Lan," she replies, moving to try and come in, I go to hold up my arm to block the pathway inside.

Rachel looks at me, confusion and annoyance passing over her face. "What, am I not allowed inside anymore?"

"I have company Rachel, and *no* you're not welcome here. I'm going to need you to leave now."

She takes in my appearance, no shirt and only in my underwear, my hair probably a tousled mess. Her face instantly turns to a mask of pure disdain.

"Oh, I see, you have that *whore* over, don't you?" She tries to peer over my shoulder to look into the loft.

I try to remain as calm as I can. "You have about ten seconds to remove yourself from my doorway and leave."

"Fine, I came by to check if you were going to your brother's for Christmas, no need to be so hostile."

I don't try to hide my confusion. "Why would you care if I was going to Jack's or not?"

"Oh, you didn't know? I decided to stay in Ohio a little longer and Mom invited me. I figured we could carpool," she adds with a smug smile, "But if *she's* with you, I don't accept trash in my car."

"Careful," is all I say, not hiding the bite in my tone.

"Oh *honey*, you should be the one being careful. We don't want a repeat of last Christmas do we?"

A flash of chaos goes before my eyes as I remember all the events of last year, shutting it out quickly before I become enveloped in it.

"Good-bye Rachel." I don't wait for her response as I slam the door in her face.

Lilah luckily stayed out of sight, either still in the bathroom or maybe she heard someone and chose to remain hidden.

"Who was at the door?" she says as she walks back into the main living area.

I pause, trying to figure out what the hell happened. Wondering if I should call my brother to figure out how she was invited for Christmas this year or if I should let it go until I see him at work tomorrow.

"*That...*" I point towards the door. "My Love, was my ex-wife. She's a big fan of you by the way."

"Yeah... I heard." She lets out a small forced laugh, heading back towards the bed. "How can she hate me so much? She's never met me."

I settle back onto the mattress, grabbing Lilah to rest on top of me again as I kiss the top of her head.

"Oh, Rachel finds a way to hate anyone if she puts her mind to it, don't worry, I won't let her near you."

I shut the lamp off, the only light venturing into the loft from the city lights in the curtainless windows. I try to shut out the memories tempting to flood back in, breathing in Lilah's scent as I drift off to sleep.

———

Mondays. Oh, how I hate Mondays. My boss is such a prick at the beginning of the week. Already shouted at me this morning as soon as I walked in. I need to find another job.

Rachel would be pissed if I quit though, she would say we don't have enough money. Granted we would have a lot more if she didn't keep redecorating the house with any savings I built. I want to see her happy though. Three and half years in and all I want is to get us back to the place we were when we met. She did seem happier as of late though. Back to singing in the shower, and being more active. Her new friend she met at the gym was probably helping. Maybe all she needed was another woman to talk with.

I needed to stop by the florist again today. I've been trying to keep up with getting her flowers every week. Along with planning date nights, even if it meant her rain-checking most times to go out for girls night.

Tonight though, tonight I planned on pulling out all the stops. Her favorite wine, roses and the movie we saw on one of our first dates on the projector outside. We haven't had an intimate at home date in a very long time. Maybe we would have sex again, I can't remember the last time we did.

Finally, home. Today was super hectic, I felt like ripping my hair out multiple times. Rachel texted me that she was out for coffee with her friend from the gym so I have time to set everything up. First a shower though. Heading upstairs to our bedroom I have a weird feeling. Like a gut-punch, but nothing is amiss. Probably leftover stress from work.

I take a shower, drying off in the bedroom, I open our shared closet to get dressed. Opting for my usual black t-shirt and jeans. I spritz on the cologne Rach got for me. Walking back out I go downstairs to grab some of the roses, pulling off a few petals. Figured I'd be cheesy tonight. I start sprinkling them over the bed, I'm about to walk out and finish setting up when I catch something in the corner of my eye.

Reaching under the bed, I pull out a baseball cap. Maybe Rachel borrowed one of mine. No. This one is definitely not mine. The navy blue and orange hat, with the Detroit Tigers logo. I would never own this, being from Ohio. Whose is this? We haven't had anyone over, and why would it be under our bed?

Waking up in a brief panic. I glance over to see Lilah curled up next to me, breathing evenly. I instantly calm myself, staring out the window at the night sky.

Chapter Fifteen

Simmer

"**U**ncle Landon, can you get this off my head!?"

Isabelle, my niece, immediately shouts my way as I walk through the front door of my brother's house for Sunday dinner. The seven year old is charging straight for me with a bucket stuck to her head.

I reach down to stop her before she runs into the lamp right next to me, "How the heck did you get yourself into this?" I ask, even though I could guess exactly what happened.

I yank the plastic off her head as we both simultaneously answer, "*Emily.*"

The older twin by only a minute is always the trouble maker, probably because she is the biggest daddy's girl and reminds me a lot of how my brother and I were as boys. Frequently running about and breaking things, pulling pranks on each other or our sister.

The second I go to hug Isabelle she starts charging down the hall shouting Emily's name. The former might be the victim most of the time but her revenge is usually ten-fold of what Emily's crime was.

I do not want to see what's about to go down as I hear them both screaming. Branch, their giant shaggy dog running off to inspect the commotion.

I take my coat off and hang it in the closet near the front door, already smelling the delectable food Nancy is working on. I decided to get here a little early, it being only four in the afternoon. I wanted to ask my brother about what Rachel said, since we were busy at work the last time I saw him.

"Hey, Nance," I say to my sister in law as I make my way into the kitchen.

She is elbow deep in dough for whatever concoction she is making for dinner, flour dusting her face and apron.

"Hey Landon! Jack is outside in the garage, no Lilah?" she asks me, noticing I'm alone. Lilah said she wanted to come but had to deal with something urgent for work in the upcoming week's issue of the magazine she works for. I tried not to be too disappointed. She would be here for Christmas anyways.

"She couldn't make it today, but she told me to thank you for inviting her. She will try to make it next time."

Nancy gives me a small smile before returning to her cooking. I head out to find my brother.

Jack is exactly where I figured he would be, working on his truck. I spot my covered motorcycle in the corner. I wonder if Lilah would let me take her out on it when the weather warms up some.

"Hey man, she giving you a hard time again?" I ask in regards to his truck which always seems to break down every winter.

Jack peeks his head around the red hood of the truck, giving me an exasperated look as he replies, "What do you think?"

"Need a hand?" I ask, though I knew Jack's answer would be the same as always.

"No, but you can hand me another beer."

Already a bottle in my hand from the small garage fridge, I hand it to him.

"I see you're alone, your girl couldn't make it?" he asks as he opens his beer, taking a drink, "I'm starting to think this girl is either incredibly hideous, a spy, or has a secret family."

I laugh as I respond, "Nope, none of those, she had something she had to deal with for work."

Jack gives me an incredulous look, "Will she at least be here for Christmas? I'd like to meet the woman who's been distracting my brother so much."

"She said she would be here," I say, rolling my eyes and opening up a beer for myself. "I do need to ask you something though."

Jack looks away from the truck at the wariness in my voice, waiting for whatever my question is. I take a drink before I get into it. He towels off his hands and walks over to sit on the work bench next to me.

"Well, I was graced by another visit from Rachel the other day while Lilah was over."

I pause, wanting to gather his expression before I continue. The puzzled and concerned look on his face confirms he had no idea she was in town.

"What the hell is she doing back here again? I at least could justify it when mom was in the hospital last month, which was still crazy. But this is what, the third time since then?" he asks.

"Mhm... and she told me she was invited here for Christmas too." Taking another long drink of my beer, I glance at Jack again. He looks furious.

"Yeah, definitely not happening, did mom invite her? I don't know why I'm asking, of course she did." He shakes his head, running a hand through his grey brown hair as he takes a long sip of his drink. "Don't worry brother, she is not going to be welcome, especially with Lilah coming too. I'm not having a repeat of last year," Jack says as he gets back up to mess with his truck again.

I glance back over at my bike in the corner, spacing out as I remember the shit show of last Christmas. There was always drama with my family and my ex-wife, but last year was definitely the tipping point for our fallout. Flashes of shouting, doors slamming and sirens are on repeat in my head until I hear the side garage door open.

"Sup, Stone brothers! I see you've started drinking without me, looks like I gotta catch up," Aaron shouts from the doorway, reading the room and taking it upon himself to lighten the air of whatever was talked about before he arrived.

"I bet you both twenty bucks I can finish three beers before either of you finish the one you're on," he says as he grabs three bottles from the fridge, almost dropping them all in the process.

Definitely lightening the mood.

———

"Dinner was amazing Nancy," Madison says from her place at the table across from me, right next to Aaron. All of us content and full from the chicken pot pie my sister-in-law made.

"Don't lie to her, Madison, it will only go to her head," Jack teases from one end of the table, Nancy on the opposite end, leaving me in between the twins. Both of who liked to stab me with their forks when I would try to take a bite of food.

"Ha, you're hilarious. Looks like you boys will be cleaning up the dishes for me," Nancy says with a satisfied smirk.

"Hey, we didn't do anything!" I say laughing and gesturing to Aaron and myself.

"Guilty by association. I'll give Aaron a pass because he asked for a third helping," she replies sweetly looking at our gruff lumberjack friend who is shoveling food into his mouth.

"I knew she liked me more than either of you," Aaron says with a mouthful and a wink.

After dinner is cleaned up, both Isabelle and Emily reluctantly having helped Jack and I load the dishwasher. Aaron and Madison headed out about half an hour ago since the former has work in the morning. I should probably head home too for the same reason, but the girls want me to join their game of darts in the basement.

"You two are grounded from darts, remember!" Nancy shouts from the kitchen where she is pouring herself a glass of wine. Jack is content with staying out of the conversation from the couch.

"Aww but Mom!" Both girls protest with their arms crossed, their eyebrows bunched together in anger.

"It's okay girls, I should be leaving but maybe we will convince your mom to let us play darts on Christmas," I say out of earshot of Nancy, winking to both of them as they grin from ear to ear and run off to play a different game.

"Well I better head home, thanks for dinner again Nance, it was perfect," I say as I pull her in for a hug.

Jack gets up from the couch and pats me on the back, "See you at work tomorrow."

"I can't wait to meet Lilah next week! Tell her we are excited and about how nice we are so she doesn't get nervous," Nancy adds excitedly as I put my coat back on and open the door to leave.

The drive home feels longer than the usual twenty minutes. I try calling Lilah to tell her how my night was but she doesn't answer. I'll try again when I get home.

"Hi Beautiful," I say into the phone after she picks up on the third ring an hour later.

"Hi," she replies sleepily.

"Were you asleep? I didn't wake you, did I?" I glance at the clock, it's a little after nine o'clock at night.

"Today was rough at work so I laid down for a nap earlier, looks like it was a full sleep instead." She lets out a small laugh and a yawn. "How was dinner?"

"It was good, wish you could have been there though. Oh, and Nancy wanted me to tell you how excited she is to meet you."

"Well, that was nice of her." Another yawn.

"Why don't I let you get back to sleep, Gorgeous. I'll talk to you tomorrow. I love you." I reply, not wanting to hang up at all.

"Okay, goodnight, Landon. I love you too."

"Goodnight," I say as I hang up the phone, laying down on my bed after I kick off my boots. I land on something hard. Reaching behind my back I find Lilah's stolen book under me. Feeling a little too awake to fall asleep, I decide to flip it open to a random page.

"There must have been moments even that afternoon when Daisy tumbled short of his dreams–not through her own fault, but because of the colossal vitality of his illusion."

Yeah, I'm not awake enough to actually read this.

Closing the book, I turn the lights off and drift to sleep.

Chapter Sixteen

Hope

A week and a day later the sunlight once again beaming in, the moment I open my eyes. Maybe I will finally get some curtains for myself as a Christmas gift. I glance at the clock on my nightstand, a little past ten in the morning. I couldn't sleep. Dreams, *more like nightmares* played on repeat. Of my past relationship and of last Christmas.

I woke up with a weight of anxiety on me, probably due to knowing I would be seeing my crazy family in a couple of hours. Everyone usually arrives at Jack's around one o'clock in the afternoon. Only my immediate insane members of our family would be there this year, our cousins came last year and quickly regretted their decision when all the drama went down. Hopefully this year won't be a repeat.

After hopping out of the shower and wrapping a towel around my waist, I head into the kitchen. In desperate need of some coffee, despite the anxiety building up. Glancing over at the dresser in my bedroom, closest to the kitchen, I zone out on Lilah's Christmas present. I picked it up Friday afternoon. After spending the morning with her, the perfect gift idea popped into my head. The small box wrapped with a red bow has been hidden in the drawer of my nightstand so she wouldn't find it if she decided to stay over. She's been at her place finishing a couple of last minute things for work though.

My phone starts buzzing, I walk over to pick it up. All the worry and anxiety leaving my body as I see who it is. *Lilah.*

"Good morning, beautiful," I say, smiling into the phone.

A pause, "Morning."

"You okay?" Worry spreads through my body tenfold.

Lilah lets out a deep sigh before answering, "I'm so sorry Landon." Another pause as she adds, "I can't come to your brother's house for Christmas."

The small present with the red bow mocks me. As much as I am disappointed, I don't want her to think I am mad, it is Christmas after all.

"Did something happen?" I ask tentatively, searching for a reason as to why she would change her mind. This past week she hadn't let on that she wouldn't be there, and she didn't say anything on the phone last night to hint that she wasn't planning on coming. Granted she never openly talked about coming either.

"I just– I just can't. I'm sorry." Another big sigh, "I have to go Landon, I'll call you later." The phone clicks off before I'm able to reply.

Great.

Walking up to my brother's front door, snow under my boots and a bag of presents for the twins slung over my shoulder. I can't help but feel a wave of sadness being here alone. I spot my parent's car, conveniently taking up the majority of the driveway so I have to park down the street.

Lilah didn't answer when I tried calling her again, or to the two texts I sent before I left the loft. The first, telling her it's okay and I wasn't mad. The second, giving her my brother's address in case she changes her mind. I knock twice on the front door. Nancy opens it shortly after and brings me in for a hug.

"Landon, Merry Christmas!" She looks past me, obviously expecting Lilah to be there but she doesn't say anything to my relief.

"No Lilah?" Jack asks as soon as I'm inside, earning a glare from Nancy.

I shake my head as I remove my coat, handing the bag of presents to Nancy to put by the tree in the corner of the living room.

"No, something came up with her family and she went home." A blatant lie, because I knew for a fact she was choosing to stay in the city for Christmas, possibly going home after the new year. She told me her parents have lived in Arizona for the last few years and they would be in Hawaii for Christmas.

"Well bummer, I was looking forward to meeting her. The girls haven't stopped talking about it all morning." As if on cue both twins run into the room.

"Uncle Landon! Uncle Landon!" both say in unison at way too high of a decibel for the headache starting in my temples.

"Look what Santa brought me!" Emily shouts, showing me her giant toy nerf gun. I glance over at Nancy, her face tells me it was definitely Jack who was in charge of gifts this year.

"She already shot me with one of her stupid darts," Isabelle says as she rubs her left arm, a small bruise already starting to form where the styrofoam dart must have hit her.

Trying not to laugh, I make my way into the kitchen, where the rest of my family members are hovering by the snack table. Casie, my sister, the youngest of my siblings, already a few glasses deep into some champagne. My dad is sitting by the corner of the table, finding enjoyment in a crossword puzzle book as usual. An attempt to avoid my mother's bitching at him, I'm sure. She always is in a special mood at family gatherings around the holidays.

"Merry Christmas son." Speak of the devil. I turn around and there is my mother, walking into the kitchen from the hallway.

"Merry Christmas," I say, trying to at least feign some politeness in my tone.

I would try to be as civil as possible today, considering the last time I saw any of them was at the hospital when my mother faked a heart attack to get me and Rachel back together.

I turn to my sister. She looks at me as if I'm a beast with three heads. My dad is the only one of the three who smiles at me. My sister and mother go back to their conversation as I walk around the table and give my dad a hug.

"Merry Christmas Dad, how's the crossword puzzle?"

"It's not a great one," he says, shaking his head down at the book. "Merry Christmas son. Your girlfriend didn't come?" No hint of judgment laces his tone, only genuine curiosity.

My father and I's relationship was never like the one I had with my mother. He was always supportive, attending my baseball games as a kid, driving me to and from practices. He was a good person with a big heart, how he ended up with someone like my mother I will never know. Unfortunately, our relationship has always been outshined by my mother's hostility.

"No, unfortunately she couldn't make it," I say as I make my way to the fridge to grab some eggnog, facing this holiday sober is not on my to do list.

"It's probably for the best," my mother says in her favorite condescending tone.

I shut the fridge, wanting to probe further as to why she would even say such a thing but Lilah's voice goes through my head, reminding me I don't need to give them power.

The thought is oddly comforting, a sense of ease takes over. I make my way back into the living room to sit next to Jack on the couch.

"Sorry she couldn't make it man," he says as he tries to fish out one of Emily's nerf darts from under his seat.

"It's okay, I'm sure some drama would've ensued if she did. Even though with our family we both know something is bound to happen before the day is over."

He laughs and gets up from the couch, "I'll be right back, I got you a bottle of whiskey I'm going to let you open before dinner." Looks like my brother intends to also not be sober for today's festivities.

At the same moment a styrofoam dart flies past my head to land on the window behind the couch, the doorbell rings. A spark of hope shoots through me, Lilah must have changed her mind and came anyway. I get up to go to the door, telling Nancy I would get it so she doesn't have to stop her cooking prep in the kitchen for tonight's dinner.

I almost trip over a stuffed cat Isabelle got as a gift from Santa as I go to open the blue front door, trying to tame my smile as the cold air pelts my face.

"Merry Christmas, Lan."

The sickly sweet smell of roses hits my nostrils.

Not Lilah, but Rachel stands on the other side of the doorframe, a grin plastered to her face as she goes to move past me into the house.

Chapter Seventeen

Strike

I don't know why I'm surprised, but somehow, I am. Rachel walks right past me. Her blonde hair swishing from shoulder to shoulder as she heads straight towards the kitchen to hug my mother. I look straight at Jack, surprise filling his face as much as anger fills mine. I gesture for him to follow me outside.

Once we are both out in the cold, our breath visible in front of us, I lose it.

"Jack what the actual *fuck?*" Not that I actually think he had anything to do with Rachel being here, I just can't hold back my anger that she is here at all.

"I promise I had no idea she would have the balls to show up, I told mom she wasn't invited." Complete shock and worry crosses his face.

I sigh, "I don't even know what to do at this moment, how the hell am I supposed to just sit in there with her like we are all one big happy family?" I say with complete exasperation.

Jack considers for a moment before he replies, "I hate to say it man but maybe to keep the peace you try to play nice for today."

That's it, the strike to light the match of the flame I've managed to keep down for the past year. Everything I've bottled up and held down for the sake of *keeping the peace* threatens to come to the surface. Not only Jack's words but seeing her here with my family yet again, as they shut me out and welcome her with open arms.

"With all due respect, *fuck you,* Jack." I shake my head, unable to calm the racing thoughts coming in. I don't want to fight with my brother, this isn't his fault, but him implying it's up to me to be the bigger person is too much. Granted he doesn't know everything.

Before I say anything else I might regret to one of the few people in my life I know truly care about me, I turn straight for the garage. Jack following close behind.

I throw the cover off my motorcycle in the corner, letting it fall to the cold cement floor. Standing there, debating if this is the best idea. Sure, I could go for a drive but my car is a couple streets over. There is nothing that beats a ride on my bike to clear my head. I haven't ridden in almost a year, just once in the spring after last Christmas.

"You're not thinking of going for a ride are you?" Jack comes up beside me, concern and fear lacing his voice.

I don't answer as I hop on, flipping the ignition switch as the lights flicker to life. Grabbing the clutch and starting her up, vibration seeps through to my bones as I put my feet down to push off out of the garage. Jack moves quickly out of my way.

The wind in my face is pelting me with enough force to hurt. The mix of rain and snow isn't helping either. Damn myself for forgetting my riding glasses or helmet in the garage. I just needed to get on the road. My brain feels like it's moving a thousand miles per hour.

My breathing feels halted, like my lungs can't take in a full breath. The events of the past couple of weeks feel like they're all falling down on me. Every moment of drama caused by Rachel and my family.

Today was the final straw, I couldn't stand to be in that house with everyone. Although they don't know everything. I'm tired of them all acting like one big happy family. I swear Jack is the only one not completely wrapped in her vice grip, but I haven't even told him the crux of it. I can barely bring myself to relive the memories to try to explain what happened. I knew today was a mistake, I shouldn't have come and Rachel sure as hell shouldn't be there either.

I don't fully know where I am headed to. The roads are nearly empty with it being Christmas and the weather is definitely not cooperating. I just needed to clear my head, if I had stayed back at the house I would have combusted, ruining everyone's holiday. Shit. The roads are slick, the rain turning more into sleet. I didn't even bother grabbing my *helmet. I need to figure out what the hell I'm going to do. I can't stand to be in the same room as Rachel.*

Fuck! That was close, lucky I didn't hit that giant ice patch. I should probably turn back. I'll pull into this park for a minute then head back to my brother's house.

The cold air is definitely not helping me breathe better, I feel like every ounce of me is wanting to burst out of my body. My vision feels tunneled and my heart is racing. I must be having a panic attack. I should head back to Jack's. Damn, even my boots feel slick on the foot pegs of my bike. Luckily I didn't go too far, only a few minutes ride back to the house.

Running off probably wasn't the brightest move, Rachel and my mother I'm sure are waiting to tear into me for handling this childishly. I'm sure even if my mother knew what happened she wouldn't care. This panic needs to subside before I set foot back there. Luckily the sleet has stopped, but the roads are still so slick and my rear wheel feels like it's locking—Oh shit!

The side of the road is the last thing I see before I black out.

———

Thinking back to last year, I realize getting back on this bike probably wasn't the smartest move. I didn't forget my helmet this time though and luckily the roads aren't nearly as slick. Last Christmas, this motorcycle almost cost me my life. I'm not trying to be as reckless as I was then, I just needed some air.

Pulling off into the parking lot of the same park I was aiming for last year, I park my bike and go to sit on a nearby snow covered bench. Pulling out my phone to send Lilah a text.

Hi Beautiful, I wanted to let you know I'm not upset with you for not coming for Christmas, it's actually probably best you didn't. My ex showed up. I wanted you to know I love you & I hope your day goes better than mine. I can't wait to see you tomorrow.

Her reply comes shortly after.

I'm sorry your Christmas isn't turning out like you had hoped. I wish I could be there to cheer you up but remember, you don't owe anyone who treats you like shit anything. Don't let them have power over you. I love you & I can't wait to see you either.

The snow is gentle and slow, not sticking too much to the roads. My mind is starting to calm down some. Taking a deep breath in, I continue reflecting back to one of the worst times in my life.

———

A stark bright light wakes me up, followed by an incessant beeping to my right. I have no idea where I am. Panic starts to creep in again. I remember I was on my bike. Heading back to the house when I hit a patch of ice I didn't see. Then it all went black. I feel a sharp pain in my side and back. It hurts to breathe.

"Oh good, you're awake!" Rachel says from my left side.

"Rachel...? What happened?" I ask her as I try to get my bearings, I must have crashed bad if I'm in the hospital. Rachel gets up from her chair, a wild look in her eyes as she reaches for my hand, I try but fail to pull away.

"You crashed your bike Lan, I knew you would try to go on a ride. I should strangle Jack for letting you go," she says as she shakes her head.

"It wasn't his fault, I pushed past him, once I was on my bike it's not like he could've stopped me."

She rolls her eyes, a wild look there. "I've always hated that bike, I figured because you hadn't rode it in a few years since we were in California and it was here, you wouldn't have really tried to go on it again." She looks off to the side, saying in a quieter tone, "I thought since your rear brake caused you issues the last time you went out on it before we moved you would have scrapped the thing already."

I'm not sure if it's the pain, or maybe whatever is being pumped through this IV but I don't think I heard her right.

"Did you say my rear brakes?" I ask, trying to keep my focus on my words and not falling back asleep.

She doesn't look me in the eyes as she says, "Yeah, I remember Jack saying something about it giving you issues or not working, you know I don't know anything about motorcycles."

I must be losing it, confusion fully taking over. "My bike never gave me issues before we moved."

"Oh, well Jack must have told me he found something wrong with it then, I don't know. Are you in pain? I'll get the nurse to give you more pain meds."

"Wait," I grab her hand before she steps away from the hospital bed, "Jack knew something was wrong with my bike?" I ask.

"Lan, I don't know. Let me get your nurse or Dr. Alex, you need sleep." She steps out of my grasp and heads out of the room.

I must have hit my head too, because I can't seem to think straight. I don't remember anything being wrong with my bike and I'm sure my brother would have told me. He definitely would've put up more of a fight with me trying to go for a ride. Dr. Alex, the usual doctor my mother sees when she's having an episode, walks in, shutting Rachel out of the room before he walks over to my side. He starts to speak but unconsciousness takes me before I understand what he is saying.

—————

Pulling back up to the house safely, I see Jack sitting out in the garage drinking a beer. A second one sitting next to him on the workbench. No one else is out here thankfully. I wonder if anyone else knew I left. I've realistically only been gone about a half hour, granted I did the same last year and almost died.

I pull my bike into the garage, then move to take a seat next to Jack. I open my mouth to apologize but he interrupts me.

"You're a real asshole, you know." He says, handing me the second unopened beer.

"Yeah, I'm aware. Sorry man." I hesitate to bring up last year, knowing I scared Jack with my accident. "Did anyone else notice I was gone?"

Jack shakes his head as he takes a swig of his beer.

"Look, I know we don't tend to bring up last year or anything regarding me and Rachel, which I appreciate by the way. But I need to ask you something I was thinking about on my ride."

"Ok." He hesitates, "Shoot." A wary look crosses his face.

I take a deep breath, reliving the memories of last Christmas once again. "Last year, after my accident when I was in the hospital. Rachel said something, I meant to ask you about it then but they had me on a ton of meds I couldn't think straight and completely forgot."

"Well yeah, you fractured and broke multiple ribs and punctured a lung. I'm not surprised you don't remember much," Jack says.

"Yeah, don't remind me," I say with a dry laugh, "Anyways, when I woke up Rachel was telling me what happened and mentioned something about my bike." I open and take a drink of my beer before asking, "Did you tell her something was wrong with my rear brake on my bike? Or about anything being wrong with it?"

Jack thinks for a second, confusion etched into his face. "No man, I hadn't looked at your bike for a while. The last time I peaked at it under the cover before last Christmas was last Thanksgiving when you and Rachel were here. I came out to grab a drink and she had the cover off."

"Wait, what? She was out here alone and looking at my bike?" That's odd.

"I didn't get a chance to ask her, she quickly put the cover back on and said something about taking a picture of it so she could list it for sale when you guys went back to California." He shrugs, "I didn't think much of it because I know she's always hated you riding."

I don't even know what to think, she's always doing questionable things and has tried to sell my stuff without telling me before. I just don't know why she would have mentioned something being wrong with my bike, she doesn't know anything about motorcycles. Maybe I was more out of it than I thought then.

Shaking my head, I hop off the workbench. "Well I guess it's time to face the music, let's go have a *Merry Christmas*." I laugh as I wrap my arm around Jack's shoulder, earning a laugh and an eye roll as we make our way back into the house.

Chapter Eighteen

Smoke

The divide in the room when Jack and I walk back inside is apparent, it's almost comical. Nancy and my nieces are in the kitchen, finishing up some cookies. You're able to tell which ones the twins helped decorate by the rudimentary icing splotches, versus Nancy's intricate snowman ones. My father is sitting alone at the kitchen table still, looking fully content to be around family, even if we are all at each other's throats lately. Then Rachel, my mother and sister are sitting in the living room. I don't think about which direction to go as I make my way straight to the kitchen table.

"Still working on your crossword puzzle?"

My dad looks over at me, a smile on his bearded face. "Of course, it's the only thing keeping me sane with all of this family's antics."

I laugh, "Yeah, sorry about my part in any of it." I run my hands through my hair, not sure what else to say.

He's looking down at his puzzle as he says, "You know I just want you to be happy son, even if I don't understand your choices. Happiness is all I want for you."

Reaching over I pat my dad's broad shoulder, "I know dad." Thinking to myself about Lilah. I think I am finally allowing myself a piece of happiness.

"Dinners ready!" Nancy shouts from the kitchen, shutting the oven as she pulls out a delicious turkey cooked to perfection. The same scent filling the air as last year.

———

Everyone is sitting around the long rectangular table in Jack's and Nancy's dining room. The sound of Bing Crosby coming from the small radio in the corner. My sister-in-law went all out as usual. Everything smells amazing, the small table in the opposite corner of the door filled with an array of different desserts, the cookies of which were definitely decorated by the twins. Rudolph looks more like a cow than a red nosed reindeer. Chuckling to myself I go to take my seat, next to Rachel who is already sitting and talking with my mother on her other side.

Rachel and I fought the entire car ride from the hotel. I don't know which is worse, the fighting or the complete silence on the plane ride here from California yesterday morning. I don't know why she is the one leading in this battle we are having. I'm not the one she walked in on.

It's crazy how much changes from one holiday to the next. We were here last month for Thanksgiving. Holding hands, laughing together. We were having some issues, sure, but I thought we could move past those. Regardless of my mother trying to convince me to leave Rachel. We hadn't had sex in a while, but I thought it was because of our arguing and the fact that she was always going out with friends when I was home from work. I never thought she would stoop as low as she d id.

The replay of last week has been on constant repeat in my head. Taunting me to the brink of insanity. I had come home from work a couple hours early to surprise her. I bought her flowers, made a reservation at our favorite restaurant in the hopes of rekindling what we at one point had. I knew something was off as soon as I spotted that brown jacket thrown onto the kitchen counter. Smelling exactly like the cologne she bought for me on my birthday, but this jacket wasn't mine. Maybe she bought me a present too? My naive brain tried to convince me.

Walking up the stairs I could hear the water running, I figured she was in the shower. I headed into our bedroom, taking off my jacket and shoes to start undressing, before I could unbutton my pants I heard her. Moaning. My brain tried to convince me it was her alone, pleasuring herself. Then I heard him calling my wife baby. The sound of them fucking filling the room over the sound of the running water. Over the sound of my heart pounding in my head.

———

After we help carry in the rest of the food from the kitchen, we all take our seats at the dining room table. Nancy labeled them with small place cards. My heart falls a little when I spot my place, with Lilah's name on the seat to my right. I go to reach for the small piece of paper. Looking around to find my more rebellious niece Emily to take her place when another hand reaches out to snatch up the card as my fingertips graze the paper.

"Oh, was your little girlfriend supposed to come today?" A glass of white wine gets set down next to me.

"Don't start Rachel," I say quietly, trying to avoid as much drama as possible for the rest of today.

Rachel sits down in Lilah's place after crumbling the piece of paper like it was a bug about to bite her. I lean over, keeping my voice low, "You think that's a good idea? Why don't you go to take the seat on the other side of my mother?" I say, nodding in the direction of the other side of the table.

"Oh, Lan," she replies with an eye roll, reaching for the glass of wine she set down. "I'm not here to start anything, you were the one who thought inviting your play thing to a family event was a good idea."

Before I respond, Jack stands, holding up a new bottle of beer, clearly sensing the tense energy coming from my side of the table.

"I wanted to thank my family for being here today. Me and Nancy love when the girls get to spend holidays with...," He hesitates for a brief second, glancing around the table before finishing, "...ev eryone. Cheers to this evening being filled with love, *support*, and understanding."

Jack finishes his toast with a pointed look in Rachel and I's direction. He's lucky I love him or I would have outright laughed when he said the word *family*. However, I am determined to be the bigger person like he suggested and try to ignore any and every attempt by my ex to rile me.

"Glad it's only family here," Rachel adds as Jack goes to sit down.

This is going to be harder than I thought.

———

Her moans mixed with his would not stop in my head even at Christmas dinner. Sitting right next to her I only see her in that shower. Normally an exciting thought, until I spotted him thrusting into her from behind, both of their hands intertwined on the glass of the steaming shower. I only feel betrayal anymore.

Being so close to Rachel at the table, my family not knowing what she's done and treating her like family, despite talking bad about her when she isn't here. I can't deal with it, I can't escape the roar-

ing thoughts in my head. The pounding of my heart mixed with the pounding of his dick inside of my wife. Those thoughts lead me to my bike.

———

Luckily the rest of dinner went by smoothly, following with present opening in the living room. It didn't bother me at all not getting any presents besides those from Jack, Nancy and the twins. I hadn't expected anything anyways. However, what I was not expecting the most was Rachel to get up and hand me a small wrapped box.

"Oh, uh thanks Rachel," I say awkwardly, "I'm sorry... I didn't bring you anything." I grab the small box from her hands.

"That's okay Lan, you can make it up to me," she replies with a wink.

Jack's brows shoot straight up at Rachel's response, earning a nudge from Nancy next to him. All eyes are on me. Even my sister stopped ignoring my existence to watch me open Rachel's present. Beneath the tissue paper inside the box, lay a small glass bottle. Cologne. The scent is different but the brand is the same from the cologne she used to buy me, *Whiskey Smoke.*

———

I thought we might have had a chance to make it work after she cheated. Thought maybe my accident was my saving grace. She was supportive, at my side most of the time during my recovery. She picked up a few shifts at her friend's coffee shop even though she hadn't worked our entire marriage to make up for some of my missed work, or so I had thought.

Instead, she was at his house. I could tell something was off but she kept denying it, saying she stopped seeing him. Swore it had only been the one time. I should have known though, finding the hat in our room years prior, despite her saying it was her girlfriend's. Her being out frequently, yet I never met her friends. Him and I wearing the same cologne couldn't be just a coincidence.

———

I tried to hold it in, smile and say thank you. I couldn't.
   Fuck being the bigger person.

"You buy this one for only me this time? Or is this an extra bottle he had lying around his house?" I say as dryly as I can manage. I look up, Rachel standing in front of me.

I knew she wasn't seeing him anymore, but I couldn't help myself.

The mix of reactions is hilarious. Jack's and my dad's eyebrows shoot almost straight off their forehead. Nancy's eyes widen with sudden panic while she simultaneously pats the twins on their shoulders and moves them from the room. My mother and sister both shout, "*What the fuck Landon!?*"

The best reaction though is Rachel's. Her mouth hangs open for but a minute before she composes herself, turning instantly to defensive anger.

"Landon what the *fuck* are you talking about?"

I know I'm not crazy, even if she's always made me feel like I am. The day after I was fully recovered from my accident, all of her transgressions came to light. I was able to freely move around and had just done laundry to help out. While putting away her things as a thank you for being so caring during my recovery. I found all the evidence she had in her underwear drawer, inside a tampon box nonetheless. I guess she never thought I'd check there. The box was carelessly in the front, I couldn't help but investigate when I noticed it was full of folded up pieces of paper instead of what should be there. It was full of letters, tons and tons of letters.

She had been fucking the man I caught her with in the shower for years. They celebrated anniversaries, and some holidays together. Him writing cards thanking her for his cologne and pictures she sent him. Almost every time she said she was with her friends, she was with him. She told him we were getting a divorce. Told him I didn't love her.

That was it. That was my final straw to ask for a divorce. I confronted her but I never told anyone else, for the fear they wouldn't believe me but also to try and *be the bigger person*. Even when my family shunned me after she told them our divorce was my fault because I didn't want to work through our *issues*. I didn't even try to fight for anything in the divorce, I just wanted to be done with her.

"Stop playing Rachel, you know I know everything."

A look of nervousness crosses her face. She gives me a pleading look, she knows I haven't told my family, not even Jack. I've given her grace this long with nothing to show for it. Time to stop being passive.

"I'm sorry Jack, I'm not trying to ruin Christmas again but I can't sit here with her anymore. She was cheating on me for years, that's why I left, why I asked for a divorce."

"Landon, I'm sure Rachel didn't do such a thing. I bet this is all a misunderstanding, if you weren't so stubborn–" My mother starts to say before I interrupt her.

"Mom, I'm going to need you to stop siding with her. She is *not* your daughter and she is not the woman she has led you to believe she is. I know I have my issues, I know the small arguments we have had in the past I could have played a better part in but I walked in on another man's dick inside her. I'm pretty sure I'm not the bad guy here."

I walk away from the living room, back towards the garage. I need to be alone, before I blow up anymore. Right before the garage door shuts behind me, Rachel follows into the cold dim room.

"Landon, what the actual hell is *wrong* with you!?"

"Don't," I say, turning around to face her. "I am sick and tired of being made to be the villain in this story. I did not give up on us, *YOU* did. I tried to make it work. I thought you changed and were remorseful after my accident but you continued to play me. I was an absolute idiot. I should have left a lot sooner than I did!"

"*YOU DROVE ME TO CHEAT!*" she shouts, "You were away working most of the time, and then you were always exhausted because of work. He at least showed me attention!"

"Are you actually kidding me Rachel? I worked during the day, was home every night and attempted to be intimate with you all the time. I constantly told and showed you how much I *loved* you! Even when you started showing distance, I blamed *myself* and attempted to fix whatever I was doing wrong."

"You're unbelievable Landon, ruining Christmas yet again because you're jealous your family loves me more. That's really what all this is about isn't it?" she says as she crosses her arms.

"There you go again, always trying to deflect the conversation away from you. Because *you* never do anything wrong right?"

"You know what Landon, I'm glad I fucked with your stupid motorcycle last year. I didn't fully know you would go for a ride, but it's a shame your little accident didn't knock some sense into you."

"*What the fuck did you just say?*" Jack says from the doorway behind Rachel.

She startles and turns around, "Oh, Jack! Uh, nothing. Go back inside." She tries to wave him off, turning back towards me.

"No, I will not go back inside. You said you were the cause of my brother's accident. I'm going to need you to get the hell out of my house." He starts walking towards her.

"Ugh, you Stone brothers are the worst. Whatever. This conversation isn't done, I hope you know that, Landon. As much as you want to move on with your little *slut,* you're never going to get over me. I'm the best thing to have ever happened to you," she says, stalking out of the garage to walk towards her rental car. Driving off into the snow.

Jack and I watch until she's cleared his street before speaking.

"Come on, I think it's time we go drink that bottle of bourbon I got you," Jack says.

Chapter Nineteen

Haze

The next morning my head is pounding from Jack and I finishing the full bottle of whiskey he got me. The rest of my family left shortly after Rachel did. Leaving me and Jack to be the entertainment for the evening.

Emily and Isabelle spent the rest of the night playing with their new toys, much to Nancy's dismay as the house quickly became a nerf gun battleground. I took Isabelle's team, Jack with Emily as we built mock forts out of the couch cushions. Nancy opted to act unamused even though I caught her smiling a handful of times. Until I accidentally hit a vase which ended up chipped, earning me a terrifying glare from my sister-in-law. She didn't stay too mad for long though. I crashed on their couch, not wanting to chance driving after how much booze we had indulged in.

After breakfast I headed out, wanting to clean up a little before Lilah comes over this evening. We talked on the phone as I drove the almost half hour home, I chose to save telling her any of yesterday's drama though until I see her in person. If I decide to go into it at all.

Surprisingly with this throbbing pain behind my eyes, I feel lighter today. Like a small weight has been lifted off my shoulders. I guess standing up to someone who has made it a point to make a portion of your life miserable will do that. I half expect to find Rachel camped out in my place, even if I made her give me back her spare key. She admitted to having more than the one, but thankfully there is no vindictive blonde in sight as I turn the key in my door and open it to the sunlit loft.

I definitely need to tidy up this place before I let Lilah in here. Mostly my clothes are strewn about and my bed unmade. First though, I need to get to the gym. Even if I feel lighter on my feet today, I want to expel any leftover anger or tension from my body before I see Lilah. Lifting weights always does the trick.

After an hour throwing around some dumbbells and a little cardio I drip with sweat. My t-shirt almost soaked through, I discard it as soon as I'm back in my place, leaving my torso bare. I hear a *woo-woo* whistle come from behind me.

I whip my head around quickly, scared it could be a certain blonde. Luck is on my side though as I spot Lilah lounging on the couch, smirking with her lower lip in between her teeth as she looks me up and down.

"I didn't realize I would be getting a show as soon as you got home," she says, getting up from the couch to walk over to me. I meet her halfway, wrapping my hand around the back of her neck.

"Didn't anyone tell you breaking and entering is a crime?" My other hand reaches around her waist to pull her closer as I look down into those beautiful steel blue eyes.

She smiles, making my heart start to pound. "Your door was unlocked." She lets out a small laugh and rolls her eyes in that sexy way of hers.

"Did you not notice my lack of presence?" I move my hand over my chest, feigning offense.

She shoves my shoulder gently with another roll of her eyes. "Of course! But you did give me a key for a reason, so I let myself in." She places her hands on my chest, looking up at me mischievously.

"I was honestly hoping to catch you in bed or in the shower so I could show you how sorry I am to have skipped out on you yesterday."

Ohh.

"Is that right?" I smirk, tucking a strand of hair behind her ear as I move in to kiss her luxurious mouth.

She meets me with her lips open, allowing me in before she pulls away.

"You taste like sweat." She laughs as she licks her lips.

I rub the back of my head, slight embarrassment taking over before I ignore it and laugh too. "Yeah sorry, I just got back from the gym. You did say something about a shower though?" I put my finger to my chin as she narrows her eyes with a knowing smirk.

I let only a beat pass before I scoop Lilah up by the legs. Swinging her over my shoulder, earning a gasp and laughing shriek as she drapes over me while I lead us into the bathroom.

Slowly letting her down once we get to the tiled floor in front of the shower. I let every inch of our bodies touch before her feet fully hit the ground. Twisting Lilah around, I run my hand up her torso, guiding up until I gently grasp the front of her neck. My other hand moving her hair behind her shoulder, giving me access to kiss her neck. I take my time, earning a small whimper.

I move my mouth up to her ear to whisper, "You said you wanted to make it up to me for not coming for Christmas right?" I feel her smile before she turns around to face me.

"I said something of the sort," she answers as her eyes take in my shirtless body.

"First though, I think you have too many clothes on," I say.

I reach to lift up the bottom of her shirt, slipping it over her head as she raises her hands. She's not wearing a bra. My heart stutters for a second as I take in the image of her. She goes to undo the button on her jeans.

"No. Me first," I say, grabbing her hand and putting it at the waistband of my sweatpants. She obliges, following the direction of my pants as she pushes them down my legs, taking my underwear with them. The sight of her on her knees almost does me in.

"*Fuck.*"

She has me in her grip.

Making her way up and down the length of me with her mouth. I'm in complete ecstasy in her control. As much as I want this to go on forever, I do not want to finish like this. My hand on the back of her head, I reach down and tilt her chin up to look directly at me.

We don't even need words, she understands by looking at me, I want her fully. As she stands up in front of me, I grip both sides of her face and take her mouth with mine, reaching left to turn the shower faucet on. Our mouths don't break contact while I use my hands to undo her jeans and slide them down her perfect ass. Leaving us both fully bare.

I lean down and grab the back of both of her thighs, lifting her up to put our faces at the same height as she wraps her legs around my waist. Walking us into the shower with balanced feet, I let the hot water fall over the back of her head as I find her mouth again. I move to put myself into her, holding her up with my other arm. Good thing I didn't go crazy on my workout today or I might be shaking a little with the maneuver.

Once I'm fully inside, the wet tightness of her claiming me, I use both hands to lift her to a rhythm matching the small thrusts of my hips. The shower filling with her moans.

Setting her down, she immediately turns her ass towards me as she bends over taking hold of the opposite wall. I insert myself back into her, thrusting harder with each of her delicious whimpers.

I'm on the brink of release but I want to be closer to her, on top of her. I lift her torso up to my chest as she faces away from me, my right hand going south as my left reaches around her throat.

"Let's take this back to the bed," I say, my voice raspy with desire.

She follows my lead out of the shower, reaching for a towel.

"Fuck towels. I need *you*." I take it from her hand and pick her up again. Thankfully the bath mat dried my feet enough.

"You're going to get water everywhere," she says with a laugh as I walk us the distance from the bathroom to the bed.

"You think that's my priority?" I reply as I lay her down on my still unmade bed. I take in the gloriousness of her before me, right before I glide inside her again. I don't think I will ever get enough of her, especially as we find release together.

———

I could lay next to this woman forever. Even on these damp sheets, the cold starting to come in full force from lying here naked without toweling off. Bringing goosebumps with it. I begin to trace Lilah's torso with my finger.

"So what all happened yesterday? You never told me everything on the phone earlier," Lilah asks, watching my hand trace her idly.

"Honestly, it was a shit show. I don't even feel like going into it all, because for once it doesn't seem to matter anymore." I contemplate, realizing I genuinely don't feel the wave of disgust, hatred and anger usually accompanied when thinking about my ex.

"Rachel, my ex, played nice in her fake way she usually does around my family. I ended up calling her on her shit and then she admitted to being the cause of my motorcycle accident. Needless to say, Jack kicked her out."

Lilah's eyes widen. I go into a little more detail about my past, the accident and me finding Rachel cheating. She already knew about the incident, just not everything about it. After I relay all of the drama, it does feel better to have talked it through. That light feeling strengthening even more.

"That's wild Landon. I'm still sorry I bailed on you but it sounds like me being there might have made things worse."

"Oh definitely. As much as I wanted you there, I'm glad you didn't have to witness any of it or be around my ex," I add, "You were there in thought anyways."

Lilah looks at me as I finish, "What you said to me, about not giving power to those who don't deserve it kept playing in my head. I honestly don't think I would have stood up for myself had you not said those words to me."

We lie there for a moment until I remember I haven't given her, her gift yet.

"Switching to a happier topic, I got you something. I was hoping to give it to you yesterday but we will just consider tonight to be our Christmas." I stand up and walk over to my dresser to open the top drawer. Grabbing the small box.

Lilah beams as I walk back over to the bed, setting her present next to her.

"You didn't need to get me anything." She reaches over to grab something out of her overnight bag at the end of the bed. "But I got you something too." Her smile is more than I could ask for this year.

I grab the large flat rectangular box from her and she picks up the small one to her right.

"On the count of three?" she asks with an infectious smile.

"One," I say.

"Two," she responds.

"Three." We both say at the same time, untying both of the bows on top of the boxes.

I lift the lid off the white box as she opens the small red one in her hands. Underneath a layer of red tissue paper, I find a leather-bound portfolio book. The brown leather is soft as butter and has an 'LS' imprinted into the corner. I open the book, it is filled with at least a hundred pages to fit photographs in. I can't help the smile spreading on my face, I do hold back the water fighting to come out of my eyes though. I don't think I've ever gotten something this thoughtful from anyone before.

I look up to find Lilah mirroring the same smile as she holds the small gold locket with a red gem in the center.

"This is beautiful Landon," she says as she looks up at me, holding the locket out. "Will you help me put it on?"

I grab the necklace. The locket is smaller than my thumbnail. I don't know what practicality this locket has but as soon as I saw it I knew I wanted to get it for Lilah.

"I saw it in a vintage shop down the street and for some reason it reminded me of you."

"I love it," she says as she reaches her hand up to grasp the metal. "What do you think?" She gestures to the portfolio at my side.

"I think this is the most thoughtful gift I have ever gotten." I look down and touch the leather. "Thank you, beautiful."

"I thought you should have something to put your pictures in. One day maybe you'll share them with more people than only me."

Lilah moves to lie on her back, staring up at the ceiling. I follow suit, pulling her onto my chest as we both lay there. She starts to breathe a little faster, like she's nervous.

"You deserve to be happy, Landon," she says, pausing as she takes a breath. "About me not going yesterday, it had nothing to do with you or how I feel about us. I hope you know that. I have a hard time fully allowing myself to be put out there. My last relationship left me extremely broken. I think I'm just trying to protect myself."

I didn't realize she's been mulling over not going this whole time. I hope I haven't made her feel guilty. It genuinely was a good thing she ended up skipping out. I want to ask her more about her previous relationship but I don't want to pry too much.

"You don't need to explain. I promise I don't hold any hard feelings about it. You need to move at whatever pace is comfortable for you." I kiss her forehead, her hair damp from the shower.

"I know, but I do love you and want you to know how I feel. I promise I will be there next time." She tucks her head further into me, nestled in between my neck and shoulder. Feeling the haze from our sex and from finally feeling a bit free, I start to drift off. Completely content and happy.

Chapter Twenty

Ember

"*H*ello!?" I look over to find Aaron waving dramatically at me, "You going to work today or keep staring off into space?" He stifles a laugh and shakes his head.

"Oh, sorry man," I laugh, running my hand through my hair. I have no idea how long I've been staring out this window.

We are on the top floor again, cleaning up anything left behind. The building is almost finished, only a couple things left to do from Dean's suggestions. Thankfully the electrical issues in the lower level are finally fixed. I know Aaron is ecstatic, considering he was the one getting most of the slack from both Dean and Jack for what was going wrong. Only another few weeks on the project as long as nothing else comes up.

"Oh *SHIT*!"

Aaron and I quickly look towards the doorway, in the direction of the shouting. We both instantly charge down the stairs, I don't trust the elevator, plus it would take twice as long waiting for it to get to us. I lose track of how many floors we get down until we find a member of our crew, Derek, holding up a loose beam in the ceiling.

Luckily the guy is tall or he wouldn't have caught it. Aaron rushes over to help him, asking frantically what happened.

Jack comes from the opposite direction up the stairs a second later. A look of panic in his eyes, "What the actual hell is happening up here!?" He shouts.

Aaron and Derek manage to set the beam down, thankfully it wasn't load-bearing. I have no idea how it would have fallen. All the beams should be pretty solid at this point considering we are venturing towards completion. Dean did want exposed ceilings though.

"Is everything okay?" A light female voice sounds from the stairwell Jack just came through.

We all look over to find Claire, Dean's assistant, standing there with her eyes wide behind those large black rimmed glasses.

"Hey Claire." Jack walks towards her with his hand extended. She meets his shake as he answers her, "Yeah it looks like we have to make a few adjustments here but all is good."

I know when my brother tells half-truths, and this is one of those times. He doesn't need Claire running back to Dean letting him know we are still somehow fucking things up. Jack and Claire look deep in discussion off by the stairs. I walk over to help Aaron and Derek set the beam down.

"Looks like a pretty serious conversation over there," Aaron notes, looking in my brother's direction.

"You know Jack is stressing about Dean, what the *hell* happened Derek?"

Derek is in his mid-twenties and could clearly not care less about construction, he never argues with Jack or any of us but always half-asses everything. He looks nervous though.

"I'm not sure man, it just fell," he says as he rubs the back of his neck where his hair ends. I visibly see how red his eyes are. This wouldn't be the first time Derek came to work stoned.

Claire shouts bye to all of us as Jack walks back over, holding a few black envelopes.

"Whatcha got there?" Aaron asks.

He glances down, "Looks like we got invited to Dean's big New Years Eve party this weekend." Jack hands me and Aaron an invitation.

"What, am I not invited?" Derek asks, hurt lacing his voice.

"Yes Derek you're invited. Dean said anyone on our crew is welcome to attend. But it is a black tie event."

"Oh, shit man yeah I probably will pass then," Derek says as he turns and walks away. Pulling out some eye drops when he thinks we can't see him anymore.

"One day I'm going to have to fire that kid," Jack says half-jokingly, shaking his head. "You guys want to grab a drink after we finish up here?"

"Is that even a question?" Aaron and I both say at the same time.

———

Map Room is packed tonight. It's only Wednesday, but I guess after everyone's holiday they needed a drink. I wonder if anyone here also had a shitty Christmas. Stacey is working behind the bar. Madison had off tonight and tagged along with Aaron. Those two are enviably adorable. Lilah and I are more of the passionate, intense kind of couple. Whereas they are the kind who seem like they've been married for fifty years already. For all Aaron's been through, I don't blame him for getting comfortable quickly. You never know how much time you have with someone.

"So, when are we going to finally meet Lilah?" Aaron looks over to me on my right. A huge grin on his face, Madison peeking around him.

"You two need to stop being so damn adorable. Lilah isn't fully ready to meet people yet." A look of confusion taking over both of their faces. I add, "She had a rough last relationship which makes her weary of meeting family and friends, she'll come around though. I just don't want to push it too far."

"So, are you going to invite her as your plus one for Dean's party Sunday?" Jack chimes in from my left.

"I had planned on asking her yes, but again I don't want to cross her boundaries. We've only been dating for barely over a month, remember?"

Everyone goes back to their drinks. Aaron and Madison jumping back into whatever it was they were grinning about before. *Has it only been a little over a month since I met Lilah?* I feel like we have known each other our whole lives, but we haven't. I definitely don't want to push her too far and make her bolt. Not that I think she would disappear on me, but I should probably tread carefully. Especially with not knowing all the details of her last relationship and why it left her scarred.

"Hey Mr. Broody," Stacey says as she walks up, another drink already poured for me.

"I don't think you can keep calling me that anymore, Stace, I haven't been *brooding* as much lately." I give her a joking glare.

She tilts her head in thought. "I guess you're right, but the name stays. Want another one Jack?" she asks looking over to him, Jack's been a little quieter today. I think he is stressing over our job's deadline.

"Yeah, I'll have one more," he answers back as she grabs another bottle to crack open and hand to him.

"You alright man?" I pat his shoulder, taking a sip of my whiskey.

For a second I don't think he's going to answer. "Yeah, I'm okay, this building crap is just stressing me out." He takes a swig from the amber colored bottle in his hand.

I feel like there is something more, I always sense when Jack is holding back his thoughts. I don't push though, considering I hate it when people push me when I am *"broody."* I look over to Aaron and Madison, giving my brother some mental space.

"Madison, you going to the big party this weekend?" I already know Aaron invited her but her happy energy is always infectious, hopefully it will rub off on my brother.

"Of course!" She immediately is beaming, I can't help but mirror her excitement. "I need to go shopping for a dress though, since it's black tie and all," she says.

Shit, I should probably get a tux.

"Aw man, I forgot about that part." Aaron grimaces, I guess I'm not the only one ill-prepared for this party.

I do hope Lilah says yes. I'd love to see her in a fancy dress, *hell* I love to see her in anything, especially my shirt when she's hanging out at my place. I need to talk to her soon to ask her to the party, hopefully a few days' notice is enough time for her to decide.

"I think I'm going to head out," I say as I down the last of the liquid in my glass. Standing up I throw on my leather jacket.

"Aww boo," both Madison and Aaron say simultaneously, making me laugh.

"I need to talk to Lilah and convince her to come to what I'm sure is going to be a ridiculously extravagant event." I pat my brother and Aaron on the shoulders, Jack's weary expression still on his face. Hopefully he doesn't let too much stress get to him before this weekend, I know we will all have to be on our best behavior around Dean and his guests.

I reach over to give Madison a side hug, "Good Luck!" She calls out as I walk towards the door into the bitingly cold air.

The next morning, I woke up early to go to the gym. The morning sun beaming in to disrupt my sleep as usual. Lilah is right where I left her, naked and asleep in my bed. Her hair tousled. She looks so peaceful I can't bring myself to wake her. I do have to head to work today unfortunately. Jack wants to make sure the building is perfect before this weekend. That way he doesn't have to lie to Dean when he asks for updates at the party.

Lilah hasn't given me an answer yet, but she didn't immediately say no last night when I asked her to come as my date. I'll take what I can get.

After I get out of the shower I walk into the kitchen, a towel wrapped around my waist. Lilah is up and cooking breakfast, wearing nothing but my t-shirt from last night. I can't tell what she is making but it does smell vaguely of burnt *something*.

"Whatcha cookin?" I ask as I walk up behind her at the stove, wrapping my hands around her waist as I peak over her shoulder at the food. If you could call it food that is.

"Well, I was trying to make some eggs and toast but I think it's a lost cause."

She turns to face me holding the pan. I back up a small step and look at the eggs, somehow they are almost cooked to a crisp. Then I look to the right of her and spy a plate of definitely burnt toast. I put my hand over my mouth to try and stifle my laugh. A sad look crosses her face but doesn't last long as we both burst out laughing.

I grab the pan and spatula from her hand and set them back on the stove, reaching around her to turn off the heat. She bashfully puts her hands over her face as we keep laughing. I grab them to kiss that beautiful mouth hers.

"Did I mention I'm not a great cook?"

"Doesn't bother me one bit love, I can be the chef in this relationship."

She lets out a small laugh, looking down like something's on her mind.

"What are you thinking?" I ask as I tap her adorable nose.

"I was going to hold out and tell you later but I don't see a point, other than to torture you." The side of her mouth tilts up into a smirk, "I'll be your date to your boss's party."

"Really!?" I try but fail to mask my complete and utter excitement.

She nods and smiles up at me.

I place my hands on both sides of her face and brush a strand of hair that fell out of the mess of a bun on her head behind her ear. Lilah's eyes will always disarm me. It's like I somehow forget how mesmerizing they are, only to be completely wrapped in them every time I look at her.

"I'm extremely happy you said yes, it should be fun." I glance down at the definitely not edible food on the counter and add, "How about we go out for breakfast this morning before I have to head into work?" My attention ventures to her bare legs. "But first…" I grab her waist and pivot her to the other side of the counter as I lift her up to sit on the edge, "I think I want a little pre-breakfast snack."

"*Ohh,*" she says with a knowing smile. I run my hands up her thighs as I get on my knees in front of her.

"Sounds like a good plan," Lilah says breathlessly as I start to savor her.

Chapter Twenty-One

Fireworks

The past two days have flown by. No more issues have arisen at the worksite thankfully. My brother is way less stressed than he has been. Instead of drinks after work to numb the day, we've been getting together the last two nights to just spend time with each other. Aaron joining every time. Madison worked the rest of this week behind the bar since she took off work today to attend Dean's party as Aaron's date. Their excitement to meet Lilah is borderline excessive.

Lilah has stayed at the loft practically every night this week. Waking up to her is the best part of my day. I love the mundane moments with her. Getting coffee, eating breakfast, seeing her get out of the shower to walk into the living room in only a towel. The latter being one of my favorite moments.

I could get used to having her around me all the time. Once I finally get her around the other people in my life, hopefully we are able to keep progressing in our relationship. I'm nowhere near wedding bells obviously but I can't picture a future without her.

"Well boys, it looks like we are all set until after the new year," Jack says.

I look away from the top floor window. Lost in thought yet again, to find my brother walking over towards the rest of the team and I, a relieved smile on his face. We gathered everyone mostly to triple check that everything is perfect and to wish everyone a happy new year. Jack handing out holiday bonuses definitely brightened up the crew's moods for being brought here on the weekend.

"Who's all joining us at the millionaire's palace tonight?" Aaron sarcastically asks the group.

"Does he actually live in a palace!?" Derek, the young kid who's always stoned asks with wide eyes.

Jack and I exchange the same look we always do when Derek speaks and I laugh, "No Derek, but his mansion might as well be from the pictures I've seen of it."

So far it looks like only Jack, me and Aaron will be attending. Luckily Jack is allowing us to take tomorrow off because of the party. Regardless, the rest of the crew is scared to face Dean apparently. I would sit this one out too if I wasn't worried about it looking bad on my brother. I'm also a little excited to show Lilah off if I'm being completely honest. She showed me the dress she got for the occasion yesterday. An almost see-through, long black one that shimmers in the light with a low cut back. I tore it off her body shortly after she had tried it on in my bedroom.

Aaron moves to stand beside me, "So are *you* bringing the flask tonight or *am I?*"

A few hours later I'm in my penguin suit and the most uncomfortable shoes known to man. I should have double checked the size when I ordered these. I don't tend to have occasions which call for a tux, I had to rent both but forgot to go in to try it all on beforehand. Thankfully the jacket and pants fit perfectly though.

I'm waiting outside in the cold for Aaron and Jack to arrive. Lilah is going to meet me here since she had to finish up a couple things for work and get ready. The doorman has been trying to get me inside for the last ten minutes, I guess Dean doesn't like his guests hanging around out front.

The estate is massive. The long driveway leads up to a gate with a security guard who is less than friendly. The main entrance to the mansion is held up by marble pillars and a *goddamned* giant wolf shaped fountain sits right in the center of the circular driveway. The pictures I've seen of this place do not do it justice. If I could have discreetly brought my camera, I would be capturing every detail. The large metal flask in my jacket pocket took up the last of my free space though.

Finally, I spot Aaron and Madison getting out of Aaron's truck. Which sticks out like a sore thumb compared to the fancier modes of transportation the valet is moving.

"Hey Landon! Looking good man!" Aaron shouts as he charges towards me, pulling me into a bear hug. Earning a few glares our way from some of the other party guests and some of Dean's house staff.

Laughing as he lets me go I give Madison a small hug and take in her fancy dress, "You look beautiful Madison." The emerald green mixed with her strawberry blonde curls makes her eyes stand out dramatically. Aaron's green bow tie matches too.

"Thanks Landon, you don't look too shabby yourself," she says with a smile and a nudge on my side.

Aaron leans in closer to me, in a much quieter voice, "You bring the goods?" He narrows his eyes.

I pat my left side, a sound of metal clanking inside the jacket against my rings, "But of course."

We all huddle together near a large bush to the left side of the entrance and take turns drinking from the flask of whiskey I brought. Not realizing someone is approaching behind us from the driveway.

"You all do know there is an open bar inside, right?" Jack says, eyeing us judgmentally. His arm wrapped around Nancy, both dressed to fit perfectly in with the rest of us. As uncomfortable as these shoes are, it is a nice change to all be dressed up for once.

"Oh Jack, don't be a buzzkill," Nancy surprises me by saying as she reaches for the flask from Madison and takes a big swig.

"Okay children, let's go join the rest of the party," Jack says as he raises his arm up for Nancy to grab onto, leading her inside.

Inside the mansion is more overwhelming than the behemoth of the wolf fountain outside. The main foyer opens up on each side, with twin staircases lining the middle. The party is spread all throughout the main section of the manor. Waiters in white shirts and black vests are navigating through the throngs of the party go-ers with trays of tiny food and champagne. With everyone in their fancy attire moving around me I almost feel like I stumbled into a party at *Jay Gatsby's*.

Speaking of the rich and mysterious, Dean spots us and immediately stops his conversation to come say hello. At least he doesn't intend on ignoring us the whole night, considering we are definitely the outcasts here among fellow millionaires and their dates. Even if we dressed the part.

"Here we go," Aaron says next to me as we walk to meet Dean where he and Jack are shaking hands in greeting.

Dean chose a white tux, to contrast with his darker complexion. Looking like he belongs to the manor's polished bronze and marble pillars lining every side of the main room we are in.

"Landon, I'm glad you could make it," he says excitedly as he reaches to shake my hand. "Where's this mysterious date your brother mentioned you would be bringing?" he asks, looking around for Lilah.

I give Jack a look, my eyebrow rising in question. He gives a small shrug.

"Lilah should be here soon. She had to finish up something with work first."

"Oh. Lilah..." he says as he looks deep in thought, "A beautiful name, I'm sure she is a catch. I hope to meet her at some point tonight." Dean looks over the rest of our group, "Well I must go greet some more of my guests, please enjoy yourselves." He finishes as he turns and walks away.

"Guess I'm invisible?" Aaron says with a chuckle. Madison pokes him in the side.

I pat his shoulder, "Sounds like an excellent time to find where the bar is, yeah?" He nods in agreement.

The next couple of hours fly by in a blur of champagne and whiskey. Only one more hour until midnight. I can't wait to welcome in the new year. Finally feeling like I have a new sense of self. Out with the *brooding* as Stacey would say, in with a small amount of newfound confidence I'll hopefully build on.

"So when's Lilah getting here? She waiting until next year?" Jack asks from my right as we lean against a wall off to the side, watching Madison and Aaron dance. Nancy tried to pull my brother on to the dancefloor with no luck, she decided to go by herself anyway. Her two left feet dancing is comical as she moves with our friends.

"She should have been here by now. I texted her not too long ago. Hopefully she won't be too much longer," I say as I take a sip of my drink. My phone vibrating in my pocket a moment later.

I'm sorry Landon... I'm not going to make it. I know I promised, but I just can't.

Fuck. Somehow I knew it was too soon after the failed attempt at Christmas, but I had real hope she would make it tonight.

Jack senses my shift instantly, "You alright?" He asks, "She's not coming is she?" I look down at my phone still in my hand and shake my head.

He lets out a sigh. "Well, it seems to me like you have two options, brother." I look over at him, "You can stay here and pretend to have a good time at this extravagant but draining party." He looks over to Nancy, chuckling slightly at her terrible dancing. "Or you meet her at her level. If she can't bring herself to come to you, you go to her."

I peel my eyes from our friends and Nancy to look at my brother, my eyebrows rising up my forehead.

"Oh, don't give me that look. You know I don't care if you leave, I appreciate you coming for my sake but go find your happiness man." He sets his drink down on the small table next to him and walks onto the dancefloor to his wife without saying another word.

I take one more second to look at all of them. Aaron holding Madison close as they sway excitedly to the fast music. While Jack grabs Nancy's hand and leads her into a dramatic and clumsy spin. Smiles on all of their faces. I grab my phone, send a quick text to Lilah and make my way through the crowd to the front door.

Luckily it wasn't too expensive of a ride here. I chose to leave my car and not chance driving after the couple of drinks I had, especially in this weather. The snow started falling on the way, a small flurry over the city starting to stick to the roads and my coat. A quick text to my brother to make sure he doesn't kill me for being here again in the middle of the night, resulting in a thumbs up from Jack. I type in the code to unlock the door.

I hope Lilah isn't here too late. After my almost forty-five minute long drive from the far West side of the city, I finally got here. Leaving us roughly ten minutes before the new year.

"Hi handsome."

I turn to find Lilah in the doorway to the top floor of my favorite building. The view of the city doesn't hold any comparison to the beauty of her as usual. That dress, her unbound loosely curled chestnut hair. Her steel blue eyes lined with black. I forget how to breathe as soon as I lock eyes on her.

We walk to meet each other in the middle of the space. I reach up to grab the back of her neck and pull her in for a slow, passionate kiss.

"You look absolutely gorgeous," I say looking down into her eyes as I savor every detail of her.

She looks down as she shuffles her feet nervously. A wary look taking over.

"What's wrong?" I ask, taking her face in my hands.

She reaches up to hold my arms. "I'm sorry I didn't come to the party tonight. I —" she starts but I lean down to steal her words with another kiss.

"Stop, you don't owe me any explanation. I love you and I respect the boundaries you've drawn. I don't want to push you further than you allow me to." I say as we pull our mouths away from each other.

"Landon. You're too understanding," she says, shaking her head. "My last relationship was a hot mess and left me terrified of finding love again. I want to tell you everything. I want to meet your friends and family, I do." She takes a deep breath. "I just can't right now."

As much as I want to ask further about her past relationship, and as much as jealousy tries to stab me in the gut at the thought of her with someone else. I tame myself quickly. I love this woman, even without knowing everything and having no idea if or when she will open up to me. I want to be there for her like I would want someone to be for me in a relationship.

"Lilah, I love you. I'm here whenever you're ready to tell me more. Until then I'll take every second I get with you." Looking down at my watch I note the time. "Speaking of seconds…"

I grab her hand and lead her over to the large windows overlooking the city. Downtown always has fireworks ready for midnight to bring in the new year. If I couldn't take her to the extravagance of Dean's estate to watch what I'm sure was an elaborate display of pyrotechnics. I would bring her to the next best thing.

As if on cue, an explosion of color ignites the sky. Lilah lights up, a smile beaming on her beautiful face. Wrapping one arm around her hips, I twist her to face me as my other hand reaches around the back of her neck, bringing her in for a deep kiss.

"Happy New Year, gorgeous."

The sound of colorful explosions and light fill the night sky as our mouths continue to tangle in each other.

Chapter Twenty-Two

Glow

The setting sun bounces off the water of the lake. Illuminating Lilah's face with a glow of golden light next to me on the steps. The early spring breeze making her hair blow over her shoulder. I think this often, but if I could freeze time and live in one moment forever, this would be it.

The last two and a half months have flown by too fast. After New Years we spent the beginning of January mostly inside the loft. Only leaving for work and immediately going back to being tangled in one another again. Jack and Aaron have been giving me shit lately about not coming out to the bar with them as often. I love spending time with them, but it doesn't compare in the slightest to wanting to be near Lilah.

We spent Valentine's Day inside, ordered some sushi and watched some corny romance movies. Both making fun of the same unrealistic plot lines. March came in with slightly warmer weather than usual which is a good break from the bitter cold the winter had been. I picked up my bike from Jack's place a couple weeks ago and have ridden it almost every day before Lilah gets home from work. She didn't hesitate when I asked if she wanted to go for a ride with me this evening. The weather is perfect, the golden sunset coming in to coat us in its light.

West of downtown near the shoreline of Lake Erie are these steps I used to always come to when I was a teenager. Granted I only cared about looking cool back then and was probably indulging in some alcohol way before I should have. Being back here years later feels different. *I* feel different. For the first time in a while I don't feel removed from myself, and only wanting to mask my feelings. Numbing myself with drinking and trying not to think about the last year.

Lilah's allowed me to finally feel secure in myself. Which is why I haven't tried to push and pry too hard into her past yet. I know we will get there.

I did get a few more details when we had a rare date out in the city at dinner last week. She finally went into a little about her last relationship. He was extremely manipulative and cheated on her, almost sounds like my ex-wife. He apparently up and left her one day, leaving her to take care of their apartment. Which is when she decided to move back to Cleveland and start over.

I can't imagine someone hurting or wanting to cheat on her. Lilah is one of the most giving and caring people I know. The amount of bullshit I have had to tell her about my life and she doesn't even bat an eye. All I know is I want to protect her with everything I have. I don't ever want her to feel pain or be hurt again.

I could get used to this life with her. Almost four months of knowing someone is crazy to feel this strongly but I'm not going to fight it. Everything about her has me hooked. Her eyes, her hair, the way she laughs to herself when she reads something funny in a book. Or the way she always touches my arm when she's near or grabs my hand if we are walking next to each other. The way her perfume of jasmine and crackling embers smells. How she tries to continue telling a story when she is falling asleep until she trails off mid-sentence.

Falling asleep next to her is my new addiction, second only to waking up to her.

"What are you staring at?" Lilah asks, looking away from the western side of the water to give me a glare. I haven't been able to look away from her for who knows how long since we got here. Luckily, I remembered to bring my camera.

"Sorry," I laugh and run my hand through my hair, "It's hard to pay attention to the sunset when it doesn't comp—"

"Do *not* finish that sentence," she interrupts me with a laugh and an elbow to the side as both of us turn to see the last bit of sunlight get swallowed up by the lake.

Handing her the bottle of wine we have discreetly covered in a paper bag I ask, "Question for a question?"

"Hey that's my thing." She glares at me as she takes a sip.

I put my hand to my chest, "Oh, my bad. I had no idea you held ownership to asking questions." I wink as she rolls her eyes at me and laughs.

"Fine," she says, handing me back the bottle.

Shifting my weight on the concrete steps, I turn to face her.

"What is one thing you've always wanted to do but never have?"

She looks off to the side, thinking. The wind picks up as the sun is fully set, playing with Lilah's hair as it flies across her face. Moonlight taking place of the golden glow of the sun.

"I've been pretty adventurous in my life but there's something I've always wanted to cross off my bucket list. I've been scared shitless to do it though..." Moving her hair out of her face she finishes, "To skydive." She looks back at me as my eyes widen a fraction.

"What?" she asks, huffing a small laugh at my expression.

"That's literally the same answer I give anyone who has asked me a similar question." I laugh and shake my head. "I've always wanted to say I did it but never could muster up the courage to actually go and do it."

"I swear you're in my head sometimes," Lilah says with a smile.

Shaking my head again because I was thinking the exact same thing. We are like two flames burning side by side. Moving in the same direction, almost blending into each other. It's definitely a change from my last relationship. I've never met someone on the same wavelength as me. It's refreshing.

"I could say the same thing gorgeous," I say, moving to her side again as I put my arm around her. She shifts to lean into me as we take in the view of the stars dotting the sky.

The next week at work is bittersweet. Our job on the downtown sky-scraper is done. Everything has been wrapped up and all issues fixed. Dean stopped by earlier to *"double check"* the work, even though he doesn't have any actual construction knowledge, only knowledge in money.

Luckily he wasn't an ass and surprisingly thanked Aaron for as-sisting his guy in getting everything fixed with the wiring near the elevators. I'm really going to miss this view. Plus a few great memories with Lilah will always live here too.

"I don't know if I'm going to be happy or start to miss you staring longingly out these windows." Aaron laughs as he pats my shoulder, once again catching me spaced out.

"Ha. Ha. You're hilarious man, anyone ever tell you that?" I jab back as we walk over to where Jack and the rest of our crew are standing around talking.

Since we're done with the actual work, my brother brought a small cooler filled with beer. We all grab one, or those who don't drink grab a water bottle to cheer to a job complete.

"Without getting all touchy feely, I just wanted to thank everyone for getting this job done. Even when it was a complete pain in the ass, you all pulled through. Here's to continuing to help with the growth of this city," Jack finishes as we collectively lift our drinks.

I walk over to Jack and throw my arm over his shoulder. "Good job brother, you put together a great team here. Without you we probably all would have fucked *a lot* more up." I clink my bottle to his as we both take a drink.

"So you going to join us tonight to celebrate at *Map Room*?" he asks.

"Are you kidding? He's probably going to be busy with *Lilah* again?" Aaron chimes in with his typical sarcastic grin.

"Oh, don't act like you and Madison aren't all over each other anytime we are at the bar and she's not working. Hell, even when she is working, you're behind the bar way more often than Stacey would ever allow either of us to be."

He smiles and shrugs as he tosses his empty bottle into the trash.

"Oh, Landon. I completely forgot." Jack says as he reaches into his back pocket and pulls out two pieces of rectangular paper. Looks like two tickets to something.

"Claire came back to give me these." Dean's assistant was here earlier with him during his inspection. "She said Dean wanted me to do whatever I wanted with them and you're definitely the bigger baseball fan out of us. I figured you could see if Lilah wanted to tag along with your sorry ass to a game." He hands me the two white tickets with the Cleveland baseball team's logo at the top. Two infield box tickets to the home opener game next Saturday.

"Damn, those are some good tickets," Aaron says from behind me, clearly curious about whatever Jack gave me.

"Thanks brother, I'll definitely see if she can make it." I pocket the tickets. "I'm down for a drink by the way, only to not have to hear you two give me anymore shit." I joke as we all pack up our stuff to head out of this building for the last time.

Chapter Twenty-Three

Glimmer

I've always held baseball close to my heart since I was younger. Late night games with my dad. Playing every weekend and after school as a kid. My interest slowed down from wanting to play the game to a love for watching it as I've grown older. Going to professional games is always a good time. Having Lilah here with me makes it even better.

Dean was generous to give box seat tickets right behind home plate. I've personally never been anywhere other than in the standing room area. The weather is perfect for a game today. Slightly warmer out with a clear blue sky. The scent of hot dogs and beer all around. Could be slightly nauseating to most people but I find it nostalgic and comforting. Lilah is already one hotdog and two beers in. She didn't know what to wear to the game so I gave her one of my old Cleveland baseball caps and a white button up jersey. She always makes any of my clothing look much better when it's on her.

Finally getting to our box after waiting in lines for the food and drinks we've already started to devour. We realized too late our tickets included some. We spot Dean standing behind a group talking to a few people. Dean's beaming smile reaches his eyes, crinkling his dark skin as he sees us. He's dressed in a light blue sports coat and slacks, definitely a contrast to the t-shirt and jeans I chose.

"Ah Landon! I'm glad you could make it. Jack mentioned he gave the tickets to you. Are you a big baseball fan?" he asks as he reaches out to shake my hand.

I reach my hand out to meet his. "Definitely. Always have loved the game since I was a kid. Thank you for the tickets, it's really appreciated. This is my girlfriend Lilah."

Turning around to pull her into view since she hung back a little when we entered the box. Her smile somewhat fading as she takes in the other people in our area. All dressed much nicer than either of us. She manages a shy smile at Dean and reaches to shake his hand as he cocks his head to the side and studies her.

"Hm, interesting," he says.

He doesn't reach out to meet her hand and just takes a sip from his glass of amber colored liquor. "Well Landon I must step away for a moment, some of my benefactors have arrived I must say hi to. I hope you enjoy the game." He nods in farewell as he steps right past us to greet a group of older men in suits by the entrance to the box.

Lilah and I share a confused look before I guide her to a couple of open seats with the best view. Most of the other attendees in our box clearly are here more for the social aspect rather than the actual game. Only two of the other six seats are taken.

"Well that was... odd," I say as we sit down.

Lilah stares off at the field as prep begins before the game starts.

"You okay?" I ask, reaching for her knee and lowering my voice slightly. "Dean is always a little off putting. That was definitely rude though, I'm sorry."

"It's okay, no biggie," she says with a shrug.

It definitely was a weird reaction though. Who blatantly ignores someone? No he didn't just ignore her, he studied her. Almost like he–

"Wait, you haven't met him before, have you?" My confusion and annoyance laced with slight concern. Did they have history or something I didn't know about? He did pause when I said her name at his *New Year's Eve* party.

"No." Lilah shakes her head, brows knitting. "I have never seen that man in my life." She looks over to me, worry lacing her eyes as she takes in my concerned tone.

"I promise Landon, I do not know him. Don't get all squirrely on me." She smiles and gently nudges my shoulder with hers.

"Squirrely?" My left eyebrow shoots upward, a laugh tempting to escape.

She opens her bag of cracker jacks and pops one into her mouth. "Yep, squirrely."

God, I love her goofiness. I settle back into my seat, taking in the glimmer of her eyes as the game starts. My concern and worry dissipate into nothing.

———

The following Tuesday I'm sitting next to Jack at our usual spots in the bar around seven in the evening. Since he and Aaron started giving me shit for not coming out with them as often the last couple of months and since we haven't begun a new project. I decided to make more of an effort to get out without Lilah since I don't see them day to day anymore.

"How was the game?" Jack asks on my left.

I take a sip of my whiskey, I've been drinking slightly less lately and already feel a buzz on my second drink.

"It was good, we won as usual. Dean was weird though with Lilah."

Jack's brows furrow. "Oh he got to *actually* meet the infamous Lilah?" He chuckles and takes a swig of his beer. "How was he weird?"

"He looked her up and down, ignored her and walked away," I say, remembering the interaction which has gnawed at my brain since it happened. Lilah doesn't seem to be too bothered by it anymore though.

"Hm, that is weird," Jack says as he squints his eyes slightly in thought. "Well Dean is a young, relatively good-looking rich bachelor. You don't think he's had a fling or something with her, do you?"

My brother knows me too well. "Yeah, that's exactly where my head initially went but I asked her, she genuinely has never met him before."

"Hm." Is all Jack responds with.

Before I'm able to question him about what he's thinking Stacey comes up to us on the other side of the bar.

"Well, if it isn't my favorite brothers. I feel like you're never here anymore, Landon," she says, refilling my drink.

"Yeah, I've been a little busy lately."

"Mhmm, I've heard. The mystery girlfriend no one has met," she says with a smirk then asks Jack if he wants another round too.

"Is Lilah going to come to the twin's birthday party next weekend?" Jack asks.

I had asked her last week about it but I didn't have high hopes though since it would be another full family event again. She did think about it for a moment before saying no at least.

"No, she isn't ready for a full family function just yet," I say, "Especially not with *our* family." He can't argue with that.

"Kinda figured," he says with an undertone I can't fully place.

"What are you thinking?" I ask him.

"Uh, nothing man. I'm happy for you, I really am. I can tell she makes you a lot less miserable than you were. I just..." he trails off, looking over at Stacey interacting with a group of loud older women her wife is drinking with.

He's never this weird with me. "Stop tip-toeing over whatever it is you're wanting to say. You and I are real with each other. Say what you're thinking."

Jack hesitates but eventually opens his mouth to speak, "I just think it's weird you two have been together for almost five months and she hasn't made any effort to meet your friends or family." He sighs as he continues, "I have a feeling she's hiding something. You mentioned she had a shitty ex, but she hasn't said anything else? She only ever stays at your place, do you even know where she lives at?"

Damn. I knew whatever was on his mind wasn't going to be good but I wasn't expecting all of that.

"Jack, I appreciate your concerns. Really, I get it. But you're not in our relationship, I don't want to push her boundaries. You know Rachel always controlled everything about our relationship. I don't want Lilah feeling like I'm doing the same by demanding she tell me everything about her past." I pause, taking a big drink. "Yes I know where she lives, I haven't been to her place but I'm not complaining because honestly, I love having her in mine. Lastly, I would love for her to come and meet everyone else in my life, I know she will. She's just not there yet." I shrug and take another sip of whiskey, the burn taming down any anxious thoughts brought on by my brother.

He doesn't respond for a minute. "I hear you man. I just don't want to see you get hurt again. Be careful alright?"

Before I'm able to respond Aaron claps both of us on our backs and pulls us into an awkward group hug.

"Looks like I walked in on a serious conversation and I feel like you two needed a hug." He laughs as he steps to my right and takes his usual seat. Madison walks around to the side opening to go behind the bar. "Also, it seems like we need a round of shots!" Aaron says loudly in her direction.

I guess I'll be drinking more than I planned for tonight.

Chapter Twenty-Four

Flicker

"*Uncle Landon*!" Emily, my more rambunctious niece, is charging straight towards me as soon as I walk into the backyard of my brother's house.

The birthday party festivities have yet to start but it looks like the girls couldn't decide on only one theme this year. One half of the backyard is filled with everything dinosaur related. A giant green blow-up T-rex, a Triceratops cake and *Jurassic Park* themed plates and cups. The other half is all Disney princesses. At least Isabelle likes the more modern badass princesses. Her favorite, which I always forget her name, lives on an island and there's a chicken. That's about the extent of my princess knowledge but the movie was fun to watch with her. The one middle ground between their opposing aesthetics is the giant red bounce house in the center.

"*Happy Birthday* Em!" I say as I grab her for a hug, handing over her present. I had to make sure I wrapped them in two different papers otherwise there would be a fight over whose present is whose.

"Hey! It's my birthday too!" Isabelle stomps over from the back door to the house. Glaring as she notices the present in Emily's hand.

"Don't worry, I got you something too." I hold out her present wrapped in pink paper. Her frown instantly shifting into the biggest smile I've ever seen as she runs over to snatch the present out of my hands before yelling *thank you!* Both of them run off to the bounce house, Branch following them at full speed as he busts into a barking fit.

Jack walks up next to me from his spot by the grill, shaking his head as he watches them. "One day they will learn manners." He laughs and hands me the unopened beer in his hand.

"They get a pass today." I laugh and crack open the bottle to take a sip.

Looking around I don't see any of the other members of my family yet. They could be inside though since I walked straight to the backyard after I hopped off my motorcycle. It's another beautiful early spring day out today, the weather is slightly warmer with clear skies. A perfect day for an outdoor get together. Hopefully the nice day keeps out any drama.

"Nance inside?" I ask as we walk the few steps back over to the grill for Jack to flip some of the burgers. I've always loved the smell of anything cooking over charcoal, brings back good memories. Branch gave up on the bounce house and is laying close to the grill, trying to catch any grease or crumbs.

"Yeah, she's getting the rest of the food ready. Mom and Dad are inside too. I think our sister is coming a little later with whoever it is she's dating these days."

Sometimes I feel bad about not getting to know more about our sister's life but it's also not like she lets me even talk to her nowadays.

I guess she's shunned Jack some too, probably since she knows we are close.

A few other parents and their seven year-olds show up over the next hour. Screaming and laughter fill the air as most of the kids jump about in the bounce house. My parents have finally ventured outside, I walk over to give my dad a hug. My mother looks at me and immediately turns to walk back inside. I haven't seen or talked to any of them since the shit-show of Christmas, I guess today isn't the day for making up.

"Don't feel too bad, I know they've gotten over their anger towards you. They said as much when I saw them last week to talk about the party," Jack says from next to me along the porch rail as we watch the rest of the party after eating and finishing with cake.

"Oh?" I ask.

"Yeah, I guess they're not ready to own up to their mistakes just yet." He takes a swig of his beer before adding, "They also have a few concerns about your dating life. They probably don't want to get into it all with you today."

Well, I wasn't expecting *that* at all. I understand Jack's worries but I don't know why they even care.

"What concerns?"

He hesitates, "The same I mentioned the other day. But we don't have to get into it man, I understand your point of view and it's not mine or anyone else's place to tell you you're wrong. You know to be careful."

I don't know how to respond, at least he gave me an out to not get into a disagreement again. If anyone else was actually in my relationship with Lilah they would understand her intentions and wouldn't question her as much. I just need to get her to meet everyone and then maybe they will calm down some.

Some hours later after the sun started to go down, we are all sitting around a bonfire in the backyard. The rest of the party guests went home not too long ago, Emily and Isabelle are inside playing with the rest of their presents. Aaron and Madison showed up a little after the girls opened their gifts. Their presence is a welcome distraction from the forced conversations my family puts on. At least we are all being relatively civil.

"I'm just saying, she wasn't that bad." I hear my sister say to my mother. Casie got here shortly before the rest of the parents left, her date has been practically silent since they showed up.

I have no idea who they're talking about. I've chosen to sit on the opposite side of the fire from them, between Jack and Aaron.

Madison is snuggled up on the other side of my lumberjack friend, enjoying some wine with Nancy. My dad is on the other side of Jack, they're talking about some potential jobs my brother has lined up for the construction crew coming up.

"No, I agree." I hear my mother say to my sister.

"Is it me or does their conversation feel a little '*spicious*?" Aaron says quietly to me. Nodding, I take a big sip of my drink, draining the bottle of beer.

My mother catches me looking in their direction, a big mistake on my end.

"Landon, can't you agree you and Rachel weren't completely terrible together?" she asks as if it's such a simple question.

"Mom, stop," Jack says.

"No, all I'm saying is they had some good times. We all had good times with her, I was talking with her the other day about it," my mother says with a smile like she's not being completely insane.

Normally my tolerance for this bullshit conversation would be slim to none, but I keep hearing Lilah in the back of my head reminding me not to give power to anyone else and they won't be able to bother me. That's the only thing keeping me calm, but at least it's working.

"Why are you still talking to her?" Jack asks, his patience for this conversation clearly showing in his annoyed tone.

"Well she decided to move back home last week. She doesn't have anyone here except us. Besides her parents of course, but since Landon has all but shunned her I think she deserves some kindness..." my mother starts to say, before my brother stands up and interrupts her.

"She almost killed him! How can you act like she did anything but torture Landon!? She controlled almost everything he did, she fucked someone else in their house and she tampered with his bike, knowing he could possibly ride it again. SHE was the cause of his accident last year. Are you really telling me she's such a *sweetheart!?*"

My eyes are wider than the ocean. The tension in the air is suffocating. Aaron whistles low and finishes his drink. I was not expecting that reaction from Jack, he hadn't mentioned Rachel and what she did since Christmas. I guess he's been holding a lot back lately.

"I'm done with this conversation." Our sister stands up with her date who awkwardly witnessed this mess of a conversation. "Come on mom, let's go."

Our mother stands and looks across the fire at me, the flicker of the flame reflecting in her eyes.

"You make your own decisions Landon, be with whoever this new young girl is who seems like she's hiding something. Or you could realize Rachel does love you and shows it in different ways." Both my sister and mother head back into the house. A few minutes pass and then my dad stands up and hugs me, a look of apology in his eyes. The sound of their car doors shutting and pulling out of the driveway filling the air shortly after.

"Well that was... something," Aaron says as he walks back from grabbing another drink for Madison and him.

"That's one way to put it," I huff a laugh and take a sip from my drink. Thankfully the subject shifts soon after and I'm able to enjoy the rest of the night air and the company I'm glad is here.

Only one person is missing.

Chapter Twenty-Five

Flare

Lilah surprised me this morning. After getting back from the gym she immediately guided me to the shower. Sadly, the surprise was not her joining me in there again. Once I was out and clothed, she blindfolded me. Before I could start thinking she was trying something kinky, she led me out of the loft and into a car. I would normally be terrified if someone basically kidnapped me but I don't think she could ever scare me.

She refuses to talk to me in the car, but at least she's sitting next to me in the backseat while *who the fuck knows* drives us somewhere. All I can do is try to keep my mind occupied to not allow claustrophobia to rear its ugly head. It's been almost a month since the twin's party. My own birthday coming up next weekend. Thirty-four came up fast. I feel like I've been through so much, yet so little. There are many things I want to accomplish but feel nowhere close to. I feel like I've made big progress in my mental state since my divorce but I keep thinking about what I want to actually do with my life.

Jack mentioned this week when I met up with him and Aaron that he signed a contract for a new job starting next week. I'm happy to be able to see them and the crew again more often but I still don't feel like it's the direction I'm meant to go. Lilah keeps mentioning I should show my photographs to other people than only her. How I should try to get them into an art show or something. I don't think my skill level is there yet, as sweet as it is of her to think so. I guess I just have to take everything day by day. The only thing certain in my life is Lilah.

About what I would guess was thirty minutes later the car comes to a stop. It sounds like we are on a gravel road. Maybe I *should* be scared and this is where she kills me.

Once we are standing outside of the car she finally moves behind me and I feel the blindfold loosen before it falls away from my face. It takes a moment for my eyes to adjust as I glare into the beaming sun above us. After my vision isn't spotty I start to take in our surroundings.

We are standing on a driveway in front of a large white hangar. Complete with a small plane taking up half of the space. There is a group of three men and two women all dressed in blue jumpsuits. I spot some lockers in the back corner and a big whiteboard which says *"Skydiving Safety Tips."* I look next to me at Lilah, a huge grin plastered on her face.

"You said you always wanted to skydive too." She shrugs, "So I figured why not cross it off your list before your birthday." Her smile is infectious. I can't help but mirror it.

"You're trying to kill me before my birthday is what it sounds like." I laugh and gently nudge her with my shoulder.

"Oh there won't be anyone dying today sir," a man with a stern southern accent and a stark white mustache matching his hair says as he walks up to us, reaching out to shake my hand. "The names Kent and I'll be your guide today as you navigate the sky," Kent says as he looks up and gestures to the cloudless blue above us. Lilah and I share a look before glancing up.

Kent turns around and guides us back towards the group gathered around a table near the whiteboard. After going through all of the safety instructions we suit up.

I swear only minutes go by as we are loaded up onto the plane with the group of instructors and Kent. The plane hasn't taken off yet but my nerves start to kick in. I envy Lilah, for saying she was also scared shit-less to do this she sure isn't showing it. She hasn't stopped smiling since we got here.

"You ready champ?" Kent asks me as he slaps my shoulder after closing the latch to the plane door.

"Eh I guess as ready as I'll ever be," I say with a laugh and look over to Lilah.

"You ready for this?" I ask her as the rest of our group starts their own conversations. All of them give us a concerned look over. I'm sure I look terrified.

She smiles at me and says, "Honestly, I'm not as nervous now that we are here. I was an anxious wreck though on the car ride."

"You'll do amazing, I'm sure." I grab her hand and kiss the back of it as Kent announces we are going to begin take off.

The ride into the airspace was a little bumpy, I started to worry my breakfast was going to make an appearance again. Luckily once we reached the desired altitude my stomach leveled out with the plane.

Kent goes to hook me up to his harness, being first timers we have to do the actual dive with an instructor. Lilah's already hooked up to one of the others in the group.

"All right! You ready kids!?" Kent shouts to the group after opening the door we are meant to jump out of.

The two women instructors jump first, with one of the other guys following right after. With how loud it is and the air almost gone from the open door my panic is starting to claw its way in. Kent and I are next. We position ourselves to the edge of the door, making it less of an abrupt jump than the others were. I feel like I can't breathe. I look at Lilah, panic nowhere in her eyes. It calms my nerves slightly.

"I don't think I can do this!" I shout to her.

Kent tries to shout something encouraging, not realizing I'm not talking to him.

"You can do this, Landon. I believe in you. Don't let fear hold you back anymore!" She shouts back at me over our instructor's words. "I'll be right behind you!"

I take a deep breath in as I go flying into the open sky with Kent on my back. My hands immediately shoot up like I'm on a rollercoaster. The feeling I thought would be in my stomach isn't there but in its place is a sense of free fall flowing through my whole body. The wind slapping my face. Through my goggles I start to make out the scenery below us. The city off in the distance but still visible. I quickly get used to the fall, excepting the weightlessness of the air. I feel free.

Before we get too close to the ground Kent pulls the ripcord for the parachute and we start to glide towards the open grass area where the rest of our group is already at. I try to look up to see where Lilah is but I can't see past the edges of the yellow chute.

The sensation of grass beneath my feet is slightly jarring after feeling light in the air. After we are safe on the ground, I finally spot Lilah and the last instructor heading our way.

Once she is on the ground and detached, I run to her and pick her up in a giant hug, spinning her around a moment before dropping her slightly to allow our mouths to melt into each other.

"What did you think?" she asks, the same smile from earlier on her face.

"That was one of the most exhilarating feelings I've ever experienced." I grab her face in my hands, inches away from her lips.

"Thank you for pushing me to do this. I've never felt as free as I do when I am with you." I press my lips to hers in a longing kiss before pulling away, "But being in free fall is a close second."

We stand there for who knows how long, wrapped in each other as the rest of the group awkwardly goes about their own conversations again. This has to be one of the best days I have ever had. Thanks to *Lilah.*

The next week the spring air is definitely bringing out more people in the city. The winter crowd is more locals at the bar trying to numb the bite of the cold outside. As soon as the flowers start blooming though, everyone from every surrounding suburb of Cleveland starts to venture here for fun. Resulting in a crowd bigger than usual at *Map Room*.

"Big crowd for it not even being four o'clock," I note to Stacey as she fills my glass.

"It is Friday though," Aaron chimes in from my right as he takes in the scenery. Hopefully no rowdy crowds venture here tonight, I don't want him getting in another fight cause some douchebag hits on Madison.

"Apparently there is some big concert over at the pavilion," Stacey says, referencing the venue on the other side of the river down in *The Flats.*

Which makes sense, usually people come here for the cheaper drinks to pregame before concerts or sporting events since drinks are super expensive closer to the river and at the stadiums.

"So I heard your girlfriend forced you out of a moving plane, Landon?" Madison asks with a smirk as she walks up next to Stacey to fill a pitcher of beer.

I shoot her and then Aaron a glare, since I know he was the one who probably phrased it that way first.

"She didn't force me." I laugh, taking a sip from my drink. "Skydiving was actually amazing. I never would have done it if she didn't set it up for us. Definitely not what I was expecting for my birthday though that's for sure."

Stacey and Madison exchange a look I can't place but before I think too much on it Aaron nudges me with his elbow.

"The heck man?" I say, nudging him back.

"When are we going to meet this girl, man? I'm getting impatient over here," he says.

I direct my glare to Jack.

"Hey, I haven't said anything since the other week," Jack says with his palms in the air facing me.

"What? I don't see why she hasn't come around even once. We don't *bite*," Aaron adds, "Or are you ashamed of us? No, I bet it's you're afraid she's going to see how much better looking Jack and I are and she's going to regret her decision to lump herself with yo-" he starts to say before I elbow him twice as hard as he did a moment ago. "Fine, fine. I surrender," Aaron says laughing as he takes a drink from his beer.

They are incredibly impatient. I know Lilah will eventually come around and meet them. She knows it means a lot to me. The doubts Jack has though have definitely been ruminating in my head the last week. I know she loves me and I don't think she's being dishonest. There is a small part of me however wanting to question why she hasn't warmed up to the idea of meeting anyone in my life though. Hell, she met the developer of the building I was working on and hasn't even met my brother. Granted it was a terrible interaction, but still.

"You know what, fine. I will ask her again to come out, even if only to the bar to meet you guys. Definitely less scary than being thrown into a family event."

"Don't let us pressure you man, you know we are just giving you shit," Jack says.

"I know, I do want her to meet everyone though. You guys mean *almost* as much to me as she does," I say half-jokingly. Earning a shake of the head and laugh from my brother and an offended look from Aaron as I stand up from the bar and take out some cash.

"Where are you going? You gonna go grab her now?" Aaron asks with a chuckle.

"No jackass, but I do have an idea. I have to pick up something first though," I say before I put the cash on the wooden bar and say my goodbyes before heading to the door.

———

I know the exact building she said she lives in. I pass it anytime I drive through *Ohio City*. Plus, I remember it from when I dropped Lilah off in those first few weeks of us dating. I don't know why I've never done this before. Probably because I was scared that she would be upset or something. We've been together going on half a year though. I think it's time to start breaking down some of those boundaries.

Lilah's building is covered in red bricks and an intricate flower mural on one side. The residential part is similar to my loft, with retail spaces on the first floor. I go to open the door to the mailroom and stairs leading to the above apartments. It's locked. Luckily, I don't have to wait long until someone leaves to slide into the small vestibule. I would have texted or called her to let me in but that would defeat the purpose of wanting to surprise her. Also, part of me is nervous she would try to say she would just meet me at my place. It's definitely past the time she is usually off work and at my loft. I figured it was a safe time and she would be here.

I shift the flowers I stopped to get before I headed this way from my right hand to my left to figure out which apartment to buzz. All of the tenants names are listed on the callbox with the associated number to dial to be let inside. I start from the top and scan down, looking for Lilah's name. Realizing I must have forgotten her last name or she somehow has never told me it, but thankfully it has both first and last names listed on the call sheet.

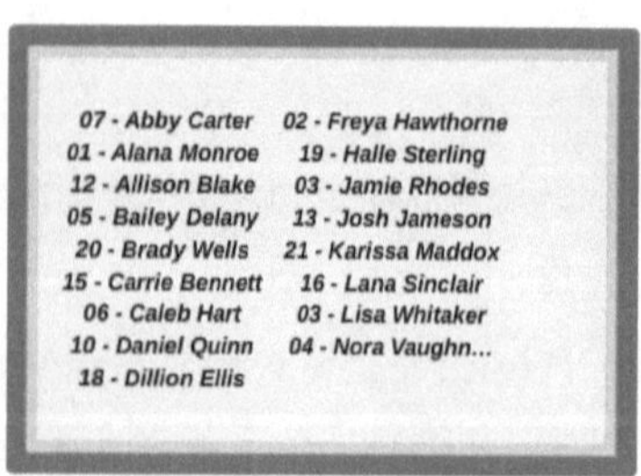

Hm. I must have skipped through too fast.

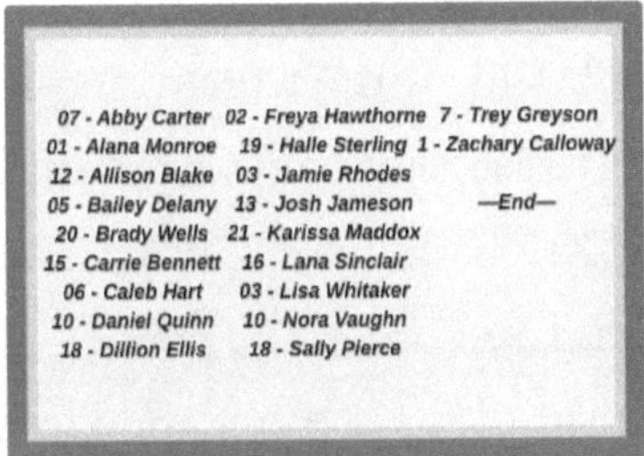

No Lilah. I walk back outside to make sure I'm at the building she said was where she lives. I'm at the right place. She just doesn't live here.

My mind starts plummeting in on itself. Why would she say she lived here when she doesn't? I almost bump into someone on my way down the street. Not realizing I'm walking the opposite direction I need to go until I'm standing in front of a mural of a man staring into a mirror, his head looking like it splits into two in the reflection while his thoughts are flying out. I sympathize with him. My head feels like it's mulling over every possibility of why she lied to me, causing a headache to form behind my eyes.

I half debate calling her but I know there has to be a logical reason for her to not tell me the truth. Maybe I did hear her wrong when she mentioned what building it was. This was months ago we even talked about it, since we both got comfortable with her coming to my place. I had only dropped her off the one time, but maybe that was down the street? When I ordered her a car the first night I met her… did I even put in an address…?

I turn away from the mural and head back the direction my car is, the flowers in my hand hanging down to the ground. I don't know why I feel defeated. It's not like this is the worst thing to happen. Maybe she didn't feel comfortable telling someone she just started dating where she lives. Maybe she's in the witness protection program? Maybe her legal name isn't Lilah?

No, I have to believe she lied for a reason. She loves me and I love her. I just need to talk to her about it once I gather my thoughts and calm this worsening headache.

Chapter Twenty-Six

Blaze

The next morning, I wake up again to beaming sunlight, this time more unwelcome than most. I have a headache already forming while Lilah is sleeping next to me. I couldn't bring myself to ask her about her apartment or why she lied. Part of me wants to forget I found out. It's not like it was something detrimental. I have to believe there was a logical reason.

She came over last night after I texted that I was home, apparently she ran late with some stuff at work. Her smile when I answered my door watered down any questions or concerns running through my mind. Selfishly, I also didn't want to potentially get into an argument the day before my birthday. We went about our evening as usual. Eating dinner in, listening to music and making love until we were too exhausted to stay up any longer.

How do I bring up the fact I spontaneously went to her place? What if she thinks I went because I didn't believe her from the start on where she lived? I don't want it to come across wrong. I think I'll save *that* conversation until after today. Not like we have anything actually planned for my birthday. Jack does want to meet for drinks later tonight though.

"Penny for your thoughts?" Lilah asks from next to me as she looks up with sleepy eyes.

The frequent irrational thought passes through that she hears everything I'm thinking. I have no idea how long she's been looking at me. I run my hand through my hair and smile down at her before I grasp her chin and lean down to kiss her perfect lips.

"Not much. Just thinking about what to do before I meet up with Jack tonight." Not fully a lie.

"Hmm, I can think of a few ideas," she replies while trailing her finger down my torso.

"Oh, I'm sure you can," I say in the same playful tone as I run my fingers through her tousled hair. "Want to grab some breakfast?" I ask, not entirely sure why I'm changing the subject from sex.

I think she senses my hesitancy. "What's on your mind?" she asks, "Other than how to spend your birthday?"

Maybe I will pivot where my thoughts are going and ease into the conversation.

"I was thinking how I'd love for you to come with me tonight. For drinks *and* to meet Jack." I chance a look at her, apprehension seeping into those beautiful eyes.

"Just one drink. And it's only my brother. I won't even make you meet Stacey or Madison if they're working. Plus the second you feel like you're at your limit, we come home and do those ideas you're thinking about," I finish saying as I tuck a lock of hair behind her ear.

I swear I count the seconds with my heartbeat before she answers.

"Okay. For you. And *only* because it's your birthday and I love you." Her smile is mesmerizing as she sits up next to me and swings her leg over my lap, straddling me. "But I do think we have time to do some of those ideas I had before." Pure mischief in her voice as she leans in and kisses me.

———

A few hours later, after we went for breakfast, Lilah had to stop at her work to handle a few things. Being alone I decided to go for a walk by the river. The weather is perfect. Since it's a Saturday the walkway by the water is pretty packed. A few couples have walked by holding hands, a group of college aged guys passing by shouting something and clearly walking with cans of beer. This is always a great time of year in this part of the city, not overly hot but warm enough to not be chilled next to the river.

Disposing of my coffee cup I got at the beginning of my walk, I spot an older couple. The man is wearing a suit jacket and fedora, the woman in a yellow dress. They're sitting on a bench watching the water and people file by. That's what I want right there. They look enamored by love. I don't know when I got this sappy. Well, I do know actually, after meeting Lilah. She's replaced every negative, self-deprecating thought with a positive one. I actually am excited for where my life is going to take me. As long as I have her next to me.

I feel the buzz of my phone while I stand here lost in thought.

Hey brother, you still good to meet at Map Room at 7?

Weird, it's from Jack. My brother doesn't usually double check when we make plans. I guess he could be thinking I made other plans with Lilah or something. I text him back and decide to get in a workout before getting ready to meet him in a few hours.

Walking to the bar I start to feel nervous for some reason. Lilah said she would meet me at *Map Room* around seven thirty. After she gets ready at her place. She apparently ran out of outfit options in the clothes she left at my place. I wish we could get there together but the most important thing is, *she said she would be there.*

Jack texted me again making sure I would be here at seven. I'm starting to feel suspicious. Maybe he's gathered everyone for an intervention about Lilah hiding things. Which clearly, he was somewhat accurate about. I genuinely don't think there is anything else she is hiding though, but *I know* her and he doesn't. I can't blame him for thinking the worst. Hopefully once he meets her, it will all change tonight.

I go to open the dark wooden door to the bar. As soon as it's open I know something is up. Being blinded for a second by the darkness of the place I blink and then see Jack, Aaron, Madison and Stacey all standing in the middle of the bar. With everyone from our work crew, Nancy and even Claire all behind them.

All at once they shout, *"HAPPY BIRTHDAY!"*

I don't know what I was expecting but a surprise party was definitely not it. I walk towards the gathering and start greeting everyone. Giving my brother and Nancy a hug, following with Aaron and Madison and then Stacey with her wife. After saying hello to almost everyone who made it out, I make my way to where my brother and Aaron are standing.

"Madison and Stacey get all of the credit. They planned the whole thing," Aaron says as I walk up.

I give Stacey a look, my eyebrows shooting up in surprise.

"Oh, don't go all lovey on me. You're still *Mr. Broody* but you deserve to be celebrated," she says with a smile.

I move to give them both another hug. After I pull away, I find myself searching for someone. *Lilah.* Did she know about this? Is that why she was hesitant at first about coming to meet Jack? Stacey catches my gaze.

"Sorry Landon, we would have invited her but we didn't have much to go off. We tried looking up whatever small magazine it was you said she worked at but couldn't find any Lilah's at any in town," Stacey says with a sorrowful look.

"It's alright, Stace, I appreciate you trying at all. She actually was going to come tonight anyway to meet Jack." Apprehension quickly takes place of the disappointment I'm feeling. How is she going to feel when she shows up to a full blown party?

"She's *actually* coming to meet me?" Jack asks, his eyebrows shooting up his forehead. Nancy elbows him in the side. He clears his throat, "No that's great Lan, let me know when she gets here."

Shit. I should give her a warning. Not wanting her to think I knew she would be walking into slight chaos. It's only five after seven giving me some time to prepare her. I go to send her a text.

Hi Beautiful. I am so excited for you to meet Jack. BUT I just walked into a full on surprise party at the bar. I still hope you decide to come but I wanted to make sure I gave you some warning first. I love you.

I put my phone away and grab the drink Stacey hands me as we all cheers to my

birthday. Everyone around us joining in.

The whole bar is blocked off from anyone else coming in who isn't a part of the party. Which is crazy for this place on a weekend. Stacey and Madison had to pull some major strings to pull this off. I spot Claire coming our way.

"Happy Birthday Landon. Dean sends his regards for not being able to make it but hopes he was able to arrange everything you needed for today," she says with a smile.

A look of confusion crosses my face. I look over to Jack and Aaron for any hint as to what she's talking about.

"Let Dean know everything worked out perfectly and thank you again," Jack says as he shakes Claire's hand before she says goodbye and heads out, not even finishing the drink she had been holding. She always keeps to herself, but with a boss like Dean I can't really blame her.

"What was all that about?" I ask my brother.

"Oh your fancy pants boss rented out the whole bar tonight for your party and gave me and Madison some money to cover for any lost tips," Stacey answers for Jack.

Looking over to Jack he shrugs and takes a sip of his drink. Maybe this is what he and Claire were discussing at the worksite awhile back. I'm actually shocked Dean would do this for me. I guess if my brother was the one who asked, he was doing it more as a favor to him for doing a great job on his building. Either way I'm incredibly grateful.

A few drinks in and an hour later and still no Lilah. I go outside to try and call her while a few of the guys from the work crew are out smoking, Derek getting stoned as usual. She doesn't answer. Before I get in my head about it, Aaron and Jack drag me back inside for a birthday shot. At least I have them and the rest of my friends here, definitely lessens the sting of my girlfriend not showing.

Who knows how many drinks later, and I feel lighter. Probably the alcohol talking but all my worries have been dulled. I haven't drunk this much in a while. Since I've been with Lilah, I've definitely cut back. I'm starting to realize exactly how little I've drank lately by how wobbly I feel.

My friends and brother are all equally enjoying themselves. My favorite songs are playing over the speakers. *Pixies, Bowie, The Goo Goo Dolls*. A giant cake with candles in a blaze is brought out. This night is perfect.

Except, it's not.

As fast as I felt numb, realizing it's almost eleven thirty and Lilah hasn't shown, dread starts to take over. She won't answer any of my calls either. Worry is starting to creep its way in.

After I convince my brother and Aaron to let me go home cause I am sufficiently drunk. I try calling her again as I start to walk. She doesn't answer. Walking into my building I pull my keys out, almost dropping them a few times.

After stumbling up a couple flights of stairs because I was too impatient for the elevator, I make my way to my apartment, actually dropping my keys this time. As I stand up I see someone sitting on the floor outside my door with a present in their hand.

Lilah.

Chapter Twenty-Seven

Combust

"*Hi*." Is all Lilah says by way of greeting. She stands up, smoothing out her creased pants from sitting on the ground for who knows how long.

She looks as if she's been crying. Her eye makeup starting to run down her face, right above her cheekbones. She's holding a wrapped box. I would assume it's a birthday present for me. If only she knew I could do without materialistic possessions, the only present I want would be for her to open up to me.

I start to walk towards my door, fumbling as I go. Damn. I wish I hadn't drank as much. I'm in no condition to sort anything out with Lilah. I hate how happy I still am to see her though. I'm honestly just glad she's okay.

"Hi," I reply back as I go to fit my key inside the lock on my door.

Lilah puts her hand not holding the present on my forearm, stealing my attention away from the lock.

"Please look at me," she says in a defeated tone. She must think I'm angry with her. I am, but not in a typical way. More upset by the fact she couldn't tell me she wasn't going to show up at the bar tonight.

"I'm not angry with you Lilah. Just a little hurt," I say as I stare into those beautiful steel blue eyes, lined red from tears. I lean down to kiss her forehead.

"I can explain," she says as I finally manage to unlock the door and we both step inside.

I need water. There is no way I'll be able to have any conversation with this alcohol swimming in my system. My head feels like I am floating in the middle of the lake. I walk towards the kitchen and grab a glass to fill. Lilah takes a seat on the couch.

"You need some water?" I ask, half stumbling over my words.

She shakes her head.

"So... Why didn't you answer any of my calls?" I ask in the least accusatory tone manageable.

"I... I just couldn't bring myself to come out there tonight," she answers as she stares down into her lap at the present in her hands.

"That's not what I asked," I try to say as gently as I can, "I understand, well I can try to understand at least why you couldn't make it out to the bar. But not answering my calls or texts started to make me nervous." I somehow manage to speak clearly. At least I think I do.

She won't stop staring into her lap. I move to set my now empty glass of water on the coffee table and take a seat next to her. Reaching for her face I pull her gaze to me.

"What's going on, love?" I ask as I hold her cheeks in my hands.

She shakes her head and resumes looking down at the box nestled on her legs.

"I. I didn't want to upset you."

"Lilah, I'm not angry." I reach for her hands, the present is still in the way. I gently grab it and place it on the coffee table next to my empty glass. "I wish you had felt like you could have told me you weren't coming tonight though." She doesn't say anything. "You haven't told me what's going on. Or why you chose not to come out tonight other than saying you couldn't."

She takes a deep breath but doesn't answer.

"Lilah. Love, will you at least give me something?" I plead.

"I... I can't," she says and pulls her hands away as she stands up.

"You're going to have to help me out a little here. What *can't* you?" I reply, standing up and moving around the coffee table. We both stare at each other in the middle of the living room.

What feels like an eternity passes and she doesn't answer. She keeps looking off to the right. At the front door. Scared she's going to try and run out I move to step into her line of vision and gently place my hands on her shoulders.

She looks at me as she says, "Landon, I can't give you what you're looking for."

I am completely confused. "What are you talking about?" I say, my grip on her shoulders my only lifeline to make sure she doesn't bolt. "What can't you give me? What is it exactly you think I'm looking for?"

Her eyes fall from mine and she tries to move away from my grip.

"Lilah. All I want from you is *you*. I love you. I know you love me. I've been patient with you, I know you hold some trauma from your past relationship, but have I pried too much? I'm sorry if I have," I say, though I know I haven't pressed her too hard for information.

Even if I have wanted to. I've always given her the space and bound-aries she's asked for. I'm starting to feel like she's never going to let those walls down.

"I love you too, Landon. But I can't," she says as she pulls away and takes another step for the door.

I grab her hand and she half turns to me.

"You can't *what*?" I ask, more desperate and an octave louder this time.

Still no answer, but she's stopped moving towards the door at least.

"Lilah. You can talk to me. Yeah, sure, I've wanted to try and pry more into why you're this secretive. But I haven't because I love you and have tried to show you the acceptance I never had in a relationship before."

She looks at me and crosses her arms. I swear I almost feel her wall building up brick by brick with each word I say. We can't live this way though. If we actually want to make us work, she has to open up at some point.

"Is this because of your ex? You've told me nothing about your previous relationship other than he cheated on you and it was toxic. Is that what's scaring you? I would never hurt you like he did," I say and reach towards her.

She takes a half step back and I drop my hand.

"If it's not that, then what is it?" I ask more exasperated. The alcohol that remains buzzing in my system makes me want to say everything I've been holding back.

"You refuse to meet my friends or my brother. I can understand not wanting to come to family events or over for the holiday's but *damn* Lilah, you can't even come out once to meet them?"

Still no answer from her but she's uncrossed her arms. I continue, the words flying from my mouth before I'm able to catch them.

"I went to your place. I know you don't live where you told me you did. Hell, I don't think you've even told me your last name," I say quietly, almost to myself.

"You've never asked," she says, finally responding with more than *she can't.*

"Fair point. But I have been trying not to push you further than I could tell you were comfortable. You're hiding yourself *Lilah.* Is there anything else you've not been telling me? Was I supposed to question when you said you lived where you did? Stacey and Madison said they tried to find whatever magazine it was you work at but couldn't, do you even work at one?" I ask as I cross my arms. Realizing for the first time maybe I should have been the one protecting *myself.* What do I actually know about this woman? *Shit.* Maybe Jack was right.

Lilah sighs and shakes her head. "Landon, I. Just. Can't. Okay!?" she says louder this time.

I throw my hands up and run them through my hair. Fully frustrated and wishing I could think straight.

"That's for you," she says and gestures to the wrapped present on the coffee table. "I have to go."

I don't have a second to respond before she's turned and opened the door. I go after her into the hallway. "Lilah!" I yell out, more concerned than angry as she makes her way down the stairs and out of sight. I debate chasing after her but I don't think doing so is going to help anything.

I walk back into the loft and sit down on the couch. Staring at the present in front of me. No, presents? There's two. Oh, wait, that's the alcohol. My thoughts and brain are swimming. I feel like my head is about to combust. I lean back to rest on the couch. Sleep claiming me fast.

———

What felt like only a minute later, I wake up to my phone going off. There's a text from Lilah. It's been almost two hours since I fell asleep.

I'm sorry Landon. I was overwhelmed & I owe you more than that. Are you still up? I think I'm ready to talk now. I love you.

My head pounds as I sit up to respond.

It's okay. I love you too. Where are you? Want to come here or meet somewhere?

A minute later her response comes in.

Want to meet at our building? If you still have access to it.

She wants to meet at the worksite. Well, I guess it's not considered a site anymore since we completed it a couple months ago. I know the code is the same because Dean wanted Jack to have access until they opened it up to the public for offices and retail space. I guess it's a good neutral ground, considering I have no clue where Lilah actually lives. I quickly reply that I'll meet her in twenty minutes. It only takes about ten to walk there but I need a moment to breathe first.

After I quickly wash my face with cold water and throw on a light jacket, I head out the door. The sidewalks are mostly empty and lit by street lamps. A few drunkards hanging about since it's midnight on a Saturday. The cool Spring night air fills my lungs. It smells of a bonfire in the distance, common this time of year since the weather mimics Autumn in the evening.

I haven't a clue what Lilah is going to say. Hell, I don't know what I'm going to say to her. Surprisingly, I'm not even angry at her for lying to me about anything, more confused and wanting answers. One thing is for certain, I love her. I'm willing to hear her out and try to move past this.

Luckily the alcohol messing with my brain seems to have calmed down since my nap and the multiple large glasses of water I chugged before I left the loft.

Glad I gave myself a few minutes to clear my head. The cool Cleveland breeze always helps to ground me.

Walking up to the square I'm almost to the high-rise I spent all those months in. I do miss the view from the top floor, that's probably where I'll take her to talk. We have some good memories there. Rounding the corner I spot something bright on the other side of the statue in the middle, my vision is still a little foggy from drinking. I can't tell where it's coming from.

As I come up closer I can just make out the source.

It's the high-rise.

And it's on fire.

Chapter Twenty-Eight

Scorch

The building is lit up in flames. It wasn't a bonfire I was smelling. The flames haven't overtaken the entire building yet. Looks like they are coming from a few floors up. From where the electrical issues initially started that we thought were fixed.

I immediately start sprinting towards the building. I don't hear any sirens in the distance. No one must have called it in yet. I can't think. I come up fast on the front entrance. Luckily no one should be inside since they would need a code...

The glass to the left side of the main entrance is busted.

I hear a woman's scream in the distance going upward.

"HELP!"

Lilah.

I don't know why she would have broken in but all I'm able to think is she's inside. I have to get to her. Avoiding the shards of glass, I step through the broken entrance. Smoke already filling the air.

"Lilah!" I shout as I cautiously head to the stairs. Who knows what floor she's on. Oh god, what if she went all the way to the top floor and can't get past the fire to get down. I start running.

I'm halfway up the third flight of stairs. The smoke is getting unbearable. I move the neck of my shirt over my nose. Knowing it won't do much to keep the smoke from my lungs but it will at least give me an extra moment before I pass out while I search for Lilah.

"Lilah!" I shout again, this time into the direction of the fire.

Everything around me is lit with amber orange and black. Beams are falling in every direction. I have to get her out before the ceiling decides to collapse on us.

"LILAH!" I manage to yell through coughs.

"Help! I'm over here!" I hear her off to the right.

Shielding my eyes I head in the direction of her voice, careful to not step in the path of the fire. I see her. She's near one of the walls of windows, luckily the glass isn't broken yet since the fire hasn't fully enveloped the area. She's sitting with her knees tucked in, holding them and shielding her face from the fire.

"Lilah!" I shout as I get closer.

"Oh my god! Landon!" she shouts as she looks up.

It's not Lilah. It's Dean's assistant Claire. Why the hell is she here? I reach down and help her up. She doesn't look to be injured. Until she starts walking with a limp.

"Have you seen Lilah!?" I shout over the roaring of the fire.

She looks at me confused, "Who?"

"Lilah. My girlfriend!" I say loudly, closer to her ear.

She shakes her head with a concerned look in her eyes. "You have to help him!" she says through a series of coughs and points off to the left near a fallen beam surrounded by flames. I can't see anyone from where we are standing.

"Who!?"

"He was trying to help me!" Another coughing fit. "Then a beam fell on him! I couldn't move it..." She's half coughing, half sobbing. "The fire started spreading near us. I tried to get away but ended up over–" More coughing.

I have to get her out of here, she's inhaled way too much smoke by the sound of it. The way I got over here remains relatively clear. Guiding her with me, I hold her up so she doesn't fall. We manage to get to the stairs unscathed. My coughing is starting to catch up to hers.

"Go get help, I'll help whoever is over there!" I shout at her. She nods and hesitates for a second, worry swirling in her smoke irritated eyes.

"Go!" I say again before I turn and shield my face to head in the direction she pointed the man was at.

Fire is rising all around me. I don't know how I'm going to get back out of here. I'm hoping there's a gap somewhere I'm able to get through with whoever it is I'm about to help. I don't know who else would have been here. Dean? But wouldn't she have said it was him. Maybe someone actually tried breaking in. I hope it's not the latter.

I finally find where she pointed out. A beam is half fallen on top of a tall man, I only see his lower half from this side. I hurry and get around the beam to where his torso and head should be. I barely make out a plaid shirt and a reddish brown beard.

Oh my god.
Aaron.

What the hell is he doing here? Quickly I move to the edge of the beam and try to lift. No give. *Fuck.* I have to get this off him. He's definitely unconscious but I don't have time to check his pulse. *I have to get this beam off him.* I move to the other end and squat down to grab the edges. Lifting up I finally manage to get it up. I pivot to the left and move it clear of his head before I let it fall.

I kneel down in front of Aaron to turn him over, his shirt is half burned and I see his skin blistering underneath. He must have shielded Claire with this side. He has a pulse. It's weak though.

"Aaron!" I shout and try to shake him.

Nothing.

I have to get him out of here or he's definitely going to die. Coughing through the smoke I manage to get him on my back. Any leftover feeling of drunkenness from not too long ago is completely sobered. Aaron is not a small man but I manage to lift him all the way up and we start to make our way to the stairs.

I have to find Lilah. Hopefully she managed to get out if she came in here at all. Before heading down the stairs, I shout her name one more time in the direction of the fire. If she's here she's not on this floor. I can't bring myself to think she's hurt or unconscious.

We round the last corner of the smoke-filled stairwell and enter the main floor. I see Claire outside on the phone through the glass panes. Firefighters are running towards us.

"There might be another woman up there!" I shout in their direction. "Her name is Lilah!"

They haven't gotten through the door yet. Time feels like it's moving at half speed. I'm almost all the way through the lobby with

Aaron on my back. It's true what they say about adrenaline, somehow, I've gotten this far with him. The first firefighter gets through the front door twenty feet from me.

Right as an explosion sounds from behind me in the direction of the elevator. Fire hits my back, Aaron taking the bulk of it as we both fly forward.

The last thing I remember is the ground before the darkness.

Chapter Twenty-Nine

Ashes

The sound of an incessant beeping wakes me up. A blinding light overhead and a sharp pain in my arm. It hurts to breathe. I feel something covering my face. My vision is blurry. I can't make out where I am. I don't remember how I got here or where I was before.

Oh god.

Lilah, she was in the building. The fire. Aaron. The explosion. All of it starts flooding my mind at the same pace the heart monitor is going. I feel someone grab my hand.

"Landon, you're okay."

It's Jack. My brother is here. My vision starts to focus on his body standing on my left. I take in the rest of my surroundings. I'm obviously in the hospital, and alive. Dr. Alex is here. My panic subsides a small fraction but continues to have hold of my emotions. I need to know what happened.

Dr. Alex walks over to my right and moves the oxygen mask from my face and checks my blood pressure and O2 levels.

"Hi Landon, glad to see you're finally awake. You're extremely lucky to be alive."

"What happened?" I ask both him and Jack. They exchange a look before Jack starts to answer.

"Well brother, you've been unconscious for three days. You ran into a fire at the high-rise. I don't know for the life of me know why you did, but you managed to save Claire. She was there to check on some last-minute things before they planned to start showings for the office space next week." He seems to be thinking over his words before he continues.

"Aaron had been heading back to the bar where we were still at after walking Madison home and he saw the fire. I guess he heard Claire inside and ran in there like you did." I swear the world shifts as he pauses retelling the events of what I thought was only last night.

"Is he okay? Jack, tell me Aaron is okay."

Jack looks over to Dr. Alex and back to me. "He's alive, Landon. Badly burnt and they had to put him in a medically induced coma for now. But he's alive."

Fuck. He's not out of the woods yet but at least he isn't dead. I let out a small sigh of relief.

"Both of you almost didn't make it. But if you hadn't gotten to him when you did, he wouldn't be here at all," Jack finishes.

My mind calms itself enough to remember why I went into the building in the first place.

"What about Lilah? Did they find her? Is she *okay!*?" I ask my brother, trying to

mask the panic which threatens to fully take over.

Dr. Alex steps to stand at the end of my hospital bed near my feet, Jack takes a seat again to my left and they share the same look from earlier.

"What's going on? Is she hurt!?" My heart feels like it's going to explode out of my chest.

Jack lets out a big sigh, "Landon, I don't really know how to tell you this..." Another look at Dr. Alex. "Lilah, wasn't there."

I let out the breath I had been holding. *Thank God.* She must have chosen not to show up, I didn't think I would ever be happy about her not showing up to something when she said she would. Besides Aaron being alive, this is the best news I could hear.

"Oh, thank God, Jack. She was supposed to meet me–" He holds up a hand, cutting me off.

"Let me finish," he says in the softest tone I've only heard him use with my nieces. "Landon... The firefighters searched the whole building and couldn't find anyone else there, even among the rubble after they put the fire out." He pauses, as if he's telling me bad news. "As soon as I got there after Claire called me, she told me how you were asking about Lilah. I assumed she was probably the reason why you were at the building in the first place. Since that's been your spot to meet her sometimes." He's explaining all of this like I need to be reminded, but I don't interrupt him.

"The paramedics gave me the belongings you had on you before they took you in the ambulance. I unlocked your phone and tried to find Lilah's contact." Another pause and look at the doctor. "Landon, Lilah's info was nowhere in your phone."

What is he talking about? I must be out of it, confusion lacing its way over the worry occupying my brain.

"What do you mean?" I ask.

"There were no texts, no phone calls, no contact at all for Lilah. I wondered if maybe you had a fight with her and deleted everything for some reason. Claire was with me and called one of Dean's contacts who works for the police department, they did some digging and..." He sucks in a breath, "There's no evidence of Lilah anywhere in Cleveland Landon."

"What the *hell* are you talking about Jack?" My brows furrow together. I'm starting to get frustrated with this conversation. "I saw her not even a couple hours before the fire. We did have a fight, which is why we were going to meet at the high-rise to talk it out." Jack looks at Dr. Alex again.

"Landon, I'm going to try and explain this in the best way I can." Dr. Alex sighs before he continues for my brother. "Sometimes, when someone goes through a traumatic experience in their life. They create scenarios or even whole personalities to protect themselves. Sometimes these scenarios include someone else created by the mind."

Okay, I'm actually getting angry. What the actual fuck are they talking about? I need to get my phone and call Lilah, of course they think I'm fucking insane. They've never met her and all of a sudden, she's missing and they don't know how to find her. I've had my own theories regarding Lilah lately, mostly about her lying about her name. That must be it, her legal name isn't Lilah, no wonder Dean's cop friend couldn't find her.

"I don't know what the fuck you two are talking about. I'm not crazy, Lilah has definitely been hiding something." I look over to Jack, "You were right, I didn't want to tell you because then I'd be admitting it to myself but she has definitely been holding some things back. We started to dive into it the other night before our fight and the fire. I have a feeling she's lying about her name, which is probably why you can't find her yet."

There goes another fucking look between the two of them. I'm about to rip this IV out of my arm and go find her myself.

"Landon, brother, *I love you* but Lilah doesn't... *exist*." He reaches out again to touch my arm, I pull away this time. I'm rarely angry with my brother but I am about to tell him to *fuck off*.

He continues, "I know this probably makes no sense to you, I'm just wrapping my own brain around it. Right after you got taken here to the hospital, I had Claire get Dean's PI to look into Lilah. He went to check your loft for any signs of her. I mentioned you had a couple cameras there and she had been staying with you a lot."

"He couldn't find any trace of her, Landon. He looked through your camera, there are no pictures of her. He searched every inch of your loft for any remnant of her DNA. There was nothing except you and a few traces of Rachel and anything else was from prior residences. He was very thorough."

My brain feels like it's falling in on itself, my thoughts all colliding together. Some of what my brother is saying starts to replay through my mind. This still doesn't make any sense.

"It's called Maladaptive Daydreaming. When someone goes through trauma, such as a bad accident, or even bad heartbreak.

Their brain starts to try and protect itself, these *daydreams* often feel very real and are vivid to the point the person having them would have no idea they weren't actually happening. I have someone here who can explain everything Landon. His focus is on the mind and trauma," Dr. Alex says as he starts to reach for the door to I assume let whoever he is talking about into the room.

I'm going to lose it. I can't listen to this anymore.

"Get out," I say in the flattest tone manageable. Jack and the doctor exchange another look and pause.

"Get. The. Fuck. Out. Now. *Both of you*, please."

Jack hands me my phone. "I love you brother, and I'm here for you, okay?" Then he stands up and both he and the doctor head out the door, closing it behind them to leave me with my thoughts.

For the first time in the last six months, I feel truly alone. My mind feels like it's lost in itself while I stare up at the white hospital ceiling. The obnoxious beeping of the heart monitor sounding loud in my head. Or maybe it's my heartbeat? I feel like I am in a fog. I know I should be angry about my brother, of all people, trying to tell me I'm insane. For some reason though I can't completely dismiss what they told me. As the beeping intensifies with the beat of my heart, I close my eyes. A replay of this last year and a half flashes before my eyes. Stopping only on specific moments in time.

Fights with my ex-wife, Rachel. Her yelling at me about how I was always hiding something from her. Waking up in the middle of the night to her searching my phone when there was nothing for her to find.

Rachel's hands on the glass of our shower, her moans mixed with his. Her yelling at me when I found them even though I wasn't the one who was cheating.

Me sleeping on the couch all those nights.

The following month at Christmas, Rachel acting like everything was fine between us, when I couldn't hold it in anymore and left on my bike.

The snow in my face right before my accident. Almost dying.

Finally realizing Rachel would never change after finding out she kept it up with him after my accident and who knows exactly how long before.

The divorce and moving back to Cleveland.

The night in the bar. The woman I had to talk to. Her chestnut hair and steel blue eyes. The smell of Jasmine and crackling embers. Her smile and laugh. Hearing David Bowie overhead while I fell completely and fully for her right there. But I was alone. Jack had left and I stayed.

Standing on stage singing Karaoke with Lilah. Everyone joined in and cheered us on... but it's only me on stage. The looks everyone was giving us. No, just me. Because I was alone.

Lilah and I broke my couch on the first night we slept with each other. No, it was just me.

The morning when Rachel showed up to my place. Lilah in the bathroom until she left. No, she was never there.

The first time I met Lilah on the top floor of the high-rise. No one else was there. I took her picture... or I thought I did. I woke up the next morning to my brother finding me, alone.

Colorado. I drove alone. She didn't have a license. She was never there. Dancing in the club. I was alone.

The baseball game with Dean. He ignored her. No, there was no one there for him to ignore.

Skydiving, the instructor kept talking over Lilah, responding when I was talking to her. But I wasn't talking to her, she wasn't there.

Christmas. Dean's New Year's Eve party. The twin's party. Drinks with Jack. My birthday party. The building the night of the fire. She never showed. She was never going to.

My panic starts to rise, my breathing becoming harder and harder as reality starts to come crashing down on everything I thought I knew. When I finally open my eyes, I know.

I know Jack is telling me the truth.
Lilah isn't real.

Chapter Thirty

Pyre

The stark white four walls of this hospital room will be the death of me. Being poked and prodded for tests to make sure my body is healing how it should after inhaling too much smoke. Would be worse if I had third degree burns like Aaron though.

I saw him yesterday. I've been in the hospital for a week and every day they refused to let me even get up to use the bathroom. Catheters are no fun. Finally they gave up and let me walk, with help of course, down the hallway to see him in the intensive care unit. He's finally awake. Madison decked his room out with balloons and flowers. She tried to do the same for me but I politely refused. The looks of pity from everyone is enough, I don't need more attention brought to me.

The first thing Aaron said to me, having been awake for only a few hours, was, *"So I heard you've gone fully nuts man!?"*

"Fuck you man, you almost died on me!" I replied in the same mocking tone.

At least he's treating me the same. Jack has been extremely cautious of saying the wrong thing around me. I haven't the energy to tell him to knock it off though. Nancy and the girls have stopped by frequently too, the girls drew me some *get well soon* cards. Emily's drawing of what is supposed to be me is terrifying. Isabelle's drawing was of Branch, his four legs all varying in different sizes. He looks more like a *Muppet* than a dog.

Jack told me our mother has tried to come see me a few times since I was admitted. He's stopped her every time. I'm glad. I don't think I could handle a conversation with her yet. I do wish I could see my dad though, but mom won't let him come without her. I didn't ask if my sister cares, she's probably glad I almost died.

Rachel apparently moved back to Ohio from California a couple weeks ago like my mom mentioned at the twin's party. I guess she hasn't figured out the perfect manipulative thing to say to me yet since there's been no sign of her.

A knock sounds at the heavy wooden door to my right, I can't see through the small window from where my bed is sitting. I wonder if Rachel is here. I should pretend I'm asleep.

The door cracks open and I see heavy black boots and a burly man. Definitely *not* my ex-wife.

"Excuse me, Landon Stone? If you're awake and up for it we need to ask you some questions." Two cops let themselves inside my room, shutting the door behind them. The burly one with a large beard stands closer while a younger and much slimmer man stands behind him, looking nervous behind his glasses.

"I'm surprised you guys actually haven't shown up sooner," I say, considering the fire was a week ago.

"Your friend, *Dean Wolf*, has kept us away as long as he could. He said you needed to *recover*. Since we knew you weren't going anywhere and seeing as he owns the building which caught fire, we obliged."

Interesting. I would have thought Dean would be on a man hunt to figure out what caused the fire. I would love to know how it happened too, though my money is on the wiring problems.

"We wanted to let you know we are investigating this case as potential foul play." The burly one continues. Shit, what does *that* mean?

"So am I being questioned as a suspect or as a witness?" I ask flat out.

The slimmer quiet cop shifts on his feet, the nervous look in his eyes intensifying. He must be new to the job. I wouldn't consider myself to look scary, he's probably afraid of Burly there.

"We are interviewing everyone who was at the scene, Mr. Stone. If you could just go over everything about the night of the fire, it would be a huge help," Burly says, clearly avoiding answering my question.

For the next ten minutes I go over the whole story, avoiding the fact I'm apparently insane and went looking for my invisible girlfriend. I stated that I decided to go for a walk. They perked up at that, obviously sounding suspicious until I mentioned the fire was already blazing before I got there. I went through finding Claire and Aaron. Carrying Aaron out of the building, well *almost* out of the building.

Once I finished they seemed content with my answers and let me know they would be in touch. The slim cop almost ran into Burly on the way out.

I'm about to shut my eyes to get some rest when another knock sounds.

"Come in," I sigh and say towards the shut door.

An older man with grey stubble and wide rimmed glasses walks in. He doesn't look like a doctor. He's wearing a thick cardigan despite it getting warmer and warmer outside every day, summer right around the corner. The man pulls up a small chair on my left and takes a seat, crossing one leg over the other and folding his hands around his knee.

"Hi Landon, my name is Dr. Harland. I've been following your journey here with the help of Dr. Alex. He said he mentioned me when you first woke up, I wanted to give you a little time before I came and introduced myself though. How are you getting along?"

Ah. The shrink. For my insane ass self. Great. I had wondered when he would stop in after Dr. Alex mentioned someone being here who could help me. *Good luck.*

"Ehh, I'm doing great, Doc. Found out I'm crazy, but other than that it's been peachy here. Dr. Alex told me you could *"explain everything,"* whatever that's supposed to mean," I say, letting the sarcasm drip over my words.

"Well, first off, I wouldn't say I can explain *everything* to you, as you say. But I am here to help you understand a little more of what's going on inside your head."

"Oh, great. Sounds like a blast." I lay my head back on the flat hospital pillow and prepare myself to be *shrunk*.

Dr. Harland lets out a rough laugh and pulls out a small notebook from his back pocket.

"Would you say you usually meet stressful times with sarcasm?" Okay, he's more of a blunt shrink then. Got it.

"I'd say most people would consider me to be *broody*. Plus I'm already on the doubting end of whether you can help me with whatever is going on inside my head, so pardon my lack of enthusiasm."

He seems to consider. "Well Landon." He clicks his pen. "Brooding and sarcasm usually go hand in hand in my experience. Let's start from the beginning. When did you start to experience your daydreams?"

"Not going to lie to you Doc, I'm not a big fan when it comes to therapy." Dr. Harland huffs another small laugh, I catch a glimpse of a smirk in my peripherals.

"How about this Landon, you just think of me like someone who is writing your life story. I'm not here to question your thoughts, only to try and make sense of why they're there. Start from when you remember the daydreams beginning and we will go from there."

Still looking up at the ceiling, I close my eyes. Picturing everything. I haven't brought myself to think of meeting her yet, only of everything after.

Reluctantly I start to recount that first night to Dr. Harland.

"I was at the bar. My brother had left to go home and I stayed back for another drink." It's crazy how real the memory feels, even though I know it was only half real. "That's when she walked in."

"The person you created in your daydreams?" Dr. Harland asks, no judgement lacing his words.

I open my eyes to sit up and look away from the white ceiling. I haven't spoken about her out loud since I woke up. Only ever allowing myself to think about the last six months in my head.

"Her name was Lilah."

A little over an hour later Dr. Harland leaves my room. I learned the frequent headaches I've been having are sometimes associated with my *condition,* as is my constant spacing out. He didn't give me any clue as to how long it would take to fix my broken mind but he didn't leave me feeling like I've gone fully insane. I guess it's not all bad.

I begin to doze off again, with not much else to do but lay in this bed. The nurses mentioned I would begin some physical therapy tomorrow or the next day. Hopefully I get out of here soon. My thoughts start to drift off but every time I almost fall asleep, I see her face. Her chestnut colored hair. Those piercing eyes. How can I feel the remnants of someone's lips on mine if they were never actually there?

A light knock at the door pulls me away from the thoughts I know will ultimately drive me fully insane.

"Hey, Mr. Broody. You up to a visitor?" Stacey peeks her head in, her long brown hair falling over her shoulder, wariness in her brown eyes but a smile plastered on her face.

"Sure, Stace. I'm always happy to see you." I've gotten used to multiple visits over the last couple of days, seeing as everyone is also here to visit Aaron.

She makes her way inside, taking a seat at the edge of the hospital bed.

"Well, at least you don't look as bad as Aaron does," she says as she takes in my hospital gown and lack of burns.

"Oh, definitely. But that was true to begin with so..." I try to joke but land a little flat. Stacey shoves my leg and lets out a small laugh.

"I guess your humor decided to come out some more huh?" she says with a smile quickly fading away as she looks off.

"What's up Stace?"

She sighs, "I've been avoiding coming to see you."

"Oh yeah? Can I ask why?" My brows furrow with confusion.

"Well, I was thinking back through the night you said you met..." she trails off, obviously not sure if she should refer to Lilah as actually existing or not, as everyone else has done when they start to ask me anything since I woke up.

"It's okay Stace, you can say her name," I say.

She hesitates, opening and closing her mouth a couple times before speaking. "The night when you stayed back after Jack left months ago close to Thanksgiving. I saw you walking towards someone. It was busy that night and there were a lot of bodies near the bar." She pauses again, like she's replaying everything in her head.

"You ordered two drinks, which wasn't like you but I got them anyway. I heard you talking to someone, but again it was extremely crowded."

"Stace, you don't have to feel guilty. I went a little crazy." I laugh, humor being the only thing keeping me from falling into a grief filled depression. "You couldn't have known I was talking to some non-existent girl."

"No, Landon. That's what I'm trying to explain, I didn't see you with anyone. At first…" My brows furrow closer together as she continues, "After I gave you the two drinks, I saw who you were talking to finally. Right before you walked to the back, there was a girl there."

"What do you mean?" I freeze, every nerve standing on edge in my body.

"Landon, you were actually talking to someone that night, but you walked off alone towards the back of the bar and I never saw the girl again."

Either I'm fully cracked in the head at this point, or Stacey is creating things in her mind too. I had to have been alone that night. Every memory of Lilah wasn't real. But, that night, us meeting. I never played it back through. All the other memories have a haze about them. Which Dr. Harland said is common with *Maladaptive Daydreams,* when you start to question the reality of them. He said the more I talk about and reframe those memories, the clearer they will become.

That night though, before I remembered the karaoke bar, there isn't the same haze. Did I actually meet someone at the bar? Did I actually meet *Lilah*?

Chapter Thirty-One

Cinder

My mind might be shot, but my body is making a quick recovery. My physical therapist, a woman in her mid-forties with short, almost silver looking hair, told me I have a one up on most people since I'm pretty active in my normal life. She seems to think I should be able to leave the hospital soon. Although she doesn't know how bad off mentally I am. When I mentioned possibly leaving soon to Dr. Harland, he didn't give me a response.

Since Stacey confused the living hell out of me with her recollection of that first night, Dr. Harland has made me relive it over and over in our sessions. He mentioned *daydreams* can be influenced by real life and people we have encountered, my case proving to be the same way. Some people fully black out during their *episodes* but since I am able to recall every moment and some are able to be confirmed with others on days I was seen texting or talking to *Lilah* on the phone. Guess I'm not fully insane, yet.

Dr. Harland seems to think I must have met someone in reality, who I turned into Lilah. I told him about the *haze* not being attached to the beginning of the night, until I was in the back of

Map Room and we decided to go to the karaoke bar, *Moonlight.* The realization does nothing to ease my nerves though. Was the girl real? Did I actually meet someone that perfect, but walked away? Only to create a whole relationship with her inside my mind. I asked Harland as much today. He only said time will tell. Whatever the hell that means.

We ended our session with me telling him to *fuck off* after he suggested I could get more clarity from confronting people and things in my life harboring trauma. Such as my mother and ex-wife.

I decided to pay Aaron a visit after my shit show of a therapy session. I've tried to see him every day. We've been close ever since we started working together, but this has definitely bonded us more. Claire stopped by yesterday to thank both of us, she's doing great and is already back to handling everything Dean throws her way. Her recovery was only a few days at some fancy clinic. Set up by Dean of course.

"Hey man, you're looking a little less rough today," I say as I walk into Aaron's room to find him talking with Jack. My lumberjack friend is still covered in burn scars, mostly on his side. The light in his eyes has returned though and he's back to his usual self.

"Gee thanks Lan, butter me up why don't you," he says with his typical humor and a wink.

Laughing, I pull up one of the other chairs. It's nice not having to be chaperoned every time I walk around anymore. Aaron's only a couple rooms away since they moved him from the intensive care unit of the hospital. The small room identical to mine looks humorous with his large self that takes up most of the bed and all the balloons Madison keeps refilling. At least he gets a room with a window.

"They say when you might get out of here?" I ask him.

He opens up one of the Jello cups he's been hoarding on the table to his left. "They think I'll be able to start physical therapy next week." He shoves a giant spoonful of red gelatin into his mouth and asks, "You getting out soon?"

I let out a small forced laugh. "Depends on when they decide I'm not crazy anymore."

"At least Dean's pulled some strings and been able to keep you here and not in the Psychiatric Unit," Jack says, stealing one of Aaron's Jello cups.

"What do you mean?" I ask my brother.

"I guess he has some connections at the hospital and wanted you to feel more comfortable so he asked to keep you here. Which is why Dr. Harland comes here instead of you going to his office in another area of the hospital." He answers through a full mouth of Jello.

Interesting. I had wondered why I wasn't in *that* wing of the large hospital. I'm not complaining though, I'm glad to be within walking distance of Aaron.

"Oh, Lan. I brought you some things from your place, since they told me you'd at least be here a couple more days." *Great.* "I'll help bring them over to your room," Jack says as he discards the empty plastic cup into the trash next to him and stands.

"Alright." I take that as my cue to walk out with him. "See ya, Aaron."

After a few quiet steps through the hallway, I break the silence. "What's up Jack?"

He's been quieter with me than he ever has been, especially the last couple of times he's come to visit. He's probably trying not to show his pity. "For real man, you've been weird with me ever since you found out I'm slightly crazy," I say as we make our way into my room.

"Landon, you aren't crazy. You've got to stop beating yourself up man," Jack says.

Well, at least my brother doesn't think I'm insane. I sit down on the edge of the bed as Jack places the large box he carried from Aaron's room onto the small table along the wall. Another short moment of silence passes.

"I'm mad at Stacey," he says as he looks down to the ground, standing against the wall with his arms crossed. He said it barely more than a whisper. I start to wonder if he meant to say it out loud.

"She didn't do anything wrong, Jack."

Shaking his head he starts to pace the small length of floor between the wall and the bed I'm sitting on.

"She shouldn't have told you something she doesn't even know is true or not. Not while you're here and trying to figure things out for yourself."

"Jack, it doesn't matter." He starts to interrupt me but I continue. "Look, I've been mind-fucked since I woke up after the fire. Luckily, as Dr. Harland has said, I seem to have a decent grasp on reality. Even if Stacey did see me actually talking to a girl at the bar that night, and say this girl was the same one in my *daydreams* it doesn't change anything." I let out a small sigh, absorbing my own words in the same breath I say them. "Let's say *she* was real. It doesn't change the fact *Lilah* wasn't. My relationship for the last six months didn't happen. I've come to terms with it. For some reason, even if I feel like my whole world just shattered. It's like I finally see clearly."

Until this moment I don't think I've let myself fully accept that. It seems to sink in for Jack too as he stops pacing.

"I guess Dr. Harland is actually helping you then, huh?" Jack asks.

"I guess it seems so, yeah." Looks like therapy isn't a complete sham, I let out a laugh.

My brother picks up the box of my things he brought from the loft and moves it to an open spot on the bed. I look inside and spot a couple of books and a... puzzle? Not sure where I had that stashed away. I can't remember the last time I put one together.

"Figured you could use some distraction from these four walls, other than annoying Aaron of course." I laugh and pick up a stack of books.

"Well I've got to meet with Dean, he's already talking about what his next project is."

"Did he forget his last one just went up in flames?" I joke.

Jack laughs and shakes his head, walking towards the door.

"You know Dean. Always looking towards bigger and better things. He doesn't seem too worried about the investigation still underway. Keep your chin up brother, I'll stop by in a couple days."

Jack walks out the door, shutting it behind him. I pull out the rest of the things he brought me. The puzzle is a no go. More than half the pieces are missing. I sort through the books I set to the side.

A book on photography, a biography on David Bowie, and a worn copy of *The Great Gatsby*. Triggering my memories, I do what Dr. Harland told me to. I replay and reframe.

My mind drifts off to Colorado. The old motel. Lying in bed with Lilah.

No, I was alone.

The deer head mounted above my head. Lilah picked up the book from a shelf on the opposite side of the room.

No, I picked it up.

She was reading it for the next few weeks.

No, I was reading it.

As much as the memory feels clearer, I can't help but feel a sense of grief. Grief for moments I thought I spent with her. Grief for the woman who never was. Before I get lost in my own head at the cinders left behind of my fake relationship, I open up to the first page and begin to read again as water tempts to break free from my eyes.

Chapter Thirty-Two

Extinguish

Two days later after my physical therapy session, I'm back talking with Dr. Harland. He's been very contemplative this session. I've been seeing him every other day since he first came to see me. He said I'm showing a lot of progress. Despite my push back the other day regarding confronting my family and ex-wife.

"Well, Landon. It seems like we are venturing towards the end of our visits here."

I had been half listening when he got here. Since he started out the session stating I will need to conquer my fear of confrontation, I perked right up at him saying I should be leaving soon though.

"I've spoken to your other doctors and they also think you are ready to venture back to your normal life. Well a new normal, but at least back to the real world out there."

"Well, sounds great Doc. Is this the last time I'll be seeing you then?" I ask. I don't hide my excitement, though I'll somehow miss my sessions with him.

"Landon, I would like to continue to see you after you leave here. I have an office downtown, I think once a week until you get reacclimated to your life and then we can drop down to once a month."

Damn. He must see my disappointment before he continues.

"I think you've shown tremendous progress, considering all you've been through. But we have a lot more to cover until you'll be ready to fully move on. I know you don't want to dive into your past but to fully understand why your daydreams began, we have to tackle those hard questions. We don't have to do any of it right now. We don't even need to do it together, sometimes talking through things with yourself is all it takes."

"Honestly, I'm not surprised. I definitely don't like or want to go down the rabbit hole of what's *fucked* me up though," I say, a little disheartened at some point I will have to face those demons.

"Look Landon, even though we definitely have work to do, both together and by yourself. I want to leave you with this."

He shuts his notebook, clicking his pen off as he continues, "I imagine finding out someone you loved doesn't exist in the same planes of reality we do to be devastating. She did represent something real though. Every moment, every memory you have with her. You were *alone,* yes. But you had yourself. You've told me stories of conquering fears. You jumped out of a plane and sang onstage to a crowd of people. You've said she helped you gain confidence in yourself, she helped you realize what you actually want to do with your life. Landon, that was all *you.* You've thought yourself to be lacking and think she made you better, but you've had the power all along to have the qualities you admired of the very person you fell in love with."

Absorbing what he said hits harder than I expected. "I've never thought about it like that," I say as he stands from his chair, smoothing his cardigan down and tucking his notebook into the crook of his arm.

"Well Landon, that's all it is. Reframing those thoughts and transforming them into productive ones. I'll see you next week. Take care of yourself, okay."

Dr. Harland walks out the door, leaving it open behind him. Moving from the chair I was sitting in I go to stand in front of the small mirror on the opposite wall of the door. I've definitely looked better, my usually trimmed beard is overgrown, the sides coming in scraggly. I'm in desperate need of a haircut too. The bags under my eyes have gotten better though since I've been here, despite everything.

Is Harland, right? Have I been the one who brought out the parts of myself I thought had been buried long ago? After my divorce with Rachel, I was left hollow. I truly didn't believe in love anymore. *Mr. Broody* through and through, as Stacey would say. But Lilah. No, only *myself*, brought me back to life. I know I should be curled up in a hole out of embarrassment. Especially after realizing Jack truly did catch me alone and fully naked at the high rise one morning months ago. There's no shame left though. I feel stronger. Sure, I go to the gym to try and make my body tough, but I'd never really been mentally tough. I let my ex-wife steal parts of me and leave me with nothing. Yet those parts were never truly gone. The last six months might not have happened how I thought. But I did do all of those things, by myself.

Fully lost in thought, not a *daydream* this time thankfully. I barely hear someone walk into the open door of my room. I see a silhouette in the mirror sitting on my bed. Turning around I realize who it is. Blonde hair and hazel eyes coming into full view.

Rachel.

"Hi Lan."

"Hi Rachel."

"What? Are you not going to question why I'm here or tell me to leave?" she says in her condescending tone I haven't missed at all.

I shake my head, crossing my arms. "Nope. You don't deserve even that much from me."

"Ouch Lan, I know you're in pain but you don't need to lash out," she says as she places a hand to her chest like I offended her.

"Did you come here just to play the victim again or was there a purpose to this visit?" I don't hold back any of the bite in my words. Seeing her for the first time since knowing she almost caused me to die on my bike is unleashing any leftover anger I've harbored towards her.

"Someone definitely woke up on the wrong side of the bed." That tone again, I swear she should get paid for it.

I don't budge from where I'm standing. She finally moves and stands by the door, surprisingly not coming closer to me like she normally would. Maybe finding out I went somewhat crazy because of some of the trauma she put me through is keeping her from crossing any lines.

"Okay look Lan, I came here because I still love you. I want to make things right with us. You know we are meant to be together."

Nope, there goes that thought.

"Rachel, what are you talking about? Is this another plan you and my mother cooked up?"

She takes one step closer. "Landon, don't be stupid. Mom won't even talk to me."

Well, that's new.

"Rachel, I don't know what you expect to happen. We were terrible together. You cheated on me, multiple times. Yet you didn't trust *me,* like I had been the unfaithful one–"

She takes another step closer but crosses her arms.

"I know," she interrupts me.

"You do?" I ask, genuinely dumbfounded. I never thought she would fully admit to it.

Another step closer. She's only a foot and a half away.

"I'll admit, I wasn't the best. But I can change Lan." She closes the distance between us, reaching for my arm.

I swallow. Completely at a loss for words. Is this actually happening? *Shit.* Am I having *daydreams* where my ex-wife isn't a narcissistic controlling tyrant?

"I'm here to take care of you," she says as she reaches up to my face. "You don't have to worry about anything. We will have to get you out of your disgusting loft in the city, you know how much I hate downtown. I just got a house out West, you'll come move in with me. I'll get someone to sort through and sell your things, especially your bed. Who knows what the hell you've been up to or who has been in that thing..."

I move her hands from my arms and take a step back. I'm done entertaining this conversation.

"Rachel. What the *fuck* are you talking about?"

"Oh Lan, don't be so sensitive. I won't get rid of *everything*, I promise."

Shaking my head, I run my hands through my hair. Why do I get a headache every time I talk to this woman? I know they aren't caused by my *daydreams*. She just knows exactly how to drive me insane. Funny actually, being told I've gone somewhat crazy and she's the only one who makes me feel like I'm fully off the rails.

"Rachel, I'm not moving in with you. We are not getting back together. You say you can change and as much as I don't believe that, it wouldn't matter. You don't need to change, we are not meant for each other and that is fine. I think it's time we both accept it and move on," I say.

A look of anger crosses over her face. Where there was once a mask of concern, there's only a look of hostility left.

"You know, you're an idiot Landon. I was the best thing to ever happen to you."

A brief pause passes, and I realize how long I had been holding onto what I thought was a marriage. It was all a sham though, I don't think she ever actually loved me. She just loved the control she had over me. Until she realized it wasn't enough. We had both been kidding ourselves.

"You're right Rachel, you were the best thing to ever happen to me. Because of you I realize the type of love I deserve and the type of love I don't deserve. You made me realize I deserve better than the vindictive, manipulative type of love you gave me. So thank you Rachel, but you have no more power over me."

She doesn't respond, and I realize I don't need her to. Finally, I feel like I have closure. The truth finally extinguishing any hurt leftover from my marriage. I let go.

She walks out the door without saying good-bye, slamming it shut on the way out.

———

The next night after my dissatisfying tray of hospital food. This time, a chicken salad sandwich. I'm reading in my bed. The doctors told me I'm finally able to leave tomorrow. I'm on the last chapter in my book when I hear the door knob turn.

"You awake Lan?" Jack peeks his head in. It's only eight in the evening.

"Yeah man, what's up? What are you doing here?" Visiting hours end soon, plus he's been spending too much of his time here lately as it is. I'm sure Nancy and the girls would rather have him home.

"Uncle Landon! Uncle Landon!" Emily and Isabelle push past their dad into the room, both wearing yellow dresses.

"Girls." Nancy says sternly after them in what could only be described as a whisper yell.

"What's going on?" I ask, laughing at my niece's excitement as they jump on top of the hospital bed. Almost squashing me.

"Uncle Landon! It's so exciting!" Isabelle shouts. At the same time Emily says, "It's a wedding! It's a wedding!"

I look over to my brother, realizing he's in a button up shirt and slacks. Nancy is in a dress a darker shade of yellow than the twins' dresses. Both of them are smiling. I don't need to ask any questions, quickly grasping at what is happening. Jack tosses me a black button up and some black pants.

After I dress, we all make our way down the hallway. We pass by the cafeteria I've only seen through the glass windows on my way to physical therapy. At the end of the hall, we reach two doors leading to what looks to be a courtyard.

As soon as we are through the doors I'm met with string lights draped along the few trees, leading to the center gazebo only big enough to fit around five people inside its white arches. The lights tempt to bring me back to that night with Lilah, or I guess it was only me, in the high-rise. I shake the thoughts. My mind returning back to the present. Aaron stands in the center wearing a suit that manages to cover his healing wounds, a wheelchair nearby in case he needs it. Looking at him under the lights you would never guess how many burn scars he has, you only see the pure joy in his smile.

We all take our places around the gazebo, Jack and I standing next to Aaron. Stacey and Nancy both in yellow on the other side.

"Landon," Aaron leans around Jack to get my attention.

"What's up man? Getting cold feet?" I joke, knowing full well he is the least bit nervous. He mentioned to me a few days ago about wanting to ask Madison to marry him, I guess they didn't want to wait any longer.

"I appreciate you being here man, I hope this doesn't feel too much like I'm throwing salt in your wounds though," he says warily.

Oh shit. He's worried being at a wedding is going to add to my list of trauma.

I reach around my brother and pat Aaron on his shoulder. "Don't be ridiculous man. I couldn't be happier for you. I'm honored you want me here."

Before he responds, we hear music sound through the small speakers lining the walls outside. Makes me wonder how many weddings they've thrown here with how perfect this all seems.

Madison makes her way down the path from the door to the gazebo. Her parents on either side. Her grin is almost as big as Aaron's. I swear I see a tear line his eyes as she closes the distance.

The officiant they managed to find begins the ceremony. Apparently, Aaron had been planning all of this since he woke up in the hospital. He got Dean's help with getting their marriage license last week.

"Before we get to exchanging the rings, would you like to say your vows?" The officiant asks Aaron and Madison.

"Yes," Aaron starts nervously, grabbing both of Madison's hands. "I know this all may seem sudden, considering we never got officially engaged, but when you have your life almost taken from you. You realize what is truly important and how you can't take the time you think you have for granted." He pauses, choking over his words as tears fill his eyes.

"Madison, you are the light of my life. You are what brought me back after everything went dark. I can't imagine another day in this life without you in it and I vow to show you that love day in and day out for the rest of our lives together."

Damn. I knew Aaron was a romantic but I didn't know how much. I find myself starting to tear up a little.

After Madison says her vows and they exchange rings. The officiant finishes the ceremony.

"I now pronounce you Mr. and Mrs. Montgomery!" They kiss and we all cheer.

The newly-weds make their way back down the aisle to the side of the courtyard where a few picnic tables are set up with food and drinks. Music begins again quietly over the speakers as the celebration continues.

Who would have thought a hospital courtyard wedding is the way to go? The perfect early summer breeze fills the air as a few fireflies glide by. Everyone dancing under the lights. Only downside to this venue? No alcohol is allowed, being in a hospital and what not. I could have fun with this group no matter what though.

I hugged Madison and Aaron as soon as we got over to the tables scattered throughout the courtyard. Both of them were still wary of whether I would be upset being here. I told them this is exactly what I needed. Sure, I could wallow in my self-pity and grief. Both of which tempt to break through the surface daily, but what good would it do me? If I've learned anything from my best friend, it's that life is too short and we need to take advantage of what we have.

Looking around at my friends, Madison and Aaron lovingly embraced in a slow dance. Next to Stacey and her wife. Jack and Nancy awkwardly move around the dance floor while the twins jump in between everyone to a completely different beat. This is what I'm grateful for. This is what will get me through it.

I don't look around and see everything I lack. A lack of love. A lack of purpose with someone else.

No. I look around and all I see is hope.

Chapter Thirty-Three

Fuse

I could barely sleep last night. Knowing today I finally leave this place. As much as I honestly will say the doctors here have helped me, including Dr. Harland, I can't wait to get back to my life. I guess nothing will really be the same when I walk out those doors though. I don't have a girlfriend. I don't expect to hear from my ex-wife again. My job is a little up in the air since I have no idea if Jack has signed another contract for our crew to begin another job yet. I'm not even sure I'd want to go back to working for him. Not that I disliked it at all, I just don't feel like it's where I'm meant to be headed.

I'm walking back from my last physical therapy session and notice my door is open. I wonder if one of my doctors was trying to check in on me. Before I round the corner to walk in the room I've called home these last couple of weeks, I sense someone. An uneasy feeling makes my hands sweaty and my heart race.

I walk in to see her sitting in a chair in the corner. The usual crazy look in her eyes is missing and for the first time in a long time she smiles when she sees me.

I walk around to the other side of my bed and sit near the edge closest to her chair. We don't hug, I think cordial smiles are enough for me at the moment. I wonder if she snuck past Jack to get in here.

"Hi, mom."

She rings her hands together almost as if she is anxious. "Hi Landon, how are you feeling?" she asks, probably in the most caring tone I've heard from her before.

As much as I want to stay angry with her for practically abandoning me and siding with Rachel, I have this nagging feeling in the back of my head. Almost like a record keeps repeating with both words from Dr. Harland and from *Lilah*, well I guess from myself on the latter half.

"I'm alright, thanks for asking. Jack told me you've tried visiting a few times." I'm cautious with what I say around her, as I always am. You never know what she's going to try and hold to use as a motive later.

"I have. I..." She pauses. she seems nervous as she continues wringing her hands together in her lap. "I wanted to come and apologize to you son."

Well, *that* is the last thing I expected to hear from her. Part of me continues to doubt any positive intentions though, despite her words.

"That's... uh, not what I was expecting you to say," I say with genuine bemusement.

She looks down at her hands and takes a deep breath before she continues.

"I've been wrong about a lot of things Landon, I... I have actually been seeing someone to talk through some of them. I know you and your brother have been trying to get me to for a while. I don't think I was ready. I saw though... saw what Rachel had done to you and I had a wake-up call." Another nervous pause but I don't stop her.

"I realized I was doing the same thing Rachel was, I was trying to control you because I wasn't fully happy with myself. The psychologist I've been seeing over the last month diagnosed me as bipolar, I've started on some medication and I feel like I can finally think clearer. I know it's no excuse for anything I put you through or enabled from Rachel but I needed you to know I am truly sorry son. I don't expect this to make you trust me again but I love you and hope we can try to move forward."

Well that was *a lot*. I think a part of me has been waiting to hear those words from her for a while. She's right though, it doesn't fully change anything.

Those words I told myself months ago, the words I thought came from Lilah play in my head. No one else has any power over me. I make my own decisions. I decide whether I want to forgive her or not.

"You're right mom." She looks up at me. "That doesn't fully change anything..." She looks back down at her hands.

"But it's a start." A look of hope shines in her eyes as she raises her gaze back to mine. "I forgive you. It's not a pass for us to act like nothing has happened in the last year or before that, but I'm willing to look forward."

She stands up from her chair and closes the short distance between us, pulling me into the first hug between my mother and I in who knows how long. I start to feel the rest of the cracked pieces within me fuse back together.

———

A few hours later I'm back in my room from visiting Aaron before I finally leave this place. He's doing amazing in his recovery. I'm sure it doesn't hurt that he's been on a high since marrying Madison. The happiness exuding from them is almost contagious. He only has a little longer here too and then he can get back to his life. To think his almost ended a couple weeks ago.

I'm packing up the small amount of things I accumulated within these four walls into my leather duffle bag Jack brought for me. The last of the items being the copy of *The Great Gatsby*. I finished it last night after celebrating with Aaron and Madison. As much as I want to leave it and be rid of any reminder of my delusions of the last six months, I realize I need to hold onto it. For a reminder that some of it had actually been real.

"Hello, Landon. You're looking well."

I turn to find Dean standing in the doorway, looking like he stepped out of a men's magazine for rich people and suits. His smile beaming as usual.

"Hi Dean, good to see you." I'm not sure where I stand with him, considering I was somewhat involved in his building burning down, even if I didn't start the fire. I still haven't heard back about the investigation either.

"Well, you're looking good for someone who almost died trying to save my assistant and your friend," he says as he crosses the floor of the small room, turning to face me again after he takes in the limited surroundings. He studies me for a second, part of me starts to question if he thinks I *did* actually burn the building down.

"Landon, I wanted to stop by to first see how you were doing. But mostly to thank you for saving Claire." I catch a glimpse of worry in his eyes. "I genuinely don't know what I would do without her. Had you and Aaron not run into that building to save her, I would be living an entirely different reality right now. I can't express my gratitude enough to either of you."

I'm actually a little shocked, I took him for the type of man who forgot his own assistant's name. I clearly have judged him a little too harshly.

"Don't mention it, I did what needed to be done. Aaron too," I say as I slip my book into my bag and close the zipper.

Dean walks closer to my side and places his hand on my shoulder. "I'm serious Landon. I owe you immensely. I've already talked to Jack about it, I told him to let me ask you." Confusion crosses my face as I wait for him to finish. "I've secured two spots for new office developments downtown, to expand on my initial plans. I wanted to offer you a higher position, within my company, to work in collaboration with *Stone Construction*."

"What do you mean?"

"I saw how much your input helped Jack, I think that input would come in handy in a broader aspect within my company. You would help oversee all of my future building opportunities. What do you think?" he asks with another beaming smile.

Today is full of surprises, I guess. It sounds like a great opportunity. But something almost tugs on my brain, telling me what my decision should be.

"Thank you for the offer Dean, I truly appreciate it."

"But?" He interrupts me, clearly sensing my hesitation.

"*But*. I think there's something else out there for me. Something else I'm meant to do. I haven't found it yet but I know if I take this job, whatever it is will pass me by."

He nods, his smile never faltering. "I understand. I'm sure we will cross paths again. I've signed Jack onto the next five contracts for my company's expansions. I'll be sure to check in with him on how you're doing. If you need anything though, here's my personal number." He hands me a sleek matte black business card, only a phone number embossed in glossy black written on one side. "I don't normally give that to people, don't go handing it out to just anybody." He winks and starts to walk out of the room.

"Hey Dean," I stop him before he's out the door, staring down at the small rectangular card in my hand. "Can I ask you something?"

He only responds with an expectant look in his eyes.

"At the baseball game a couple months ago. When I saw you, I introduced you to someone." I recall that day, another hazy memory starting to feel more clear. "I said I was with my girlfriend but no one was actually with me, why didn't you question me or say anything?"

He looks off to the side, considering for a moment.

"Well Landon, I've met some very eclectic people in my life. I've learned sometimes it's not for us to question others. Sometimes we have to leave them to figure out things for themselves." Another short pause as he looks down at the expensive watch on his wrist. "I guess at that moment I felt like there was something you needed to figure out for yourself, so I wasn't going to interfere." He shakes my hand and leaves, heading out into the hall without a good-bye.

———

Jack offered to drive me home from the hospital, but I felt like I should do this myself. Considering the last time I was at my loft I wasn't alone, well I wasn't alone in my mind at least. I've been standing in front of my door for the last ten minutes. Debating on if I'm going to be okay when I open it. There's not only a loft on the other side, but the place where I lived with the thought of Lilah. Most of my memories of her are in there.

The new couch, after the first one broke. After I must have broken it. The shower, the kitchen counter, the bed. All of it is covered in the false memory of her.

I can't stay in the hallway forever though. I have to cross the threshold, otherwise I will never be able to fully move on. I take a deep breath and insert the key into the lock, the door opening a crack before I push it all the way and step inside.

Everything in the loft looks the same but somehow different. Two used coffee cups are sitting on the counter from when I didn't clean up the morning of my birthday. The bed still unmade. I sit my bag down by the entry table and go to hang my jacket in the closet, not needing it anymore with this weather. As soon as I open the door I can't help but notice a white button up shirt, with a pasta stain on the front. I really did eat all of that fettuccine by myself then. Looking down at the crescent shaped scar on my hand I feel my emotions coming to the surface. Everything hits me at once, being in here again.

Moving to sit down on the couch, I lean my head back. Trying to do some of the breathing exercises my physical therapist showed me. Breathing in for a count of six, holding for six and then letting the breath out for six more. I do this a few times until my nerves aren't taking over my body. I look around, realizing I desperately need to tidy up this space. Maybe cleaning will help to focus on what was real and what wasn't. I'm about to get up and grab the vacuum when I realize there is a box on my coffee table. A present sitting on top of a stack of magazines. The present Lilah had gotten me on my birthday.

Did I actually go and buy myself something, wrap it and then give it to myself? I am *fucked*. At least I don't deny it. Dr. Harland said I'm further along in my journey than anyone else he's seen in his career with *Maladaptive Daydreams*. Most take months before they barely start to accept the fact they have been imagining things.

I pick up the wrapped box, feeling the edge of the paper. I notice one of the magazines the box was sitting on is open. The article almost jumps out at me.

"A Story of Love and Loss," by Lilah Harting

Damn. This must be where I came up with her name. The article says exactly what she recounted to me here in my living room on my old couch. About how heartbreak is the truest sign of love. I find that hard to believe, but then again *I* am the one who created my own heartbreak this time. I can't help but think the love I had, imaginary or not, was the most powerful thing I have ever felt. Maybe someday I will have it for real.

Feeling the box in my hand I close my eyes and do what Dr. Harland instructed me to. Replay the circumstance, take note of anything hazy, and then replay again to discover the reality.

The last night I saw her has been the hardest for me to recall since moving past our first encounter. Which apparently is normal seeing as it was the last time my *daydreams* made an appearance. I picture Lilah sitting outside my door. Us fighting. Her handing me this present and then leaving... forever.

I open my eyes and tear open the paper, lifting the lid off the box. Sitting inside is a set of cream-colored curtains.

You've got to be kidding me.

At least my delusional self has a sense of humor. All of the mornings I woke up, both alone and with Lilah, well I guess all of them were alone actually. Where the sun blinded me awake. Who knows how long I've had these curtains hidden away, waiting to surprise myself with them.

Laughing to myself I get up and walk over to the wall of windows by my bed. The sun glaring in as usual. Staring at the street below, people walking to and from the businesses nearby. The lake off in the distance. I realize, I'm not going to hang these curtains. I'm done not seeing the light in my life. For a while, I created a false sense of light, another person to bring me back from the dark.

But it was all me, like Dr. Harland said. I showed myself how to overcome fears, how to see the positive in things. I showed myself how to truly start to love what is within me.

Chapter Thirty-Four

Ignite

The last month has gone by quickly. Getting back into a new version of normalcy has been easier than I thought it would. I had some money in savings from working with my brother so not joining Jack back at the construction company hasn't hurt me yet. I've tried to take advantage of this time to focus on myself and recover.

I physically feel stronger than ever, back in the gym often over the weeks gone by. Mentally getting there too. I find myself continuing to space out sometimes but I am aware of it and am able to snap out of it quickly. No *daydreams* thankfully. The worst time is at night, a lot of my dreams have that face with those piercing blue eyes and perfect lips woven into my subconscious.

I haven't been drinking as often, I haven't even brought myself to go back to *Map Room* since being out of the hospital. It doesn't help that Aaron or Jack haven't had time to go back either. Aaron and Madison decided to take a quick honeymoon once Aaron was released from the hospital.

We finally heard back from the cops regarding the investigation into the fire. It was deemed an electrical accident. No foul play. Dean has been going full steam ahead with his new developments since then, Jack is supposed to take a trip to Columbus to meet with Claire next week. Dean decided to make her the new head of communications for his company after I turned it down. I'm glad. She deserves it.

It's Sunday today and the weather is gorgeous. I haven't gone on a long walk around the city in a while. Deciding to take advantage of having no other plans for the day. I brought my new camera with a newly empty memory card. I went through all of the pictures when I deep cleaned the loft. Every picture I thought I took of Lilah not in existence, I did find a few city shots which weren't bad though.

The breeze is blowing through my hair, the sun shining on my face. I've started to really notice the little things that make life not feel terrible.

I make my way towards the square. I've seen it a couple of times since the fire. It's almost as if it never happened. The building we spent many months working on is non-existent. I will always miss the view from the top floor. Making my way down a side street I haven't walked down since it was snowing out. I see an older couple walking on the opposite sidewalk. They were holding hands until the man raised his arm up, twirling the woman around as she laughs loudly. Her smile is infectious.

A year ago I would have rolled my eyes and thought it to be annoying, that show of affection. Back when my brooding days were in full force. When I was in love, well when I *imagined* I was in love,

I would have pictured me and her in that couple's place. I should feel sad right? Knowing I don't have that, at least not yet. But I don't entirely. I quickly take a few photos of them laughing and in love.

I walk past the next couple of buildings, the sun shining bright. I have to shield my eyes with my hand. Once I get some shade from a tree planted in the sidewalk I look at the closed down building next to me. A little run down and looks like it used to be a restaurant or a bar. There's a small neon sign halfway hanging up in the window next to a for sale sign. I have to tilt my head to read it.

Moonlight.

It's the karaoke bar. Part of me thought I had completely imagined this place. I couldn't find anything about it online and eventually gave up. Putting it aside as part of my *daydream* from my first date with Lilah. It's real. Well I guess it *was* real. I wonder when it closed down.

I step closer to take a look at the sign for a phone number, maybe I can at least find out what happened to it. I start to type the number into my phone before I notice the name of the property management company. *Wolf Industries.* Dean owns this building. I delete the number I started typing and instead pull out the small black card I kept in my wallet with only a phone number on it.

I start to dial.

Four months later, fall is in full force and I'm standing in the doorway of *Moonlight. My* photography studio. Dean didn't hesitate before selling me the space. For way cheaper than I think he could have gotten for it too.

I've spent almost all of my time here. Stacey and Madison have come often to help me make the place *aesthetically pleasing*. Apparently, my taste wasn't trusted with the decor. I'm not complaining though, they did perfect. The walls are all white. The exposed ceiling a matte black. Jack got Aaron and the crew to help with adding in some gallery walls in the center of the space, creating multiple sections for people to walk through. Tonight is the first showing.

I plan to have artists of all kinds in here to showcase. This first show is all mine though. I still haven't shown anyone else my pictures. The cityscapes, the candids of people. The one picture I decided to make the center of the show.

"Well, well, *Mr. Broody* cleans up nice!" Stacey shouts and lets out a whistle.

She's dressed up for tonight too, like our whole group. Madison is in a light pink dress. Matching Aaron's bowtie he keeps fidgeting with. Stacey and her wife are both in black, a stark contrast to the Hawaiian button ups the former is usually in. Jack is who surprises me the most, wearing a full suit, the only other time I've seen him this dolled up is at Dean's party almost a year ago and his own wedding.

"Hey brother, this place looks amazing," Jack says as he makes his way over, leaving Nancy and the twins to look through the photographs already on display. Most of the show remains undercover still.

"Thanks Jack, couldn't have done it without your help," I say as I give him a hug.

"What the heck?" Aaron says as he continues to fidget with his bowtie, "You don't show me any love?"

"Of course man, get on in here." I laugh and wave him over as he grabs us both in a giant bear hug.

"Hey, no breaking the star of tonight," Nancy says as she walks over and hands me and Jack a glass of champagne. A waiter with a tray filled with more walks over, everyone else grabbing one.

"Here's to an amazing night celebrating Landon, the best brother, friend and the best photographer you can ask for," Jack says in a toast as we all raise our glasses. I swear he's gotten more sentimental too after everything that has happened over the last year.

It's finally eight o'clock, time to open the doors. I aimed to keep this show more intimate but over the next hour the room is filled. We pass our capacity limit. Then I spot a familiar face in the crowd and it all makes sense, Dean. He must have made it his personal mission to make sure tonight wasn't a bust for me.

I'm standing in the back center of the open space on a raised platform, a makeshift stage to honor the old karaoke bar here. Behind me is the centerpiece of my show, covered by a thick red curtain, Stacey said it would add to the dramatic effect. She was definitely right.

Everyone quiets themselves when they see me there. I grab a microphone from on top of the speaker sitting on the platform.

"Thank you all for being here. If you told me a year ago this is where I would be standing, I would think you've gone crazy." I shake my head and laugh. "Some of you I'm sure know my story, tonight isn't about me though. Tonight is about rebirth, about finding your-self through the worst moments." I take in the room, the people standing around listening to the words I say. For the first time in a while, I stop searching for that one face, those blue eyes.

"This centerpiece of the show is special to me and my journey, to me it shows the true beauty in not worrying about if anyone else is watching you. I hope out of anything any of you take away from tonight, it's to go find what sets your soul on fire."

As I finish my speech, I pull the curtain away. The photograph is in full view of everyone. It's snowing in the square downtown, the woman's smile illuminating the whole image with its magnetism. Her steel blue eyes and perfect lips. Her chestnut hair. She's twirling in the snow. There is a blurry aspect to the picture, making you feel as if you're spinning with her. A golden locket with a red gem flying subtly on her neck.

The title of the photograph is written on the small sign next to it. *Lilah.*

A couple months ago when I was gathering my pictures to figure out which ones I wanted to showcase, I found it. On my old camera, the one I used before Lilah came into my life, or I guess my mind. Amongst the earlier cityscape pictures and a few other candids that were terrible, I found her.

As soon as I saw the picture, I knew. I knew the moment my *daydreams* started. It was a few days before I met the real woman in the picture again at *Map Room*. I mentioned this all to Dr. Harland at one of our monthly visits after I made the discovery. He thinks when I met that woman in person at the bar it solidified who I would come to imagine as Lilah. Meaning I might not have gone through all I did if I hadn't met the woman that night.

I've come to realize I don't regret anything, or wish any of it hadn't happened though. Even if those interactions weren't real, those memories and moments I made by myself have given me what I needed to get to where I am.

Amongst all the dark, I saw the spark that lit my way out.

Epilogue:

Name

A little after eleven the crowd finally starts clearing out of the gallery space. Leaving only our main group. The showing was a bigger success than I could have ever asked for. I've sold over half of my photographs, leaving space for the next artist I host in *Moonlight*.

We've definitely all had a lot more to drink than we have in a long time. Both Stacey and Madison start chanting about having an after party at *Map Room*. The one place I haven't brought myself to return to after everything. I've basically stopped drinking at all, minus a few drinks over at Jack's house for our cookouts. Which now include the whole family.

Things are still a little weird with us all but we are making progress. My mom and dad both stopped by tonight, they aren't big on crowds but they told me they were proud of me and both gave me a hug. My sister has continued to be reluctant to talk to me, but I didn't expect to mend everything broken all at once. Some things will take time. Maybe we will talk at Thanksgiving in a few weeks, I won't be declining my invitation this year.

I don't know why I haven't been able to push myself to go to that bar though, when I'm fully ready to jump right into everything with my parents and sister. After tonight though I think I can maybe take that final step. Especially with my chosen family supporting me the whole way.

I tried to convince everyone to walk the not-so-short distance from *Moonlight* to *Map Room* but all of the women out-voted me on account of their heels and because it's snowing for the first time since last winter.

We all haul out of the car, Nancy driving us since she has to head home to get the twins to bed. She's the only sober of us, so I'll leave her to make the responsible choices.

It's Saturday night. Resulting in the bar being packed. Our previous usual spot is taken, leaving us at a table in the back. The owner jokes to Stacey and Madison about helping out behind the bar since they're here, earning a *fuck off* from both of them. We all grab our drinks and take seats around the table.

Aaron is recounting a story from when he and Jack were in Columbus not too long ago helping with Dean's latest development, I'm half listening because I've heard this story what feels like five times. I've started people watching since I'm able to see everything in the bar from this seat, even better than my once favorite spot at the wooden bar. The crowd isn't too rowdy, just loud and having a good time on the weekend.

Heroes by David Bowie starts to play over the speakers and I let out a small laugh, how poetic. I look down to grab my drink and take a sip of the remaining amber liquid when something catches my eye at the entrance of the bar.

I look towards the front door at a group walking in. The woman in the center. My breath stops as I get up from my chair. I need to get a closer look, it can't be. I make my way towards the bar. Needing a refill anyways.

She's with four other people all moving as one, I can't fully catch her face. I make out a glimpse of her chestnut-colored hair. I get my drink and stay put about halfway along the bar. The mystery girl making her way closer and closer. She's laughing about something one of her friends is saying. That smile, I'm able to only make out the side of her face.

Her group is only a couple of people away. The two guys next to me get their drinks and move along, leaving only one of her friends in between us. I swear I haven't breathed since I stood up.

I feel like a stalker. I probably look creepy. I should go sit back down. Even if it is the girl, I should just leave it.

Her friend moves. Leaving her and I standing next to each other at the bar. We lock eyes for a split second before someone next to her drunkenly falls and pushes everyone over about half of a foot. She almost trips. I can't let her fall. I grab her arm and steady her.

"Oh, thank you," the girl says as she looks down to make sure she didn't drop anything.

"Of course," I say.

She finally looks up at me. Those piercing steel blue eyes. Those perfect lips. The smell of Jasmine and crackling embers. The golden locket with a red gem in the center. It's all there. *Fuck.* I don't actually know this girl, I have to remind myself.

Somehow though I know she's going to be the death of me.

Breaking the brief moment of silence, I reach my hand out.

"Hi, I'm Landon. What's your name?"

Acknowledgements

IGNITE has been a true labor of love. A dream I never thought would be possible. From the bottom of my heart I want to thank everyone who made this dream come true. To my husband and love of my life, Josh, for your unwavering support throughout this entire process. I truly could not have done this without you, especially because that conversation in that bar years ago would never have happened ;) so many characters have been inspired by you and your strength through life. This story would not exist without you. Thank you for being the best friend, lover and husband anyone could ask for.

I want to thank everyone who has shown true excitement in wanting to read this story I created. Every comment or message you send showing your support truly lights my soul. Of course to my parents for always believing in my writing, and Mom thank you for being one of my first readers. Your phone call crying after your first read through will always live in my memories.

A special thank you and shout out to my fellow Cleveland author and friend, Allison Kennedy, for helping me navigate through this process of being a first-time author. To the city of Cleveland, a place that has helped awaken the best in me, I will be forever grateful & will always call this city home. I do have to thank the fictional character Nick Miller too, for the completely unrealistic plotline of publishing a book and for quotes that live rent free in my mind. Such as, "I'm not convinced I know how to read. I've just memorized a lot of words."

Lastly, to my grandma Lou Dean. You may not be on this same plane of existence anymore but you will always live within my heart. My love of books may never have existed had you not taken me to bookstores as a child. Sitting in those aisles, scanning through which Junie B. Jones to get for hours because I just couldn't decide. For you to then tell me to get both. Anytime I set foot in a bookstore, I think of you.

To sign off, I want every reader to take away this...
Go find what drives you. Find what sets your soul on fire.
And in the words of my late grandma, Lou Dean Atchavit...

Be Bold.

Be Daring.

Be Fabulous.

Be Happy.

www.ingramcontent.com/pod-product-compliance
Lightning Source LLC
Chambersburg PA
CBHW051214130726
47988CB00001B/92